W9-BSD-160

JACKPOT BAY

ALSO BY MARTIN HEGWOOD

Massacre Island

The Green-Eyed Hurricane

Big Easy Backroad

JACKPOT BAY

Martin Hegwood

ST. MARTIN'S MINOTAUR NEW YORK

 For information, address St. Martin's Press, 175 Fifth Avenue, New York, N.Y. 10010.

www.minotaurbooks.com

Library of Congress Cataloging-in-Publication Data

Hegwood, Martin.
Jackpot Bay : a novel / Martin Hegwood.—1st ed.
p. cm.
ISBN 0-312-28096-3
1. Delmas, Jack (Fictitious character)—Fiction. 2. Private investigators—Mississippi—Gulf Coast—Fiction. 3. Gulf Coast (Miss.)—Fiction. 4. Mississippi—Fiction. 5. Casinos—Fiction. I. Title.
PS3558.E4233 J33 2002
813'.54—dc21

2002069940

First Edition: November 2002

10 9 8 7 6 5 4 3 2 1

For

Linda, Eliza, and William

ACKNOWLEDGMENTS

I'd like to thank the following persons for their help during the writing of *Jackpot Bay*: Senator Tommy Gollot of Biloxi for sharing his knowledge of the Mississippi Coast and the history of legalized gaming in Mississippi; Michael Hatch, my British friend who helped my family and me in so many ways and led our escape from France; Chuck Patton, former Director of the Mississippi Gaming Commission, who gave me an overview of the industry; Larry Stroud, former attorney for the Mississippi Gaming Commission, for patiently explaining many aspects of casino security; and Judge Joe Webster and Ann Harland Webster, my longtime friends, for providing me a refuge when I needed one. I'd also like to thank my editor, Joe Cleemann, for his sure and steady hand in guiding me through.

JACKPOT BAY

ONE

"Would ya just listen to all that racket outside? If them rednecks don't haul ass, and I mean *real* soon, I'm gonna go down there and personally whip the hell outta every last one of 'em!"

Johnnie the Dime was bursting with high blood pressure, and both his face and his bald head were as pink as a boiled shrimp. He swept his fat fingers through the scraggly wisps of moistened hair that clung to the base of his skull, and then used the back of his hand to wipe away the drops of sweat that had trickled down into his eyes.

"I just turned and walked away from this great setup I had out in Vegas. Just walked away from it, I tell ya! I bring my ass back down here to give these shrimp pickers some good-payin' jobs, and *this* is the way I get treated? You tellin' me I gotta put up with *this* crappola?"

What I had to say to Johnnie was going to be tough enough, even without the swarm of singing protesters out on the street below. "Mr. Koscko," I said, "I won't take much of your time. Bayou Casualty needs to do a security audit of your casino."

He glared at me and looked like he needed to clear his throat and spit. "Now, ain't that just swell? They already done one of them audits before we even opened for business. Y'follow me? That ain't been six months ago. Sent in that smart-ass broad.

What's her name?" He glanced at Clyde who was standing at the window. "Hey, Clyde, ya listenin'? I'm talkin' to ya."

"Yeah, Uncle Johnnie?"

"Get ya ass away from that window and stop teasing them people. They won't never shut up if they think ya listenin' to 'em. That gal that did the audit on this place a few months ago. What's her name?"

"You talkin' about the one with the great legs?"

"And the smart mouth," Koscko said. "What the hell's her name?"

"Name's Tara something."

"It's Tara Stocklin," I said. "But, Mr. Koscko, she never got a chance to finish her work here."

"That's because she didn't know what she was doing. She was too busy runnin' around trying to get laid."

"You want I should shut the windows, Uncle Johnnie?"

"You crazy or something? I'm already about to suffocate in here. Look, you . . . what's your name again?"

"A.J. Delmas," I said. "People call me Jack."

"You one of them Delmases from around here?"

"He's from around here all right." Ever since high school, Clyde's had this edge to his voice when he talks to me, or even about me. Like he's always bad wanting to try to get a piece of me.

"Dammit," Johnnie said, "I wasn't talking to you."

The air conditioner was broken and the morning sun was at just the right angle to light up the room and overpower the ceiling fan. We were in the downtown office of Jackpot Bay Casino. The casino itself was seven miles away, all the way down Beach Boulevard to where it dead-ended into Bayou Caddy. The office occupied the top floor of a two-story, turn-of-the-century building that featured twelve-foot ceilings and wide-planked wooden floors. A steamy breeze coming through the open French doors carried a strong fragrance of cinammon from the bakery next door. So the room not only felt like an oven, it smelled like one too.

"Delmas, I been in this business forty years. Y'unnerstand? I don't need no insurance company telling me how to run a casino."

"All we know is that you've been losing too much money to theft," I said, "or maybe to cheating at the gaming tables. The company wants to bring in an expert to check procedures on the floor, calibrate the slots, check cash flow procedures. It's just routine."

Koscko grunted and pulled a roll of bills out of his front pocket. He peeled off a fifty and held it up. "Clyde, why don't ya run on down to that Dollar General Store and get us a couple of box fans."

Clyde was still standing at the window, behind Johnnie the Dime's desk, looking out over the crowd like he was the Pope or something and, when his uncle wasn't looking, cupping his hand behind his ear, acting like he couldn't hear all the singing and chanting. Back in high school Clyde was a couple of years behind me, a hood from that tough part of Biloxi near the projects who used to drive over to Bay St. Louis just to get into fights. But even in those days he knew better than to try to mess with me.

He had been out in Las Vegas with his uncle the past few years working as a blackjack dealer at the Golden Nugget, but he still looked like a small-timer. Always would. He's a big guy with a Fu Manchu, pumped-up arms, but soft around the middle, constantly reaching for the comb he kept in his back pocket.

"Go on and get them fans," Koscko said. "I'm about to burn up."

"I've done called the air-condition repair guys. They oughta be here any minute."

"Don't argue with me! You're in charge of making stuff run around here. We need some relief right now."

"But I've done called . . ."

"Just go get the damn fans. Okay?"

Clyde twisted about a quarter turn, just enough so that his back was to his uncle, and he flipped off the crowd. About what you'd expect from some eighth-grade punk, not a full-grown man. The gesture set off a big roar that caused Johnnie the Dime to spin his chair around, and Clyde held out his palms to proclaim his innocence.

"Quit messing with them holy-rollers and get ya ass in gear."

The singing outside intensified. I never knew the hymn "I Shall Not Be Moved" had so many verses. "Listen to all that," Koscko said. "Y'know what them dummies are down there protesting? They think the lead singer on this Snow Mountain Band is the Antichrist. Y'ever heard anything so stupid? One idiotic story shows up in one of them rags they sell at the checkout counter and them Bible-thumpin' dummies fall for it."

"Maybe I oughta call them air-conditioning guys again," Clyde said.

"I heard they're angry because you scheduled the concert on a Sunday," I said.

"Yeah, that too. I told some of my buddies back in Vegas about that Sunday business and they nearly busted a gut laughing. Hell, this place ain't changed one bit since I was in high school."

I didn't have time to argue the point, but Johnnie Koscko was dead wrong about that. The Mississippi Coast is changing every day whether I like it or not. You can see the change firsthand if you go twenty miles to the east and take a drive through all that new traffic along the beach in Biloxi. You'll have plenty of time to take it all in, because it'll be so crowded you probably won't be able to go more than fifteen miles per hour. High-rise hotels have gone up where shrimp boats used to unload their catch, and these days the pastel glare of casino marqees crowds out the soft orange glow of the moon when it's low in the eastern sky over Deer Island. The whole place has nearly been pushed to the limit as far as I'm concerned.

But of course the civic booster types, including my own brother, have got a different take on it. Their idea of progress is to pack a million people into this place. And, hell, maybe they're right. Maybe the real estate salesmen and bankers and retailers and convention directors are right. Rising real estate values are everything. Just sit back, world, and watch us grow! I'll admit it, I'm stuck in a time and a way of life that will never be here again. But I'm just hoping that down here we can hang on to at least a piece of what we have now.

"So let's say ya set up all this high-priced security and ya catch somebody cheating," Johnnie said. "What then?"

"You file charges at the police station and they start the prosecution."

"Oh, that's brilliant. That's what your insurance company's got to say about it? That's just a great way to let the whole world know that we're an easy mark. Get caught cheating at the Jackpot Bay and all ya do is pay fifty bucks to some justice of the peace. Listen, I cut my teeth in Vegas back in the old days. Y'follow me? I know how to handle cheaters so they don't come back."

Clyde smiled and started cracking his knuckles. "Damn right."

The door behind me burst open and in stormed this tall, thin man. Short sandy hair, almost a crew cut, and a single diamond in his right earlobe. His lips were pressed together in a tight line. "Mister Koscko, I simply cannot put up with this any longer! I've got Snow Mountain coming here in two days and the accounting division is telling me I can't hire a limo to bring them in from the airport. That is nothing but bush league, pure and simple. We're talking about the hottest band in the world."

"Do what ya gotta do, Rulon," Koscko said. "You're in charge of this weekend. I already told ya that a hunnerd times."

"Well, maybe you better tell those accountants. They questioned the limo, the flowers, the food, everything. I thought we had an understanding. I thought you'd let me get whatever I need."

"Ya got plenty of shrimp?" Clyde asked. "Shrimp and crawfish, that's what the crowds down here want."

Rulon glared at Clyde and put his hands on his hips. "Oh, and I suppose you want me to spread them out on folding tables covered with butcher paper."

"This ain't no fancy crowd," Clyde said. "They ain't interested in none of that finger food those French chefs you hired come up with."

"Well, it might just be a little fancier crowd than you think. I've got some special people coming this weekend."

Clyde sniffed. "You mean ya lined up the Gay Pride Alliance for their convention?"

"Mr. Koscko!"

"Knock it off, Clyde." Koscko lowered his head and rubbed both temples. "Who ya got coming?"

"Gretchen La Pointe just called me and asked me to make sure we stock some Glenlivet Scotch. She's bringing the Earl of Stropshire to the VIP reception."

Johnnie turned his eyes up to Rulon and started grinning. "Earl? Like from England?"

"So who's this Gretchen woman?" Clyde didn't have a clue.

"You mean an earl as in high roller?" Koscko's spirits were rising.

"I don't know if he's a high roller or not," Rulon said. "But I'm sure some of his friends are."

Johnnie clapped his hands and started laughing. "That's what I wanna hear! Good job, Rulon. We start getting Gretchen La Pointe and some of her jetset buddies comin' in here and we can make this the classiest joint on the Coast. You go order all the Glenlivet they got."

"So you'll speak to accounting?"

"Sure, sure."

A rousing chorus of "Onward Christian Soldiers" cranked up outside. Rulon glanced at the window and winced like he was seeing somebody chewing up tin foil. "Would you like for me to go outside and put a stop to that noise?"

Clyde laughed out loud, and Johnnie the Dime lightly bit his bottom lip like he was trying not to snicker at a child who had just said something cute. "I'm sure they'll be through singing in a little while. You just run along and order that scotch."

"Well you let me know when you get tired of listening to it and

I'll do something about it," Rulon said. "Oh, and Clyde, when do you think you can get the air conditioner fixed?"

"You ain't gonna melt, sugar." Clyde puckered his lips and made kissing motions at him.

"Aw, come on, Clyde. Leave him alone, dammit."

"I've got a lot to do," Rulon said, "and I can't do it in an oven."

"Get him one of them fans, too," Johnnie said. "We got us a rainmaker here. Gotta get him a good place to work."

"Do you think you could pick me up a bag of ice while you're out running your other errands?" Rulon asked.

"You can get your own damn ice."

"Hey! Would you shut up?" Johnnie stabbed his finger at Clyde "Rulon here's the manager, whether ya like it or not. Get him what he wants."

Rulon smirked at Clyde, wheeled around, and flitted out of the room. Even from where I was sitting, I could see the muscles in Clyde's jaw working.

"Mr. Koscko," I said, "can we talk about this security audit?"

"Now lemme get this straight. Are you telling me what I think you're telling me?"

"The company is bringing Tara Stocklin back down here, if that's what you mean."

"Like hell they are."

"Mr. Koscko, she comes highly recommended. I know that you had some personality conflicts with her earlier. That's why I'm here."

"She's a damn pushy bra burner, and I ain't worked my ass off my whole life to have to take no orders from somebody like that. Y'unnerstand?"

"Bra burner?" I asked.

"You ain't never heard of that?"

"Not in the past twenty-five years or so."

"You know what I'm talkin' about." He jumped up out of his chair and dashed to the window. "Hey! All you holy-rollers out there! You call that singing? You come back this weekend and you'll hear some first-class singing!"

The singers had moved on to a new hymn, one I didn't recognize. Koscko gripped the railing of the balcony like he was trying to bend it into an arc. He straightened to full height and swung his right arm upward to give them the "Up Yours" gesture, which drew a roar of boos and some laughter. He rifled through both his pants pockets as stepped back to his desk, cursing and grinding his teeth. "Some homecoming this is."

"I can make sure that group don't come back tomorow," Clyde said. But Johnnie the Dime had started fumbling through a drawer on the side of his desk, running his hands through a mishmash of pens, pencils, and paper clips. "Or maybe you'd rather get your manager Rulon to muscle 'em outta the way for ya."

Johnny ignored his nephew, didn't seem to have even heard him, and slapped a few pennies down on the surface of the desk. "A sprinkler system!" he snapped his fingers. "That's what we need. Clyde, I want ya to call somebody and get one put in today. I'm gonna get rid of them Bible thumpers one way or another."

"May I get a cup of water?" I asked.

Koscko went back to rummaging for change with both hands and used his head to point me to the cooler in the corner. "Go get me them fans before I pull out a gun and start shooting at them fools down there."

The water was icy and I drank the first cup too fast so it shot a quick pain into my head. Clyde left the room while I was filling a second cup. He slammed the door on his way out. The phone rang and Johnnie the Dime started this loud and bawdy conversation about some boat he was wanting to borrow for a few days the next week to take out some women he had lined up. I stepped to the window just as the singing stopped.

The people down on the sidewalk were all standing, their heads bowed, as this dark-haired linebacker-type in a white shirt and a bright red tie led them in a quiet prayer. I recognized him from the

TV news of the past few days. The Reverend Billy Joe Newhart, pastor of the newly formed Narrow Path Independent Bible Church a few miles north of town above the Interstate toward the little town of Kiln. Newhart was new in town, all I knew about him was that he was one hell of a salesman. They called him "The Fireball from Tomball" after the town in Texas where he grew up.

Over on Beach Boulevard, half a block away, kids in cars cruised past the antique stores and gift shops, the restaurants and bars, slow as a walk and silent except for an occasional stereo with throbbing bass speakers. Some were headed for the beach, some were just riding. I was twenty feet above the street, high enough to see the sunlight sparkling on the bay and the gray profile of Cat Island at the southern horizon. As soon as I could get through with this baby-sitting I was doing, I'd be headed there on my sailboat.

I had wanted to be on the gulf much earlier that day. I had planned to go in and tell Johnnie Koscko that the security audit he had bitched about enough to get it stopped a few months earlier was about to start up again, and that he'd have to suck it up and stay out of the way. Should have been quick and easy. But I knew that was asking way too much from Johnnie the Dime and nephew Clyde. It was asking for some degree of class and maturity.

I just had to go out and start getting more clients. Daddy always warned me about being too dependent on one customer or one client. But it's such an easy trap to fall into. Bayou Casualty had just made me their main man on the Mississippi Gulf Coast. Made it official, that is. I had already been handling most of their stuff over here for nearly four years on a day-to-day basis. They called and offered me a guarantee of five days' worth of pay every month whether they use my services or not. All I have to do is agree to take whatever jobs they send me as long as they give me a week's notice.

My brother Neal called this setup a retainer, but he's a lawyer so he uses words like that. I call it a cushion, and it's enough for me to get an office outside my house without worrying about making the monthly rent. Neal's been nagging me to do that for a year now, telling me how an office in my house is a red flag for an IRS audit. And I don't want any part of that.

So I was glad to get the deal from Bayou Casualty. Still am, I guess. But lately they just haven't had all that many cases over here that need investigating, so they've got me running all kinds of errands. Like trying to make sure two grown people like Johnnie the Dime Koscko and Tara Stocklin don't get into some hair-pulling, eye-gouging fight when she comes back to town.

Tara had been down here three months earlier, and she and Johnnie developed a hatred for one another. So the company figured they needed to at least give him a heads-up that she was coming back. They could have done it by phone, but since I'm their man on the Coast and getting paid anyway, I got the call to break the news to him.

They also wanted me to pick up Tara at the New Orleans airport and get her checked into her hotel and take care of her for a few days while she did her preliminary investigation, which is a joke because if there's any person on earth, male or female, who can take care of herself, it's Tara Stocklin. In fact, if she and I were going to be spending any time together, I was the one who might be needing the help.

"All right, Delmas," Johnnie said as he hung up the phone, "when's that bitch coming back over here?"

"Mr. Koscko, you're going to have to treat her with some courtesy. Especially in front of the staff."

"Yeah. Right. Who's she been screwing over there at Bayou Casualty?"

I took in a deep breath and let it out real slow. "I don't know, and I don't care. All I know is that the company will have her over here and ready to go within the next twenty-four hours. She'll have security credentials and full authority to investigate your books, the operations on the floor, and any other areas insured by Bayou Casualty."

Johnnie the Dime had started squeezing the arms of his chair. "And what if I say no?"

"I think you ought to know that if the company is going to continue to cover your casino, you're going to have to let her do her job. The State Gaming Commission won't allow your casino to operate unless you're fully insured for liability, including theft by employees or patrons."

Koscko slammed his fist on the desk hard enough to knock a few of the pennies to the floor. He pushed up from his chair, and started toward the window. But after he took two steps, the singing stopped and he flapped his hands in disgust at the open window. He stepped back to his desk, softly cursing about Jesus freaks, and plopped down in his chair and threw his feet up on his desk. He started squeezing a blue rubber ball hard enough to smooth out the skin on the back of his hands.

"If you're finished preaching to me," he said, "I'll explain a few things to ya. I been in the casino business for forty years. Before I ever went to Vegas, my daddy and my granddaddy worked down here in Biloxi workin' as blackjack dealers and floor managers for the Golden Nugget down on the Strip. This stuff is in my blood. Y'follow me? I've been working every casino in Vegas for the last forty years. So now they go and legalize gambling in my old hometown. It's like a dream come true. I'm back and I'm gonna take the Jackpot Bay and make it into the classiest joint in the eastern United States."

"I understand what you're saying, Mr. Koscko."

"No, I don't think ya do unnerstand what I'm saying. I don't just work for Jackpot Bay, I own the place. I been working my ass off all my life, and I finally got what they call an equity position in a casino in my own hometown. I'll stomp the hell out of anybody who rips this place off."

"So," I said, "we shouldn't have any problems. We're going to help you find out why there's been some leakage in your cash flow."

"I could find it myself," he said.

"The company wants Tara Stocklin to do it."

He blew out a breath and ran his fingers through his hair and rubbed the back of his neck. "Aw, Jesus on a bike."

There was just enough resignation in his voice to where I sensed I had acomplished my purpose, so I stood to leave. Time to get out before he changed his mind and decided to fight the company's decision to call Tara back into town. But just about the time I turned toward the door, damned if the crowd outside didn't crank up again, this time with a bullhorn. And I could see his blood rise once again.

"TESTING . . ."

He leaned toward the window as if he had to strain to hear. "Is that a bullhorn out there?"

"BROTHERS AND SISTERS, THE LORD IS WITH US TODAY! CAN I HEAR AN 'AMEN'?"

"A-MEN!" screamed the crowd.

"I'd know that voice anywhere," Koscko said with a groan. "That's the radio preacher. Crazy son of a bitch is on the radio ten times a day raisin' hell about something. Usually about this place."

"IT'S TIME TO TAKE A STAND FOR THE LORD. IT'S TIME TO LET THE DEVIL KNOW THAT JESUS IS LORD IN BAY ST. LOUIS! NOT GAMBLING, NOT DRINKING! NO, NOT OLD SATAN HIMSELF! BUT THE PRECIOUS LAMB OF GOD!"

"AAA-MEN!"

"You know where that preacher says he's from?" Johnnie asked. "Get this. He's from Tomball, Texas. Y'hear what I'm sayin'? TOM-ball friggin' TEX-as! Musta had him plenty of rattlesnakes to handle in *that* place."

"I guess so," I said. "I'll call you when Tara . . ."

"Well, I'm gonna call the cops about that bullhorn." He reached for the phone book. "They said that crowd could sing all they wanted to, but noisemakers ain't allowed. I give a thousand bucks to the sheriff's barbecue, I oughta get me some service around here."

"I'll let you know when Ms. Stocklin gets here."

"God, the shit I gotta put up with," Koscko said as he squinted at the small print in the phone book. "First I got this crazy-assed rock band coming in who won't let me pay them with a company check. Gotta have cash. And you think I can just put that cash in the Hancock Bank and get them to transfer it? Hell, no. They want me to hire an armored car and drive it all the way up to Nashville. Ever heard of anything so crazy?"

I shrugged my shoulders.

"AND ABRAHAM WANTED TO SAVE THE CITY OF SODOM FROM THE WRATH OF GOD SO HE ASKED, 'WHAT IF THERE ARE FIFTY RIGHTEOUS PEOPLE IN THE CITY?' "

Johnnie the Dime kept right on talking to me as if he didn't hear a thing. "And then Clyde, he gets his butt up on his shoulders because I give the manager's job to Rulon Hornbeck instead of him. Hell, Clyde's my nephew, and just about all the family I got left, but that don't mean he don't have to work his way up the ladder. There's a lot to learn about this casino business. I mean, he's a pretty good floor manager, but it takes a lot more than that.

"Plus, if you want to give the place a touch of class, you gotta hire a homo. That's what the rich folks expect, y'know. Rulon, anybody can see that he's light in the loafers. But he got his training over in Monte Carlo. I'm telling you, that's what these society types want. You wouldn't happen to have a quarter, would ya?"

"Well, I don't know anything about society types." I dug into my pocket.

"None of you people at that damn insurance company know first thing about runnin' a casino. That's what I'm trying to tell ya. You'd save us both time and money if you'd just listen to me."

"ONCE AGAIN ABRAHAM SPOKE TO GOD, 'WHAT IF ONLY FORTY

ARE FOUND THERE?' DO WE HAVE FORTY RIGHTEOUS PEOPLE HERE IN BAY ST. LOUIS TODAY?"

"I don't make the rules," I said. "I just deliver the messages. Will two dimes do?"

"Forget it, I'll just drink some of that water." He got up and stepped toward the cooler. "I mean, like this business with Rulon Hornbeck. He knows where I stand. He makes a pass at me, and I give him a sex-change operation right there on the spot with my pocketknife. Y'unnerstand what I'm sayin'? I can't stand to be around 'em. And Clyde, he *really* hates the homos. But, don't ya see, Rulon's done gotten in good with Gretchen La Pointe, the queen of Gulf Coast society herself."

"AND IN VERSE THIRTY-ONE ABRAHAM ASKS, 'WHAT IF ONLY TWENTY CAN BE FOUND?' "

"And now she's got some duke or earl or something coming in from England. We show this earl guy a good time over here, show a little class, and pretty soon the word gets back to the high rollers in Monte Carlo and they start comin' over. That's what Clyde can't see. We gotta get Gretchen La Pointe and her crowd coming in here. Not that polyester bunch that comes in with a handful of coupons and heads straight to the half-price buffet line."

He reached into his pocket and pulled out a little brown bottle and popped a pill under his tongue. He knocked back a paper cup full of water and swallowed hard. "I swear, puttin' up with all this crap is gonna kill me. I'm popping these high blood pressure pills like they was breath mints. But I'm gonna make this work, no matter what it takes. You watch, when I bring in a few more acts like Snow Mountain, them Bible thumpers out there will disappear. I been waitin' for this chance a long time, and there ain't nobody gonna get in my way."

"I've got to be going," I said as I stood.

"BROTHERS AND SISTERS, COULD THE PROPHET ABRAHAM FIND TWENTY RIGHTEOUS PEOPLE IF HE CAME HERE TO THIS CITY TODAY?"

"Tell ya what, Delmas. You find out who that Tara Stocklin's been screwing over at Bayou Casualty, and I'll make a call out to Vegas and line the guy up with something better. A lot better. Maybe then he'll tell her to hit the road, and I can get her outta my hair once and for all."

TWO

That afternoon I sat on a padded stool at the bar on Concourse B of the Louis Armstrong Airport, waiting for Tara's overdue flight and watching an Astros game. The flight was held up in Las Vegas at take-off, so she missed her connection in Denver and was already an hour and a half late. But what the hell. That's one reason they put bars in airports.

I ate half a bowl of extra-salty peanuts and tossed back a couple of Diet Pepsis and was about to walk down to Gate 14 when this New York Life salesman who had also been watching the game bet me a Samuel Adams draft that I couldn't name the starting defensive line of the old Dallas Cowboy Doomsday Defense. I didn't really want a beer that time of day, but I just couldn't pass up a freebie like that.

Johnnie the Dime might have been right about Tara and the Bayou Casualty brass. The vice president who had brought her down here in the first place was this Porsche driver who was into tanning beds and plastic surgery and regularly hit on every woman in the building. The type who makes a fool of himself trying to pick up stewardesses at thirty thousand feet when they're pushing meal trays up the aisles. The kind of guy who, without a doubt, would have zeroed in on Tara. After he hired her, she had barely had time to get settled in Bay St. Louis and take a good look at the casino before he got zapped by lightning on the back nine at the English Turn course downriver from New Orleans. It was what we in the insurance business refer to as an act of God. Turns out the dumbass must have taken Lee Trevino seriously; they found a half-melted two-iron on the ground beside him.

Less than two weeks after lover boy bought the ranch, Koscko had run Tara off. She's the best at what she does, the tops in the country in casino security, and Koscko didn't have a good reason to get her fired. He just didn't like her. I had a feeling he and Tara might have had some earlier run-ins back in Las Vegas, but I was just guessing. I never heard him say that. Anyway, all of that happened about the same time that Bayou Casualty was trying hard to get in on some of the casino business on the coast, and Jackpot Bay was their first customer. So they went along with Johnnie the Dime and canned Tara.

That was around the first of the year. And now the Jackpot Bay Casino is losing money faster than a dot-com technology stock and nobody seems to know where the money's disappearing to. So Bayou Casualty's bringing her back now that what she said turned out to be right. And I had the feeling that Johnnie the Dime was about to wish he's never messed with Tara Stocklin.

I recognized her when she stepped out of the passenger tunnel, but that's mainly because she was wearing this short yellow dress with a split up the side nearly to her waist. She's tall with a magnificent set of legs and she knows it, so she takes every opportunity to display them. They're long and smooth and perfectly tapered. Against the light yellow dress, they seemed almost caramel brown with a midsummer tan. The sharply defined muscles of her thighs and calves are so tight they ripple when she walks. I remembered the legs.

But she had dyed her hair and cut it short since the last time I saw her. When I say short, I mean maybe two inches long all the way around. She had colored it blond, a bright yellow blond, but the yellow was just at the ends. Underneath, next to the scalp, her hair was nearly black. A punk style, the kind you see on the nose-ring crowd that hangs around the malls. She wore a blue eyeshadow with a light sprinkling of sparkle dust, and she had a new row of diamond studs lining the outside edge of her left ear.

Definitely built for speed.

“So, how are things going down here in Gritsville?” she asked as she fumbled through her purse. “Fish still jumpin’? Cotton still high? Everything okay at the trailer park?”

“Just bought Mama a pair of shoes. They fit her okay, but she’s having a hard time getting used to them, what with it being her first pair and all.”

There’s nothing more tiresome than trying to undo the damage that’s been done to us over the years by Hollywood and the evening news. So I said to hell with it a long time ago and gave up trying. I mean Tara had just flown in from a city whose idea of class is a rented stretch limo and a hundred thousand flashing lights, where you’re considered aristocracy if you’ve lived there ten years. So why should I give a rip what she thinks of Bay St. Louis?

“If you don’t mind,” I said, “would you please buckle your seat belt?”

“You sound like that silly recording on the plane. But at least there aren’t any kids in this truck. There was one on the flight, y’know, and he was, like, driving my ass crazy. I mean he never shut up. Hell, I was this close to shoving his little ass out the door. They ought to keep kids locked in a closet until they turn eighteen.”

“I felt the same way until I had one of my own.”

“Well, no way that’s happening to me. Too many ways to prevent it.” She lit a cigarette and cracked the window. “Let’s go get a drink before you take me to the hotel. After that flight I feel like I’m about to jump out of my skin.”

“I guess we could go to Dan’s Boiler and get a beer. Depends on what you want.”

"Let's go to Jackpot Bay," she said. "I want to see what they've done with the place, y'know, see if they've spread any sawdust on the floor yet."

"There's not all that much to see this time of day."

"I want to take a look at the new manager."

I didn't care too much for sitting in some casino and hearing all those bells, but Rulon Hornbeck really was worth showing to her. "This guy came over from New Orleans a few months ago after he dumped his live-in boyfriend. I hear it was a pretty bad scene. He's supposed to have worked the big casino in Monte Carlo for several years. He's not exactly what you would think Johnnie Koscko would want."

"So he didn't hire that Neanderthal nephew of his? What's his name?"

"Clyde Dubardo."

"Yeah," she said. "I thought Clyde would be, like, running the place by now."

"So did Clyde."

She flicked her ashes out the window. "So how is my old friend Johnnie the Dime anyway?"

"Mr. Koscko seems to be under some pressure right now."

"Oh, really? I thought he'd have taken care of the cheating by now. Maybe he's just not readjusted to redneck country yet. Doesn't have any deserts around here, y'know, where he can bury the cheaters. So what does he do with them? Take them out to, like, the Gulf and dump them overboard?"

"As much money as the casino's losing, I doubt that he's caught any yet."

Even with the air conditioner on, it was hot where the sun came through the window on my side. I had trained a vent to cool my face and the air was icy against the moisture on my neck and cheeks, but it was spot cooling only. My undershirt was sticking to my back and the waistband of my briefs were cutting into me. I pulled at my knit shirt to peel it away from my skin. Tara turned on the radio and kept punching the seek button, not finding whatever it was that she wanted.

We bounced along the rough concrete where Interstate 10, which had been mostly a series of bridges coming out of New Orleans, touched briefly on semisolid ground so low we could smell the sulfurous swamp gas. It was a mile or so before we got to the Pearl River bridge. At the state line marker at the top of the bridge, eighty feet above the water, the swamp spread out for miles below us, a maze of bayous winding through a forest of cypress, thick as a hedge, with Spanish moss clinging to the treetops like a thin, low-hanging layer of light gray smoke.

"Oh, wow! Look at that! Looks just like the Everglades. Are there any alligators in there?"

"You could walk across that swamp on their backs," I said. "You could step from gator to gator and never get your feet wet."

"Do you guys down here learn to talk like that in high school? Got some course called Redneck Bullshit One-Oh-One or something?"

"I believe that particular phrase came from a three hundred-level course."

"So you ever go hunting for them?"

"I don't hunt alligators. Been spotlighting once, and that was enough for me."

"You've got a boat, don't you?"

I lied and shook my head no. I knew where she was headed, and I wasn't about to take her gator hunting. Not in my little fourteen-foot aluminum MonArk or in anything else. Tara is an adventure freak. I knew she went skydiving over in Pascagoula the last time she was in town, but that's pretty tame stuff for her. She's rappeled in Costa Rica, flown an ultralight over the Grand Canyon, and fished for mako sharks up in Montauk. She said last time she was here she was training to audition for *Fear Factor*, this TV show where people go on camera to do the stuff they fear the most in front of the whole world. I wondered what the hell Tara

Stocklin would be afraid of. Almost asked her, but decided I really didn't want to know.

The Pearl River swamp ends abruptly when you leave Louisiana and drive into Mississippi, and the border between the swamp and the pinelands is a sharp one. The pine forest along the side of the interstate is broken by intermittent stretches of rolling pasture where cattle have ranged since the 1700s when French settlers named Ladner and Dedeaux and Necaise and Favre let their wild and wiry cattle roam these woods. Unnoticed, unfenced, and unmolested, they wandered until there was a need for meat or hide. During my lifetime, that same pastureland, dotted by haystacks and roamed by black-and-white Holsteins, has provided a calming, peaceful, and pretty view for drivers on old Highway 90 and now its successor Interstate 10.

But a few years ago the casino billboards went up. Maybe billboard isn't the right term to use. Those damn things are as big as the side walls of airport hangars and are set on telescoping steel columns that could support water towers. And they're lit up at night, bright enough to illuminate a high school football stadium. Sometimes they put up rows of five or six of these, identical in size and color, each hawking the same casino and usually giving the dates of headliner acts that will be coming to the coast over the following months. Has the same effect on the scenery that a can of spray paint would have on a Rembrandt.

Fifteen minutes after we crossed the river, a quarter mile before the Bay St. Louis exit, we came to one of these monster billboards set off in a hayfield. But this one wasn't advertising any casino. Across the top was the number of the toll-free Salvation Hotline, 1-800-I'M SAVED. The left half was a rendition of an open Bible with "Narrow Path Independent Bible Church of Charismatic Believers" written across the face in Old English script and below it in black, block lettering "THIS EXIT." The right half of the billboard was a close-in facial shot of a smiling Reverend Billy Joe Newhart, his head slightly tilted to the right. He has the coloration of a Cherokee with glossy black hair and deep-set brown eyes. A good-looking man with a square jaw, a dimpled chin, and big shoulders.

"That's why Koscko's been so edgy the past week." I pointed to it.

"Is he worried about, like, going to hell or something?" she asked.

"Does he act like it?"

"So who's the stud up there on the billboard?"

"That's the Reverend Billy Joe Newhart. He's been leading protests outside Johnnie's office every day for the past week."

She reached for another cigarette and tapped it against the dash as she crossed her legs so tightly they looked braided. There was a toe ring I hadn't noticed before. "I hooked up with a preacher one time. He had tapped into the collection plates and sneaked out to Vegas for a little R&R. Throwing money around, buying drinks for every unattached woman in the bar, that kinda thing."

"How'd you know he was a preacher?"

"Saw it on his credit card. I wasn't really interested until I saw that. And then I was like, oh wow! I just had to see what it would be like."

"Uh-huh," I said. "So anyway, Reverend Newhart has been stirring up his congregation about the Snow Mountain . . ."

"Don't you even wonder what the preacher was like in bed?" She kept her eyes trained on the billboard until we passed it.

"Let me guess," I said, "the guy was really into the missionary position."

"That's about the only way we didn't get around to trying." She took a drag from the cigarette and stared straight ahead. A smile played around the corners of her mouth as the memory kicked in. "That preacher on the billboard, you think there's a chance he'll be hanging around Koscko's office the next few days?"

"He'll be outside on the street along with a few dozen of his congregation," I said. "You'll hear them."

"So you think maybe I ought to call him on that toll-free number instead?"

We turned into town off Highway 90 at Beach Boulevard at the foot of the long drawbridge that spans the bay. We first passed a group of hundred-year-old cottages with gingerbread galleries, then on to the art studios, antique stores, and restaurants of Old Town, set high above the beach on a hurricane-proof bluff, shaded by live oaks and scented with wisteria. A flock of gulls had come in close to shore to forage and were especially loud and irritable, and a white-over-red shrimp trawler spewing gray diesel exhaust sounded its deep whistle to open the bridge. If you lifted a fishing village from Maine's Midcoast and set it down intact on the warm-water shore of the Gulf of Mexico, you'd have downtown Bay St. Louis.

We followed the pocked, sand-colored concrete road along the beach, past turn-of-the-century Victorians with their turrets and stained glass, past 1930s-style Mediterranean mansions of white stucco and red tiled roofs, down through the flat, sandy, scrub pine stretch of beach where I live in a camp house set on poles. The new Jackpot Bay Casino sits at the road's marshy endpoint, where Bayou Caddy feeds into the Mississippi Sound and where waves sometimes splash over the seawall and onto the road and fishermen with their spinning rigs stand on the edge of the pavement to cast for speckled trout.

Another casino had moved in there some years earlier when Mississippi first legalized gambling and when the boom was in its first stages, when nobody thought they could possibly lose money by setting up their own gambling palace. And so the speculators and first-timers came with visions of mansions and Mercedes convertibles, and, since they were blinded by the glittering vision of all this gold, they neglected to take a hard look at the numbers.

Or even if they bothered to do an analysis, they used as their business models some predictions of future growth that were so outlandish they would make even a real estate salesman laugh.

That first group of investors who set up at the end of Beach Boulevard had bulkheaded the shoreline along the mouth of the bayou and jammed concrete pilings, three-foot by three-foot square, at a slant out into the water so they could tie off the casino barge in a permanent mooring since, for some unknown reason, casinos in Mississippi can only be built on floating boats or barges. That casino went bust after a few months and they towed the barge and most of its equipment to some town on the Mississippi River in Iowa, where they have two-hundred-dollar betting limits.

Months went by and then years. Tall sprigs of Johnson grass sprouted from the cracks in the concrete parking lot, the sign above the entrance became a target for bored teenagers with slingshots, and the black paint on the metal hand railings faded and gave way to rust. The old owners had given up hopes of a comeback and the place was scheduled for a tax sale when Johnnie Koscko came to town and bought the whole place for back taxes. To remove any clouds on the title that might be floating around, he gave the owners another ten grand or so of what my brother called sympathy money. He filled in the cracks, slapped on some fresh paint, and got a license from the Gaming Commission in record time.

When we turned into the parking lot, I noticed that the tags on the cars and pickups were mostly from Mississippi. Some came from as far away as Meridian or Jackson, but most were from Hancock and Harrison counties down here on the Gulf Coast. A good number of the other tags were from Louisiana, and I saw one from Texas and three from Alabama. Koscko's plan to make the Jackpot Bay an international gambling destination still had a long way to go, but he sure was making inroads in Bogalusa and Slidell. At least the place wasn't empty like it had been when that other casino was here.

A pair of tour buses were making the wide turn, about to pull up to the stopping area under the steel girdered porte cochere at the front door. Their yellow flashers were pulsing and diesel exhaust squiggled from their tailpipies. The man who stepped to the passenger door of the lead bus looked like Clyde, but I was a good distance removed and looking through my filmy windshield.

"So they've got Clyde greeting the buses?" Tara asked.

"No wonder he's been so hostile," I said. "That's quite a step down from manager."

"Hey," she said. "Maybe not."

I didn't know much about the pecking order at a casino, but I couldn't imagine that standing outside and breathing bus fumes while checking in a bunch of buses would be a prized position. I didn't want to show how much I didn't know, so I let her remark slide.

"Pretty good crowd," Tara said. "The word must be getting out about the Snow Mountain concert."

"You know more about the casino business than I ever will," I said. "How in the world did Johnnie Koscko get them to come down here for a concert?"

She opened a tube of pink lipstick and leaned her face near to the vanity mirror behind the sun visor. "I hear that some of his old mob buddies had some favors to call in. They thought they'd give this place a little jump-start."

"Old buddies? I never knew the Las Vegas mob was sentimental."

"Get real, Jack. They'll come in here and make a big splash. Then they'll take their part of the cash and run. They might have had a few laughs with Johnnie the Dime out in Vegas, but to them money's money."

"Are you saying some Las Vegas group owns this place? Koscko talks like he owns all three rings of this circus plus the elephants."

She ran her tongue across her front teeth, still looking into the mirror. "You don't find one-man shows in this business anymore. One maybe two at the most. They're all incorporated these days. This joint's nothing more than a setup for a few players in Vegas to turn a quick buck. They'll pull in some crowds with groups like Snow Mountain, keep the place open and keep the creditors off their ass until they can double their money, and then sell out before the banknotes start coming due. They do it all the time."

I didn't have the same take on the situation that Tara did. Johnny Koscko didn't talk like a man who was trying to make a quick hit and get out. But maybe I was reading him all wrong. Or maybe she knew something I didn't.

When incoming waves hit the seawall at the edge of the parking lot they rebound into the waves behind them, so instead of the timeless, soothing rhythm of waves lapping on sand there is the constant splatter and slosh of water against concrete which makes the smell of the sea even stronger. The breeze at water's edge was cooler than it had been inland and was blowing in hard enough for a pair of gray-backed gulls to hang motionless just above eye level fifty feet offshore. A wooden shrimp boat, a Biloxi lugger rigged with skimmer nets, purred as it drifted by the casino barge and left Bayou Caddy, headed out the channel for a night of shrimping out beyond Marienne Pass.

But Tara didn't notice any of this. She was studying every detail of Koscko's new combination sign and marquee, a free-standing giant tall as a three-story building and rising from the very center of the parking lot. It featured a big pot turned on its side with gold coins spilling out of it, bordered with neon tubing, a pattern of green and gold. The word "Jackpot" was written above the pot with "Bay" written below it. I had been out on Cat Island the week before, a good ten miles out in the Gulf, and I could see the thing plainly, could pick it out even among all the other lights on shore. The only good thing about it was that it was tall enough and bright enough to serve as a navigational marker for any boat trying to find the mouth of Bayou Caddy.

"Not bad," Tara said. "In fact, it's pretty cool."

"Oh, I don't know. I think they could have found room to stick a few hundred more lights somewhere. Maybe up and down that pole."

"It's a casino," she said as she pulled a litle 35-mm camera out of her purse. "What the hell you expect?"

The lighted messages on the marquee alternated between the Larry Raspberry and the Highsteppers show and the Snow Mountain concert. Tara lined up the image through the viewfinder, snapped two quick shots, and stuck the camera back into her purse. "Let's go inside," she said. "It's so humid here I feel like this dress is stuck to me."

As we walked I handed her the laminated ID card she'd need when she started the security audit. She glanced at it before clipping it to the side of her dress at the highest point of the slit that ran up the side to mid-thigh. "I guess you've told Johnnie the Dime that I'm back?"

"He didn't take the news very well," I said. "What's the problem between you two, anyway?"

"Koscko's the one with the problem."

I grasped her arm and stopped walking. "I'm supposed to keep you two from going to war with each other for the next week or so. It would help if I knew why he's so pissed at you. Why don't you help me out here?"

She smiled and brushed her finger across my lips. "I'm here to do a job and I don't want him or anybody else getting in my way. And that includes you, even if you do have a cute ass."

"Come on, Tara."

"I'm serious. It really *is* cute."

"Why does Koscko want to get you out of here?"

"Because I've been in Vegas for years and I know, like, all his secrets."

"What kind of secrets?"

"Like his real story back in Vegas," she said. "Like where he got his name."

THREE

So are you going to tell me about his name or not?" The plate-glass door opened to let us walk through. I instinctively paused for her to proceed, which drew a strange look.

"Maybe later," she said. "Let me get a few chips first."

"I thought you were about to die for a drink."

"They'll bring me one at the table."

"You better take off the security badge if you plan to gamble."

Jackpot Bay Casino was too new to have become seedy. There were no worn paths on the carpet, the paint was still shiny and still had a sweet smell. The curtains had neither faded nor begun to droop, and the cigarette smoke had not yet yellowed the walls or settled into the air-conditioning system. It was new enough and fresh enough that nobody noticed Johnnie the Dime's cheap and thin carpets, or his pressed wood furniture, or the loose seams in his vinyl wallpaper.

It was an afternoon crowd, most of them early-bird retirees from the assisted-living center over in Ocean Springs who all came in on the same bus, every one of them hunched over a slot machine. I went to a stool at the bar and ordered a Barq's and Tara went straight to the craps table just beyond the brass rail that separates the bar from the gaming area. That table was the only real action on the floor, and eight loud players were standing around making two-chip bets and working this tightly packed brunette cocktail waitress into a case of sore feet and exhaustion.

The shooter was a fireplug in tan Sans-A-Belt slacks and an aqua and yellow tropical shirt with gray hair almost shaved on the sides and a tattoo on each forearm, sure signs of retired military. He was a loud, laughing, life-of-the-party type who kept holding the dice up to this big-busted redhead at his elbow for a kiss. Had a strong run of four straight rolls without making point before finally crapping out with a six/one combination. He was rewarded with a squeeze from the redhead and a round of applause, which he acknowledged by killing what was left of his drink and holding both arms straight up.

He passed the dice to Tara, who had been standing back and observing the action until then. She held the dice next to her ear and shook them, looked over at me, and started smiling. She took in a deep breath and let it out slowly, like some cocky late-inning reliever with a big lead who was about to step to the mound to throw his 98-mile-an-hour heat.

The table had 2X odds and a skinny stickman with a wispy moustache who was paying a whole lot more attention to the rear end of the roving cocktail waitress than to the game. Tara set her chips on the rail in a stack. Laid two chips on the Pass Line, gave the dice a final shake, and hit a natural seven for even money.

She left the original two chips where they were. She put one of her new chips onto the "Any Craps" line at seven-to-one and put the other new chip on the "Any Eleven" line at fifteen-to-one. So if she hit another seven, she'd break even. And if she crapped out she'd lose at the "Pass Line" and at "Any Eleven," but win seven at the "Any Craps." If she hit an eleven she'd lose the other three bets she had working, but the odds on the "Any Eleven" are fifteen-to-one. Sure, they were sucker bets, but she was just having a little fun. At the worst she could roll four, five, nine, or a ten and have a hard point to make. But with a point of six or eight the odds that she would bust would only be six-to-five in the house's favor.

Tara rattled the dice around in the cup a long time and started doing a little dance, which the guy in the tropical shirt liked a lot. So did the stickman. Tropical shirt started dancing along with her as she held the dice cup over her head and shook it like a maracca.

The crowd started clapping in unison. She began shaking the cup along with their rhythm as it grew faster and faster and faster. The clapping and the shaking became a steady rattle and the crowd started whooping and hollering.

The noise rose in volume and pitch. Got so loud the blue hairs over at the slots actually looked up from their slot machines. When it peaked, Tara swept the cup downward and slammed the dice against the opposite railing. The stickman announced that Tara's spot was an eight. She immediately put her maximum of four chips on a "Free Odds" side bet.

She made point on her second roll. The crowd, which had doubled in size, cheered and whistled. She scooped up her chips, kissed tropical shirt on the cheek, and handed the dice to a kid in jeans who was so entranced by the whole thing, and by her in particular, that it took him a second or two to realize she was talking to him. The crowd pleaded for her to stay, to at least finish her roll, but but she begged off. Dropped several chips in front of the stickman as a tip. They applauded as she walked away.

"That was some show," I said as she sat on the stool beside me.

"A craps table is one hell of a a rush when it goes right." She laid her hand on my knee and squeezed. "Next best thing to sex."

"That good, huh? No wonder these places make so much money." She rubbed the top of my thigh. "Can I get you something?"

She leaned in close and whispered in my ear and told me exactly what I could get for her, in unmistakable detail. Made my pulse jump a few beats. "I was talking about something from the bar," I said.

She laughed and kept fondling my knee as she ordered a Summer Storm, this pink, fruity house drink that comes in a big stem glass and is served with a straw. There was a squeal over at one of the slot machines, and when I glanced over there I saw Clyde decked out in a navy blazer and a tie, his floorman's badge clipped to his breast pocket. He was standing with his thumbs hitched in his pants pockets, working over a jawful of gum and looking at us.

"Tara, maybe we ought to talk about this somewhere else. Clyde Dubardo is watching us."

She smiled and I felt a tickle as she moved her fingers up the inside of my thigh. "Well let's give him something to see."

I caught her hand. "We better act like professionals as long as the client is watching. Koscko would love to have some reason to get rid of both of us."

"Screw him." She sipped her drink and reached for her purse. "I was just trying to have some fun."

"The craps table is the most fun you're likely to have in here." I swept my hand to indicate the gaming area "So what do you think about the Jackpot Bay Casino so far?"

"What do you know about slot machines?"

"They're hungry little bastards that flash in your face and ring in your ears until you feed them."

"Look around out there," she said. "Count up the white lights you see on top of some of the machines."

I looked out over the floor and noticed several such lights at various points around the floor. I had never paid any attention to them before. "I see six. What does that mean?"

"It means the floor boss isn't keeping up with business. Every one of those white lights means the machine is either out of chips or not working. Either way, six machines showing a service light at the same time is way too many."

"I don't guess it's possible that they've had six winners," I said.

"Not all at the same time. Not unless somebody's working this place over with a monkey's paw."

"What's a monkey's paw?"

The bartender, who had been sneaking peeks at Tara's legs as he ran the blender, set the frothy pink drink in front of her with something of a flourish.

"It's a flasher you can stick up in the machine that you can set off by remote control. It triggers a photoelectric switch that opens the money chute." She took a long sip of her drink. "You really don't know squat about this stuff, do you?"

"Never claimed to."

"So I guess they just hired you for your looks."

"I've already told you why they hired me for this job."

"Oh, yeah. You're the peacekeeper. That means you're supposed to keep me happy, right? You know how you could make me happy?"

I had to smile. The woman was relentless. "Weren't you going to tell me about Johnnie Koscko and how he got his name?"

"Hey, at last they decide to service the machines." She pointed to this chunky, mannish young woman. Dull blond hair, long on top but so short on the sides it appeared to be shaved. She wore a light blue shirt with the Jackpot Bay logo above the pocket and a pair of twill pants with a cell phone clipped to the belt. She was carrying a pair of canvas bags, one in each hand. "Take a good look at those bags."

"They look heavy," I said. "What's in them?"

"Those are chips to refill all those empty slot machines. You notice anything wrong?"

"Look like good, strong bags to me."

"The damn bags aren't even sealed. God, it's no wonder this place is losing money." She pulled lightly on the straw. "You need to try one of these."

"Let's get back to where Koscko got his name."

"Fine, if that's what you're interested in." She pulled out a pink plastic lighter.

"I already know his last name's not really Koscko," I said. "It's Koscovanovich. He's a Slavonian from over in Biloxi. He calls himself Koscko because he thinks it sounds more Vegas."

"That sounds like something he'd do," she said. "But I was talking about the Johnnie-the-Dime part. You know where that came from?"

"I'd guess it's a mob name. Sounds like he's a guy who maybe can make a phone call and get things done."

"Is that what he's told you?"

"I've never mentioned it to him. It never has seemed like the right time for me to ask if he got his nickname because he could make a phone call and order a mob hit."

"This drink is really good," she said as she took a long sip. "Is that a Coke you're drinking?"

"I'm not in the mood for anything stronger," I said. "So has the name got something to do with how much he bets?"

She lit a cigarette and looked toward the rows of slot machines. "Koscko was a mobster wannabe who worked for years as floorman at the Nugget. Somehow he got to know Dean Martin and when the old Rat Pack was in town he ran their errands, fetched their drinks, that kind of stuff. So naturally he met some of the Mafia types. The reason they kept him around was because he could get on the phone and line up women for them. That's why they call him Johnnie the Dime. Doesn't have a thing to do with any mob action."

The bartender came over, but Tara shook her head, so I waved him off. Maybe she was right. I could see where Koscko wouldn't want that story making the rounds in his old hometown. Wouldn't help his tough guy image one bit.

"Have you told that story to anybody over here?" I asked.

"Nobody except you."

"It's probably best if we don't spread it."

"Yeah, sure," she said and pointed across the room. "What the hell's happening over there with Clyde?"

Clyde and this young man in a long-sleeved white shirt had squared off, and the guy was giving Clyde a nonstop earful. I couldn't hear much of what he was saying, but I did make out the word "thief" a few times. The guy was clean-cut and broad-shouldered, tall as Clyde but not as bulky, and was punctuating every other word with a stab of his finger just inches from Clyde's nose. He was getting louder and redder by the minute.

"Might be a sore loser," I said.

"I'm sure Clyde'll handle this in his usual professional manner."

"The guy doesn't look like he's drunk."

"You mean the guy in the white shirt," she said, "or are you talking about Clyde?"

Across the way, the guy stuck his finger a little too close and Clyde snatched it. He twisted it downward and the guy screamed as he went to his knees. Clyde grabbed the back of the guy's collar and pulled the guy's hand around behind him in a half-Nelson and jerked him up from the floor.

I jumped off my stool and hustled toward them as Clyde began shoving the man toward the front door. The man stumbled and almost lost his balance but Clyde pulled him upright and kept pushing. I fell into step beside them.

"Hey, Clyde," I said, "take it easy."

"Stay the hell outta this, Delmas!"

"Let go of me!" the guy shouted.

"Why don't you just let this man walk out of here on his own power?" I said. "It'll be a lot better to discuss this outside without the show of force."

"Damn you!" the man shouted. "You're gonna give me that money!"

"Let's calm down," I said.

"He owes me seven hundred dollars, and I'm here to collect it."

"You're crazy, man," Clyde said.

"Naw, *you're* the crazy one if you think you're gonna stiff me and get away with it!"

"Come on, you two," I said. "You're disturbing all these other folks in here."

The guy in the white shirt stomped Clyde's foot. This broke the grip and triggered a loud string of curses. He grabbed for his injured foot and got his head down just quick enough to avoid a wicked roundhouse swing.

The guy stepped toward him, fists flying in wide circles, wild swings delivered so hard I could almost hear them whipping through the air. A left, and a right, and a left. Clyde leaned away from this steady advance and was a little off balance as he threw up his forearm to block and caught a fist right at the elbow, a punch with so much force that it knocked him backwards. He stumbled and fell hard, flat on his back. The guy charged like he was going to jump on top of Clyde.

I crouched and lunged and blindsided the guy. Locked my elbows and shoved hard, like in the old blocking sled drills. Caught him chest-high with both hands and knocked him sideways straight into a craps table. The three players around the table and the stickman yelled and scattered. Their stacks of chips flew off the railing into the air like Mardi Gras beads, and two oversized cups of beer hit the floor, splattering suds and golden liquid across ten feet of carpet.

The railing caught him just above mid-thigh. His momentum flipped him forward and he fell onto the table face-first. I jumped behind him and laid across his back, pinning his chest against the green felt surface. He strained and pushed and growled in frustration as he tried to elbow me off him.

"I'll KILL him! I'll kill that son of a bitch!"

"Hey, come on, man," I said. "Calm down!"

"That no-good lyin' thief!"

"Get outta my way, Delmas!" Clyde had picked himself up and was standing beside us. He was reaching into his coat.

"Back off, Clyde," I said. "Don't make this any worse than it is."

"Move ya ass outta the way, dammit!"

"You pull a gun and they jerk the license for this place. How you think Uncle Johnnie's going to take that the day before the Snow Mountain concert?"

"You cheated me, Clyde! You know you did!"

"Would you shut up for a minute?" I said.

"Hey, everybody!" the guy yelled. "Listen to me! This place'll cheat ya outta your last nickle!"

"Shut him the hell up," Clyde said.

"Y'all better get outta this clip joint if you know what's good for you!"

I pressed the heel of my hand against the side of his face. "That's enough, man."

"This is none of your business, Delmas."

"Clyde, do you know this guy?"

Everybody in the place had stopped gambling and was staring at the three of us. The only sound was the soft ringing of a few unoccupied slot machines. Clyde snorted and straightened his tie. "Get him the hell outta my sight," he said as he turned his back to us. "Everything's okay, folks! Sorry for the inconvenience. Have a free round on the house!"

The young man was exhausted and breathing hard, damp with sweat and still shaking. "He's not gonna get away with this."

"What's your name?" I asked.

"Robert Earl."

"I'm going to let you up, Robert Earl. Okay?"

He nodded his head. I eased off his back, keeping both hands up in case he tried something. He pushed himself off the table like he was doing a pushup.

"Don't even think about trying anything funny," I said. "I'm going to walk you to the door, and I want you to leave."

"I can walk myself."

He stood and rolled his shoulders and wiped his hand across his mouth. Clyde was on the other side of the room sitting at one of the slots along the far wall, resting both hands on his knees and staring at us. Robert Earl clenched his teeth and stared back, wasn't backing off one bit.

"You go on home and cool down."

"He owes me seven hundred bucks."

"So get a lawyer and sue him," I said, "but for right now, it's over."

Robert Earl's eyes smoldered just below the flash point as he glared at Clyde. "You wrong, mister," he said in a lowered voice. "It ain't over. Not by a long shot."

FOUR

Hey, I am so totally impressed!" Tara smiled as she nibbled on her bottom lip. "You ready for that drink now?"

"Can I get you something, sir?" the bartender asked.

"Let me start out with a glass of water, and then bring me the biggest draft you've got."

She reached out and rubbed my arm just above my elbow. "My earlier offer still stands."

The bartender set down a frosty schooner of beer on a round cardboard coaster with the Heineken logo. He twisted the top off a plastic bottle of Kentwood water and handed it to me. I slugged down half of the bottle in a single breath.

"Where'd you learn to handle yourself like that?" Tara had started running her finger up and down my forearm.

"Learned the basics in the Army MPs." I killed the rest of the water. "But I've had a lot of practice since then. And for some strange reason, this practice usually comes in a bar somewhere."

"You love it, don't you?" She took a final drag off her cigarette and crushed it into a green plastic ashtray.

"You mean fighting? You're asking me if I love fighting?"

"I mean any kind of action, especially if there's a little danger involved. You really get into it, don't you?"

I shrugged off the suggestion. I never had thought about it that way, or at least I don't remember ever thinking about it. Nobody had ever asked me straight out if I enjoyed danger. And if they had asked me I would have tilted my head back and given them my best incredulous look and said of *course* not. That's what we civilized and college-educated types are supposed to say, isn't it? At least that's what my ex kept on telling me.

But somehow this private eye business that I have come to love keeps putting me into these situations that no seemingly sane person would want to be in. In a typical month or two I get threatened, chased, beat up, and shot at more than a normal person will in a lifetime. But for some reason I never could explain to myself, much less my ex-wife, I keep going back to it. I mean, how crazy is that? How crazy is it to work in a business that routinely requires you to carry a damn gun to protect yourself?

And yet the closest I ever came to going really crazy was not when I was pulling some eight-hour shift watching the door of a motel room and peeing into a coffee can so I wouldn't miss the three seconds it would take for somebody to go in or out of the room. No, the greatest threat to my sanity came right after I got married when I spent those two godawful years behind a desk in Memphis working in this bank owned by my then–father-in-law and putting up with all those buttoned-down, money-grubbing, back-stabbing shit hooks with their MBAs and their leased Volvos.

"After we finish these drinks," Tara said, "why don't you drive me to my hotel?"

"You never did tell me which one you're staying in."

"Which one's the closest?" She laced her fingers in mine. "I wouldn't want to make you wait too long."

That caught me off guard, and she could tell it. I couldn't think of an instant comeback, so I just gave her hand one quick squeeze and smiled at her. I mean, what was I supposed to do, play hard to get or something? And how the hell do you do that anyway? Even a few seconds later when I had gathered my wits, everything I thought about saying sounded pretty lame, and that got me to feeling a little flustered. So I just sat there with this dumb smile running my finger around the rim of the big beer schooner.

My ex-wife once told me about a book titled *The Rules.* It told girls how to catch a guy by playing it cool, by holding out and making him run the obstacle course. That book popped into my mind, and I wished like hell I had a copy in my pocket. I'd have sure ducked into the men's room for a little speed reading. I mean, I bad needed to find out what kind of strategy you're supposed to use when you all of a sudden find yourself on the other side of the ball.

"When I was here a few months ago," she said, "you were about to go see your ex-wife."

"That's not exactly right. My daughter had been down here on a visit, and I was just taking her to Dauphin Island because that's where her mama wanted to pick her up to take her back home."

"So what about it, did you screw her or not?"

"I don't know why I'm even telling you this, but it's over between her and me. She's about to get married to this doctor up in Memphis."

"So I guess that means you're over those hang-ups you had about cheating on her."

"We weren't married, so I didn't have any hang-ups."

She squeezed my hand. "Could have fooled me."

The eye contact was getting pretty intense. The girl wasn't shy, not by a long shot. All of a sudden I got real thirsty, so I called time out and quaffed about half of that big schooner. Knocked it down so fast that it made my molars hurt and gave me this mild head rush.

For a second or two that seemed to clear things up some. The thought passed through my brain that maybe I had been reading Tara all wrong. She had been so blatant that she was probably just messing with my head and I didn't realize what she was doing. Hell, for all I know that's just the way northern girls are, playing mind games and all. Yeah, maybe she was just all talk and if I started coming on strong, it would back her down.

About that same time, she pulled this cherry out of her drink and started running her tongue all over it as she winked at me. And, son, there wasn't even one *little* bit of backing down in those blue-gray eyes. But after I killed the rest of that beer, that look wasn't so disconcerting anymore. Not at all. In fact, I was almost getting used to it. Another one of those cold beers, and I could see where this might even turn out to be fun.

"Excuse me." The voice came from behind us. "Could I speak to you for a second?'

Tara apparently never heard a thing. She kept gazing at me as she squeezed the cherry between her front teeth and popped off the stem. It was bewitching is what I'd call it.

And that ain't all bad.

"Aren't you the man who was involved in that fight a few minutes ago?" There was a tone of impatience.

I turned and damned if it wasn't the new manager of the place. He had walked up to us without me seeing or hearing a thing. Earlier in the day I hadn't noticed him being so tall, at least two inches taller than I am.

"It wasn't really a fight," I said, "and can we talk about it later?"

"Don't I know you?"

"I don't think so," I said.

"Didn't I see you in Mr. Koscko's office?"

Tara giggled and started tickling my ankle with her big toe. Made the hair on my leg rise. Rulon caught the gesture, but pretended he didn't see it and just stood there until I gave in.

"Tara Stocklin," I said, "this is the new manager here. What's your name again?"

"Rulon Hornbeck."

"Well, Rulon, you're about to get to know Tara real well. She's the security auditor who came here from Las Vegas to check out this operation."

Rulon took Tara's hand, kissed it just below the knuckles, and pressed it against his cheek as he spoke. "*Bienvenue au Casino de Jackpot Bay, mademoiselle. Vous êtes belle et je suis à votre service.*"

"*Merci, monsieur,*" she said. "*Où est l'hôtel le plus près?*"

He smiled and winked. "*Ç'est urgent?*"

"Hell, yes, it's urgent," she said. "I've been trying to get this guy into the sack for the past hour."

"Well, the nearest hotel for such an emergency is out on Highway 90 at the turn off to the interstate."

"She's got a real sense of humor," I said. "Ought to be on the casino comedy circuit. Is there something I can do for you?"

"Haven't I seen you in here before?" Rulon asked her.

"You weren't around the last time she was here," I said. "What do you need?"

"As I said earlier, I hear that my floorman got into an altercation of some sort a little while ago."

"So Clyde's the floorman," Tara said. "That explains all the unattended machines."

"He got into an argument with a customer and tried to shove him out of here," I said. "I just tried to calm things down some."

"That was no customer, I'm sad to say."

"I need another drink," Tara said. "You want me to order you one of these?"

"I may need for you to give me some kind of statement about what happened," Rulon said. "This isn't the first time Clyde's tried to act like a tough guy and showed his ass in front of the whole world."

"I don't know who was at fault. Don't know what happened before Clyde grabbed the guy. He may have deserved to get kicked out for all I know."

"Time out," Tara said, "do you want to try one of these Summer Storms or not?"

Across the room, Clyde was standing behind the stickman at one of the craps tables. He cut his eyes in our direction a few times, but tried not to appear to be watching us.

"Is it true he pulled a gun?" Rulon asked.

I shrugged and signaled the bartender for two of the fruit drinks.

"I don't think he ought to be allowed to carry a gun," Rulon said. "He's got a hair-trigger and one of these days he's going to shoot somebody."

"I didn't say he pulled any gun."

Our drinks came and Rulon told the bartender that the house was picking up the tab. "I should think your company would worry about the lawsuit if he shot somebody."

"Good point," I said. "Let me think about it for a while, and we can talk about it tomorrow."

Rulon lowered his eyes toward my feet where Tara had started playing with my ankle again. "You do that," he said with a frown. "I'll just go back to the office and leave you two alone so you can think in peace."

He stepped back and for a moment regarded Tara as if he were trying to recall when and where he had seen her before. Then he turned and took several quick little steps toward the casino floor, pausing long enough to rearrange the chairs at a table by the brass railing. Clyde had not moved from his position behind the craps table, and was standing with his hands clasped in front of him, staring at Tara and me.

"You were right," Tara said. "Rulon's not what I though Johnnie the Dime would want as a manager."

"Koscko's convinced himself that Rulon'll add a touch of class to this place. Thinks he'll bring in some high rollers from Europe."

Tara tossed back her head and laughed out loud. "Oh, God! That's a good one. So he thinks that guy we just talked to is going to bring in the whales? Is that what he told you?"

"Apparently Rulon worked in a casino in Monte Carlo."

"Really?" she asked. "Which casino was it?"

"Who knows?"

Her shoulders shook with soundless laughter as she reached for another Virginia Slims. "Koscko is, like, absolutely delusional."

"By the way, what's a whale?"

"Have you ever been to Monte Carlo?" she asked.

I shook my head and reached for the big red drink she had ordered for me. "Is that by any chance where you learned to speak French?"

"I worked there for three years. It's the top of the pyramid when it comes to gambling. Believe me, the Jackpot Bay Casino will never even be in the same league. There's no way this place could ever compete even with some of the bigger places in Biloxi, y'know, much less some world-class operation." She flicked the lighter three times and got nothing more than sparks. "Take a look around. How many of those people at those slots with their polyester pants and their big plastic cups would come back if the management decided that the men had to wear a jacket, or if they raised the table stakes to twenty bucks a pop? I mean, Koscko's just talking crazy."

"You still haven't told me what a whale is."

"A whale is a high roller, y'know, a big spender. An Arab oil sheik, that's a whale. Dot-com billionaires, big-time investors, those types. The kind who anchor their hundred-foot yachts in Monaco Harbor and ferry to shore by helicopter."

"You see any in here?" I asked.

She kept laughing as she flicked her lighter once more and still couldn't get a flame. "Johnnie the Dime needs to stick with the all-you-can-eat crowd."

"He's got some British earl who's supposed to be coming in for a few days, and the head honcho of Bay St. Louis society has told Koscko's new manager that they will be making an appearance here. And then there's the Snow Mountain performance. Maybe Johnnie figures everything's looking up."

"Take a deep breath and think about what you just said." She tosssed the useless lighter into a trash can behind the bar. "A British earl, Johnnie the Dime Koscko, and the Snow Mountain rock-and-roll band. Does it sound to you like they fit under the same tent?"

"What do I know?" I said. "Are you telling me they don't have rock-and-roll bands at the Casino de Monte Carlo?"

A woman screamed from somewhere across the room, a panic scream, shrill as a referee's whistle. It set off a chorus of screams and shouts that rippled across the floor. Robert Earl, the guy who had been in the shouting match with Clyde, was back. Standing tall in the main aisle between the flashing, ringing banks of slot machines, holding a snubbed-nose revolver in one hand and a boxy, large-caliber blue-steeled automatic in the other.

And he had both of them raised and ready to shoot.

FIVE

Robert Earl pointed the big automatic straight up and pulled the trigger. The blast reverberated through the room, setting off a stampede of squealing, crying gamblers. The guy in the tropical shirt who had been at the craps table with Tara bolted toward the back of the room, dragging the busty, screaming redhead behind him.

The rest of the players raced to the exits, spilling their plastic change cups, knocking their chairs over, and splattering their beers and Cokes and margaritas against the flashing red and yellow and green faces of the slot machines. I pulled Tara down to the floor.

The smell of burnt sulfur and cordite drifted across the room. The juices kicked in and my heart began pounding as I took a quick mental inventory of places to hide, of escape routes through the maze of machines. I tried to think of something I could get my hands on—a whisky bottle, a carving knife, a bar stool—anything I could use as a weapon if he got close enough. But that was a hell of a long shot. Nothing I could reach was any match for that cannon he was holding.

He walked slowly down the aisle toward the middle of the gaming area, calm as a beachcomber, oblivious to the few slow and old gamblers still in the room as they made their pitiful and lonely bids to get out alive. A fat woman in stretch pants and a foot cast from recent surgery lumbered toward the red lighted exit sign still clinging to her rattling cup of chips. A shriveled, gray, wide-eyed Navy vet in a white cap with *USS O'Brien* across the front and scrambled-egg yellow braiding on the bill, strained forward in his wheelchair, grunting as he shoved the wheels as hard as he could, but making no better time than a baby could make on a tricycle.

Tara and I were blocked off from the exits, couldn't get anywhere without a long run across way too much open space. We stayed low and when Robert Earl turned his back to us, we scooted behind the bar. The bartender was on his hands and knees peeping around the end of the bar, keeping his eyes trained on Robert Earl and pulling his head back in every time it looked like Robert Earl was turning in our direction. We stayed on our feet, crouched low, and looked at him over the top of the bar.

"There's not a gun back here, is there?" she whispered.

"If there was, that bartender down on the floor would have already have it in his hand."

She reached down and pulled off her shoes. "The next time he turns around I can run over behind that row of machines."

"And do what? Forget it, you're going to just sit here until the cops come."

"I can get behind him."

She had begun breathing hard. Her eyes were wide, pupils dilated. But there was no fear. In fact, she had almost that same look I saw when she had been closing in on me at the bar just minutes earlier. Hell, she was loving this whole scene.

Robert Earl reached the center of the room. He stopped and looked all around. The few people still in the room were hunkered down behind whatever was closest. The only sound was the constant trill of bells from the slot machines. He put the revolver in his hip pocket, keeping the automatic in his right hand. He slid back the chamber, slipped his finger inside the trigger guard, and raised the pistol.

"He's about to shoot himself," Tara whispered. "Oh, wow!"

"Stay low, dammit! That gun's an automatic and he can wheel around and pop off three or four rounds at us before you can blink."

"Clyde Dubardo!" Robert Earl shouted. "You sorry, cheatin' piece of shit! You get your ass out here and give me my money now!"

He looked up, spotted one of the spy cameras on the ceiling, took aim, and blasted the thing into fifteen hundred pieces. We ducked behind the bar out of reflex. Damned if an M9 fired in an enclosed room, even a big one, doesn't nearly burst your eardrums. The dozen or so people still pinned down at various spots around the main room shouted like fools and gave away their positions, but he paid them no mind.

"Hey," I said to the bartender as quietly as I could, "don't they have any guards on duty?"

"We got a buncha rent-a-cops. No telling where they are."

We eased back up to peer over the top of the bar. "Have you got any kind of weapon we can use?" I whispered.

"I've got a four-inch knife with a plastic handle I use to slice lemons and stuff. You're welcome to it."

Somebody hit a switch and killed the overhead lights and the room darkened, lit only by the flickering pink and yellow lights of the slot machines, not much brighter than the glow of nightlights in a baby's nursery. Robert Earl was facing us, but not seeming to look at us. The big pistol was dangling at his side. Behind him, Clyde ran into the room at full speed, hit the floor, rolled over a couple of times, knocked over a table, and scooted behind one of the machines. Robert Earl turned toward the sound, but probably didn't realize it was Clyde. At least he didn't act as if he did.

Judging from the way Robert Earl had casually lifted that gun and popped that overhead camera dead center, I knew he could handle a pistol. He had taken some training somewhere, because he didn't even flinch when the blast from that shot nearly burst everyone's eardrums. So if Clyde was planning to be a cowboy, he may have picked the wrong corral. Trouble was, if he stayed where he was and started shooting at Robert Earl, he'd also be shooting on a straight line toward Tara and me.

"Robert Earl!" I yelled. "Drop the gun!"

"What the hell are you doing?" Tara said.

"Nobody's been hurt, Robert Earl. Let's keep it that way!"

"You tell Clyde to gimme my money, and then everything will be all right!" He moved his head around trying to figure out where I was in the dim light. "That's all I want!"

"Let's keep him talking until help gets here," I whispered to Tara.

"Now that the whole world knows where we are," she said, "we don't have any other choice."

"Look straight behind him." I pointed toward Clyde who was on one knee, peering around a slot machine. He was holding a revolver, pointing it straight up. The lights from a neon sign reflected off the silver barrel. "Do you really want Clyde to start shooting in this direction?"

"Oh, shit! What is that fool doing?"

"We don't need any gunplay," I said. "This bar won't stop any bullets."

"It's all right, Robert Earl!" Tara shouted as she raised up and looked over the bar. "It's all a misunderstanding!"

"He owes me that money!" Robert Earl's voice quivered, just on the brink of tears. In the dim, pink light, the shadows on his face gave him a gaunt and haggard look. "It ain't right, dammit!"

"You know this guy?" I asked the bartender.

"I've seen him around," he said. "He might even work here. Maybe in the business office or something."

"Do you have any idea what he's talking about?"

He shook his head no.

"Just lay down the guns, Robert Earl." Tara's voice was warm, soothing, almost inviting. "Nobody will get hurt, and you'll get your money."

Robert Earl had started wiping his face and eyes with his hand. He walked toward us, out of the shadows, to a blackjack table not thirty feet from us and leaned against it.

"You mean it?" He was sniffling and cleared his throat. "You promise?"

"I promise," she said. "Just be cool, man."

"I don't want to hurt nobody. I just want my seven hundred dollars."

"You'll get it," she said. "Just lay down the gun."

Robert Earl eased the automatic toward the felt surface of the table, looking at Tara and me. He was breathing through his mouth, and he started nodding his head. "Okay. Okay. I'll pay for the overhead camera I shot up. That's gonna cost me more than I'll get from Clyde. But I just want that thieving son of a bitch to have to count out seven hundred . . ."

"DROP IT, ASSHOLE!" Clyde yelled as he popped up, squared off, and drew a bead.

There was an instant tightening around Robert Earl's eyes, instant resolve, instant rekindled anger. He gripped the big gun, twisted his shoulders toward the voice, jerked his head around, trying to zero in on the source of the challenge.

"NO!" I screamed. "DON'T SHOOT!"

SIX

In the dim light, the shots from Clyde's gun glowed like yellow showers of sparks from a blast furnace. The first one might have hit home; it staggered Robert Earl. But it didn't put him down. The second shot took out a row of stem glasses in a rack over our heads, raining shards of glass down on us, tinkiling like wind chimes and sending Tara and me back to the floor. Two more shots came in rapid order and the echoes of the blasts bounced off the walls. Then it stopped.

Tara pushed up from the floor, but before she could stand I grabbed her arm and pulled her back down. "Don't stick your head up over that bar," I whispered. "He may still be out there with that gun. And if he is, he's probably good and pissed by now."

"I think Clyde took him out with that first shot."

"Shhh!"

The room stood silent except for the irregular chiming of the slots, sounded like a xylophone being played by a two-year-old. I crawled to the end of the bar, stayed low, and eased forward just far enough to see the gaming area. Robert Earl was down on the floor, on his side and struggling to raise his head. The pistol was a yard or two away from his feet. Clyde was still across the room at the edge of the bank of slot machines, but he was now standing and had a two-handed grip on his pistol which was pointed at the downed man. Robert Earl groaned and fell flat, the side of his face thudding against the floor.

I ran to him and checked for a pulse. Clyde came over and kicked the pistol across the floor as he kept a steady aim at Robert Earl's head, like Robert Earl was going to jump up off the floor or something. He was still alive, but he was losing a lot of blood and since it was a chest wound, there was no way to apply either tourniquet or compress. He was unconscious but still breathing, so CPR wouldn't help. I tapped the side of his face and shouted at him and tried to wake him up, to keep him from slipping away.

Robert Earl Bailey, thirty-two, died at the trauma unit of Gulf Regional Hospital in Gulfport at 6:42 P.M. from a combination of traumatic shock and loss of blood from two bullet wounds to the chest.

Bailey was a native of Picayune, Mississippi, and a graduate of Hancock Central High School, where he was a class favorite and two-sport letterman. He had joined the Marine Corps right out of high school and spent three years in Camp Lejeune as a rifle instructor. Clean record, no priors. Not even moving traffic violations.

Robert Earl Bailey earned an associates degree in accounting from Jefferson Davis Community College three years ago and was in the payroll department of Mississippi Power Company over in Gulfport until Jackpot Bay Casino hired him as head of purchasing six months earlier. He was described by his coworkers as "pleasant" and "mild-mannered," but several noted that he had "been keeping to himself lately."

Bailey had been married for six years. He and his wife, Brenda, had two daughters, Tiffany, three years old, and Amber, eighteen months.

He was a churchgoer, devoted to his children, and a big fan of the New Orleans Saints and the Mississippi Sea Wolves hockey team. He had resigned from his position with Jackpot Bay Casino eight days before his death.

All sheriff's offices are about the same to me, no matter if I'm in Chicago or Memphis or Hancock County, Mississippi. There's always the smell of coffee brewing in some cheap plastic coffeemaker. There are phones ringing nonstop and hard-soled shoes tapping on concrete floors. The walls are always gray or pale green, and the place is always too cold to suit me.

There's a staleness, this filmy feeling from air that has been recycled so many times, and it gives me the urge to open every window and door in the place and air it out. There are the same slurred protests of the drunks who have never had more that two beers, and the same shrill outrage of some woman swearing out yet another assault complaint against a husband or a live-in, a complaint everyone knows is going nowhere. Denver, Atlanta, or Bay St. Louis—it's all the same.

I was seated in the hallway in a steel chair with a worn-out, padded vinyl seat, waiting for the detectives to finish taking statements from everyone who was present at the shooting. Tara and the bartender had already given theirs and left. I had given mine too, such as it was, and I was waiting for my brother to talk about the call I had already received from the front office at Bayou Casualty. Johnnie Koscko had beaten the front office to the punch and had already called Neal to sit with Clyde while the DA took his statement.

So it was the craps player in the tropical shirt, the veteran in the wheelchair, the stickman from the craps table Tara had played, Johnnie Koscko, and me. We were lined up outside the interregation room sitting in armchairs that had the look of surplus stuff from the Keesler Air Force Base, drinking canned soft drinks and thumbing through two-year-old *Outdoor Life* magazines. Johnnie the Dime and the white-haired veteran in the wheelchair were bitching about the state of the world, speculating that the dead man might have been some kind of al Qaeda terrorist in disguise.

"So, I tell my friends in Vegas I'm going back home to the quiet life," Koscko said. "Gotta get out of Vegas, I say. Gotta get get back where things are normal. Y'unnerstand? Normal. Yeah, normal my ass!"

"We shoulda learned our lesson at Pearl Harbor," the vet said. "But, hell no. And then we get caught with our pants down again with that World Trade Center. Jeez, we ain't gonna never learn."

"So, what happens?" Johnnie says. "I try to start up a classy place and some wacko comes in and starts shooting up the joint."

"From what I understand," I said, "that wacko you're talking about was a man named Robert Earl Bailey. And he was on your payroll up until a week ago."

"Well, who do you think I've gotta hire nowadays? You can't even check 'em out. You start askin' a few questions before you hire somebody, and the next thing you know they're suing ya for ever'thing you're worth. Y'unnerstand what I'm sayin'?"

"If it wasn't for them damn liberals on the Supreme Court," the vet said, "we could cut out all this stuff."

"That man was saying Clyde owed him some money," I said.

"So, I guess that gives the guy the right to come in and start shooting up the joint?" He pointed to the vet in the wheelchair. "Hell, there were innocent people all over the place. Am I right?"

"These thugs don't give a rat's ass about innocent people," the vet said. "It's just like them camel jockeys that blew up the Pentagon. What we gotta start doing is crackin' some heads."

"I'm trying to run a class operation. Y'follow me? I got a duke from England coming in. What if he'd a been in there today. Whadda ya think he'd go back and tell his buddies? This kinda stuff don't help me not one bit."

"They start crackin' a few heads and it'll cut out this monkey business," the vet said.

Koscko glanced down at his watch. "What the hell's taking them so long?"

"Mr. Koscko, your nephew just shot and killed a man. They usually ask quite a few questions when something like that happens."

"There ain't no telling how many lives got saved this afternoon," Koscko said. "Some lunatic busts in there popping off hot rounds left and right. I'm tellin' ya, if them passengers that them terrorists hijacked had been carryin' a few guns on 'em, them jets wouldn't have ever got close to that World Trade Center. That or the Pentagon, neither one."

"All I'm saying is that the detectives are going to have to ask him a lot of questions."

"Hell, Clyde didn't have no choice. Y'unnerstand? They oughta be givin' him a medal, but they're acting like he's a murderer or something. Having a few guys out on the floor who can take care of theirselves, now that's the kind of security a casino needs. Not all that high-priced crap like seventy overhead cameras that don't work half the time."

The guy in the tropical shirt bumped his head back against the wall and blew out a hard, loud breath. "I'm gonna spend my whole three-day weekend in a damn police station."

"Hey, no problem," Johnnie said as he scribbled on the back of a business card and handed it to him. "Go back to the Jackpot and give this to my manager. That's good for fifty bucks' worth of chips on the house."

The guy read the card and broke into a smile. "Sure thing, buddy. Thanks."

"Hey, you need to come to the big concert tomorrow. That is if they let me outta this place in time to get things set up. These headliner acts, they're all a little crazy, y'follow me? This Snow Mountain bunch has got this special way they want me to handle their money."

I shook my head to try to shut him up.

"They want to take the cash and . . ."

"Put it in the bank," I said. "Can we talk for a minute?" I tilted my head toward the far end of the hallway to indicate it was time for a private conference. I turned in that direction before he had time to ask questions.

"Those guys don't need to hear about any financial arrangements with that band," I said.

"What? Ya think these guys might try to knock over the place?"

"Tell me what you know about the guy who got killed," I said. "I understand he worked in your bookkeeping department."

"I don't even know them bean counters. I farmed out all that hiring shit to this group called Workforce, Incorporated. If Bayou Casualty's so damn worried about money being stolen, that's who they oughta be talkin' to. Y'unnerstand me? Hey, that Workforce group, they're bonded. Go after them."

"Yeah, sure," I said. "Who was his supervisor?"

"Why you need to know that?" Koscko lit the cigarette that dangled at the corner of his mouth. "Hell, the doc told me to quit smokin' and all this mess has got me started again."

"I've got to send a report back to the company."

"Here's a report for 'em. This nutcase comes in my place, starts shooting it up, and my floor manager blows him away before he can shoot a buncha customers. That's all the report you need. What're you gettin' at?"

I glanced back at the other guys as I pushed both palms down to try to get him to keep it quiet. "The guy had almost laid down his pistol when Clyde popped up and blew him away."

"Is that your story?"

"Mr. Koscko, the whole thing is probably on the surveillance tape."

"Screw him! He was a friggin' lunatic!"

"I'm not saying what's right or what's wrong, I'm just saying they've told me to start my investigation of this Robert Earl Bailey because they think there *might* be a lawsuit. It's just a precaution."

"Now you listen to me," he pointed at my face with the two fingers holding the cigarette, "that Bailey guy was the one who was in the wrong. If they want to sue me, let 'em sue. We'll take it to court and whip their ass."

"Mr. Koscko," I said, "you never know how a jury will react. The guy left a young widow behind, not to mention two small children."

"So you're sayin' we oughta settle out of court? Is that what I'm hearin'?"

"I don't know yet. That's why I need to do a report."

"Report? That's all I ever hear outta you guys. Hell, you already got that Tara Stocklin writin' up enough reports to fill up a storeroom."

"That's a different matter," I said.

"Come to think of it, she's probably behind this whole thing. She's the one who wants to settle, isn't she?"

"What on earth are you talking about?"

"That's exactly where this is coming from," he said. "She wants me to look bad, so she's sayin' we oughta admit we done something wrong."

"Tara's not involved with this."

"The hell she ain't! She's behind this whole thing!"

For the next few minutes, I tried to explain how there was a good chance a Hancock County jury might just find that Clyde, a casino employee, had been a little trigger-happy, how they might want to take care of those two baby girls whose daddy got shot when he was trying to collect some money he claims was owed to him by a big, rich casino. But I could almost see my words bouncing off Koscko's head. He glared at a spot on the floor and his jaw muscles flexed as he silently talked to himself.

"That gal's had her stinger out for me for a long time," he said.

"Nobody's out to get you, Mr. Koscko. Tara Stocklin doesn't even know about this stuff."

"Hey, I ain't nobody's fool," he said. "You better keep ya pants zipped up and listen to what I'm tellin' ya. I'm fightin' any damn lawsuit. Ain't gonna be no settlement."

"For all I care, you can get your ass sued from here to Islamabad. But if you expect Bayou Casualty to defend you in any lawsuit, I'm going to have to get some cooperation."

"Clyde didn't have no choice. He had to take that maniac out, and that's what he did. Period. End of story." He took a deep drag off his cigarette and thumped the ashes to the floor. "You and that Las Vegas slut better get on board with that idea, or your company'll never get another casino account, here or nowhere else. Y'hear what I'm tellin' ya?"

SEVEN

The door to the back room opened and Clyde walked in, grinning, chewing gum, and flashing a thumbs-up to his uncle. He whipped out his pocket comb and swept it straight back through his hair. Neal stepped into the room right behind him looking grim. Johnnie turned away from me and stepped over to give Clyde a big bear hug.

"What did they say?" Johnnie asked.

"They said I was a good shot."

"Clyde, let me warn you again," Neal said in a low voice. "You don't need to say anything about this to anybody. Especially not to the newspapers or the TV."

"So did they clear you or not?" Johnnie asked.

Clyde glanced at Neal then back at Johnnie and shrugged his shoulders.

"They haven't decided," Neal said.

"Well what the hell am I paying you for?"

"I'm trying to keep your nephew out of jail."

This female detective I had never seen before opened the door of the interregation room and called for the vet in the wheelchair. The bartender and the guy in the tropical shirt sighed in unison and sagged in their chairs like punctured beach balls.

"We need to get some things straight real fast," Neal said to

Clyde. "You could be facing some serious charges, and you need to start acting like it."

"Whaddya mean?" Johnnie said. "This has gotta be an open-and-shut case."

"I'll talk to you about it later," Neal said. "Right now, I'm talking to my client."

"The guy had a damn M9 automatic, for chrissake," Clyde said. "He shot the ga'damn thing in a crowded room and then he tried his best to shoot me."

Neal got to Clyde in two quick steps and clamped down on his shoulder. He had a look in his eyes that I had seen only once before, and that was many years ago. "I'll talk real slow this time," he said. "You shot a man in front of twenty witnesses. Any rookie cop could see that the guy was about to lay his weapon down. And you just jump up and blow him away. This thing might not be over yet, so shut the hell up."

My brother is six feet five inches, weighs about two seventy. Played offensive tackle up at Southern Miss and still works out four times a week. I've only seen him go ape-shit one time, and that one time I ended up flat on my back after crashing through a picket fence. Just before he threw me through that fence, he had given me the same look he was now giving Clyde.

"There's still a fifty-fifty chance the DA will go after an indictment," Neal said, "so if you say one wrong word and I find out about it, you can get yourself a new lawyer."

For just a moment, a moment you'd never notice unless you were watching his eyes, Clyde showed fear. But he snapped right back and took a real chance when he knocked Neal's hand away. "Get ya hand the hell offa me."

"I mean exactly what I just said. One wrong word and you get a new lawyer."

"C'mon," Koscko said, "let's get outta here."

"You hear me, Clyde?" Neal said.

"Mr. Koscko, you and your nephew need to wait right over there by that door." Roger Partridge, the sheriff, had just stepped out of the interregation room. "Don't leave this area, please."

"We gotta get back to work, Sheriff. Clyde's done told you all he knows."

"We'll let y'all leave just as soon as we can. But there's some people out in the lobby you don't need to see right now. I'd appreciate it if you'd stay where you are."

"You talkin' about reporters?" Johnnie asked. "I've been in the casino business a long time. I can handle the press."

"Mr. Koscko, what I just told Clyde goes for you too." Neal had cooled down, but only a little. "Don't be talking to the press. All you need to say is 'No comment.' "

"It's not the press out there in the lobby," the sheriff said. "It's the dead man's wife."

Clyde flexed his shoulders and stuck out his chin. "I didn't do nothin' wrong. I ain't about to start hiding from people."

I still didn't know Robert Earl Bailey's full story. But I knew that Clyde had shot him while he was in the act of surrender. I was an eyewitness to that. And now the cocky greaseball was walking around with his chest poked out like he had just won some prizefight. That smirk just flew all over me, and I stepped in front of him. "You sit your ass right over there like the sheriff said."

Clyde stared at me, smiling, chewing gum on one side of his mouth. His uncle reached out and held him by his arm. Real smart move by Johnnie the Dime, because I was looking as hard as I could for any excuse to mop the floor with that nephew of his.

"I want you to cut out the bullshit and tell me exactly what happened back there in that casino."

The brown eyes of my old fishing buddy Roger Partridge had an edge to them that didn't used to be there. Three years earlier he took a job as a deputy when Hurricane Georges broke up his shrimp boat and left him with a need for temporary work. But the sheriff who hired him turned out to be dirty and got killed in a drug deal that went bad, a deal that went down real close to the spot where the Jackpot Bay Casino was now standing. All of a sudden, Roger found himself named as interim sheriff of Hancock County. At first, he didn't look all that comfortable in the job. Even with his square jaw and deep-set eyes, he didn't look like a cop. But over the past year or so, Roger had grown into the uniform.

"I can't tell you any more than I already have." I was in the chair in front of Roger's desk. Neal was standing beside the door.

"You're an eyewitness to what might've been a homicide, and you're refusing to tell me what you saw? Neal, would you explain to your brother the finer points of obstruction of justice?"

"Didn't you already give a statement?" Neal asked.

"Of course I gave a statement. I don't know what else I'm supposed to do."

"Hey, what the hell am I thinking anyway?" Roger said. "Aren't you representing Clyde?"

"I am as of now," Neal said.

"In that case, would you mind waiting out in the hall until we get through in here?"

Neal picked up his briefcase. "My client wants to know when he can get his pistol back."

Roger pulled his eyeglasses to the end of his nose and gave him a warning look. "Your client can stick that gun up his ass."

"Hey, I had to ask."

Roger pointed to the door and followed Neal out with his eyes. "And make sure they don't go out into the lobby until I get back out there!"

"Don't I get to call in a lawyer for myself?" I asked.

"We've been friends a long time," Roger said, "but don't try to use that to hold back on me. You didn't say diddly squat in that statement and you know it."

On the wall behind his desk there was the usual collection of commissions, citations, framed press clippings, baby pictures, old high school football team photos, and shots taken at the dock featuring strings of mackerel caught on good days out at Cat Island or the Chandelieurs. One shot shows a Jack Cravelle Roger landed, which was a state record at the time of the catch, a record that lasted all of three days. Another photo shows this deep blue sailfish landed during the Mississippi Deep Sea Fishing Rodeo over at Gulfport. I was in the football team photo, kneeling on the front row, and I was also in one of the fishing shots, holding up one end of the string of Spanish mackerel.

"I'm not sandbagging you," I said. "I just can't tell you anything else that I can back up. I've got my opinion, but that's all it is. Just an opinion."

"So what's your opinion? Come on, dammit. Am I gonna have to break out the rubber hose or something?"

"Johnnie the Dime says he gave a thousand bucks to the sheriff's barbecue."

He pulled the glasses off and his eyes narrowed as he pointed them at me. "You trying to say something? If so, just come out with it."

"He's a mobster, Roger. He was tight with the wise guys out in Vegas."

"We raised twelve grand for that barbecue and gave ten thousand of it to the Boys' and Girls' Club. Lots of folks around here gave money. And the last time I looked, the company that's paying you is in pretty tight with Koscko themselves."

"I want you to know that he said that he ought to be able to get something done over here because he kicked in a thousand bucks to your barbecue. He was acting like a big shot. I'm not saying there's anything wrong. But if you deal with him in the future, you need to know that he'll run his mouth."

"I'll give the damn money back to him."

"Don't make it a bigger deal than it is," I said. "I just thought you needed to know what he was saying. You know I'm not accusing you of anything. But you're an elected official now and you need to be careful."

He jammed the glasses back into place and picked up the file in front of him. He was irritated, easy to see that, but he needed to hear what I was saying. When Neal went through that state senate race the year before, I got a real feel for how anything can be used against you and just how many fools out there are willing to believe any crap they hear.

"Can I tell you what I really think about that shooting without having to add it to my statement?" I said.

Roger tilted his chair back, tossed the glasses onto the desk, and closed his eyes as he pinched the bridge of his nose. "Why the hell are you being so slippery?"

"I can't tell you anything I can't swear to," I said. "You know how I feel about Clyde. Hell, you remember him from high school just like I do. I don't give a damn if you bust his ass or not."

"Even though you work for his uncle?"

"You could piss me off here," I said. "I work for his uncle's insurance company. They're paying me to do a two-bit security audit. That doesn't include going to bat for Clyde Dubardo in any criminal investigation."

Roger kept his eyes closed and nodded his head.

"We had talked the guy into laying his gun down," I said. "Everything would have been slick if Clyde hadn't challenged him. We had the bomb defused until Clyde jumped in and set the whole thing off."

"So why can't you just say that on the record?"

"How am I supposed to testify about the look in a man's eyes?" I said. "There's no doubt in my mind that it could've ended without anybody getting shot. But the fact is that he had already fired his gun. And if he had been able to turn around fast enough, he would have sure as hell shot Clyde."

"Did Robert Earl Bailey place his gun on the craps table? It's a yes or no answer."

"Don't you have the whole thing on tape?" I asked. "Didn't the surveillance camera catch the whole scene?"

Roger looked up at the ceiling and started drumming a pencil on the arm of his chair.

"That's the problem, isn't it?" I said. "You don't have any of it on tape. That camera in the ceiling that he blasted all to hell and back was the one that would have covered that area."

"That cheap son of a bitch Johnnie Koscko had about half the number of cameras covering the floor that he should have," Roger said. "Usually there would be two or maybe even three in the area of the craps tables. We should have had camera shots from all different angles. But we don't have a damn thing. Not even any long-distance shots."

"So are you going to charge Clyde with anything?"

"The DA's decided there's nothing he can do," he said. "He's not even gonna take it to the grand jury. You've got a guy who's mad as hell and has already been kicked out of the place. He comes back with two guns and fires off a round in a crowded room. What can you do?"

"If he had wanted to shoot somebody, he would have shot them. None of those gamblers were in danger of getting killed, at least not by Robert Earl Bailey."

"You think the DA wants to go before a jury and try to tell 'em that?" he said. "Hell, ever since the rag-heads hijacked those airliners, anybody who even looks like a terrorist is fair game. Besides, he was still holding the gun when Clyde popped him. Even a half-assed lawyer could make a case of self-defense."

"I'm afraid I can't help you," I said.

Roger snapped the pencil in half and hurled both pieces across the room. I ducked as they sailed over my head and hit the wall behind me.

"Whoa! Why are you so pissed about all this?" I said. "I know Clyde's a damn fool. But don't forget that this Robert Earl guy walked into a crowded public place and started shooting. The casino didn't handle it all that well, but the guy wasn't exactly innocent."

Roger ran his tongue along the inside of his cheek as he held his glasses up to the ceiling lights. "Do you remember when we were growing up there was a guy used to come into town called Preacher Bob Burch?"

"Of course I do. What's he got to do with any of this?"

Back when I was growing up, everybody knew Preacher Bob but nobody knew exactly where he lived. It was somewhere six or eight miles up in the county near the Caesar community, out in the scrub pines down a rutted, red dirt trail that led off the two-laned asphalt state road to Picayune and other points north. Daddy pointed out that trail to me one day when we were driving to Hattiesburg. It curved off and disappeared into the pine trees and showed no signs that anybody lived on it except for the gray metal mailbox nailed on top of a fencepost at the edge of the highway. Had the name Burch written on it in black paint. They were country people, outsiders. Only ten miles inland from the coast, but it might as well have been a thousand.

Mr. Burch fixed whatever needed fixing for the public schools in Bay St. Louis, so he came into town a lot. He was a wiry, sun-dried man with hard-muscled arms and rough hands and was missing the top joint of his ring finger, all signs common to pulpwood haulers. He wore the same thing every day, a pair of faded denim overalls and a plaid flannel shirt. When it got too hot, like in September when school had just started, he'd leave off the flannel shirt and instead wear a T-shirt under the overalls. He was a smiling, avuncular man, and sometimes he'd bring us kids a paper sack full of muscadines that he had gathered out in the woods, and we'd eat them at recess.

"He'd set up that speaker on the sidewalk and start preaching," Roger said. "He did it every Saturday."

"Aren't we talking about Clyde Dubardo shooting some guy in the Jackpot Bay Casino?"

"You remember how he used to wave that Bible around?"

On Saturday afternoons, Bob Burch would scrub down and change into his Sunday clothes, black suit pants worn smooth at the seat and above the knees and held up by suspenders. I never saw any coat, but he always had a starched white shirt, and a red tie with this horseshoe stickpin stuck through it. He would slick down his hair with a sweet-smelling lotion and polish his black, round-toed shoes, and he and his wife would drive their Ford F-100 pickup into town.

Preacher Bob had this squawk box that he must have ordered from some catalogue. It was a heavy contraption, a speaker mounted in plywood painted with black lacquer and connected to a hand-held microphone at the end of a curly cord. He hooked it up to an electrical outlet in the barbershop at corner of Main and Lameuse and held an open, leather-bound Bible in his left hand as he'd preach sermons to the guys waiting for a haircut inside the shop and anybody who was walking along the sidewalk. During the preaching, his wife would hand out religious tracts to anybody who would take one.

I can't remember anyone stopping to listen to Preacher Bob except for tourists looking for antique stores, and they didn't hang around long. He never got very loud, and his sermons only lasted fifteen or twenty minutes, and he never had the urgency of the revivalists who would come into town in late fall of each year. The amazing thing was that he never asked anybody for any money. Never was any collection plate. He didn't even ask folks to go to any particular church. He just preached, and didn't seem to care if anybody even heard him.

The regulars in the barbershop got so accustomed to his Saturday morning sermons that they didn't notice them. Sometimes I'd ride my bike downtown and sit on the curb a block away in front of Justice's Drug Store and watch him. When he'd get through and start packing up his speaker and the tracts, the owner of the barbershop, a man named Henry Dees, would open the machine and take Mr. and Mrs. Burch a couple of cold Coca-Colas in 6 ½-ounce green bottles.

"About the time you went off to college," Roger said, "Preacher Bob and his wife started bringing their daughter into town with them. Do you remember her?"

"Sure. Mr. Burch played the guitar and the little girl would sing hymns. Always reminded me of Shirley Temple without the dancing."

"She was their baby," Roger said. "Her name was Brenda. They had other children who were already grown when Brenda was born."

"You're bound to be going somewhere with all this," I said.

"Little Brenda got to be a real good piano player. And grew up to be real pretty. She still plays for weddings and receptions and things around here. She works part-time at the bank opening new accounts."

"So she's still around here. Did she ever get married?"

"She married Robert Earl Bailey," he said. "Apparently little Brenda's husband just got killed over seven hundred dollars."

On the couch along the wall of the lobby of the sheriff's office sat two women. One of them was young and petite with long brown hair, curled at the ends, pulled back and held in place with a white bow. She was bent forward with her face buried in her hands. She didn't look up when we walked in. Roger and I went in first, with Johnnie Koscko, Clyde, and Neal right behind. The rest of the witnesses had left half an hour earlier. The other woman, big and strong with dark blond hair that showed a lot of gray, was rubbing the young woman's back, chewing gum and staring straight ahead at nothing in particular.

"You don't have to stay with me," the young woman said. "I know they need you back at work."

"Don't you worry about that. Ain't no big crowd coming into

the store this time of night. Besides, they close in an hour or so. There ain't a thing in this world that could get me to leave you here by yourself."

The young woman wore a denim skirt, soft and faded, ankle length, with a pair of white canvas rubber sole shoes, the kind we used to call sneakers. The other woman also had on an ankle-length dress, with her hair tied up in a bun. The clothes worn by those you often see in the parking lot of the shopping center handing out pamphlets or selling peanut brittle.

The older woman noticed us and said something to her younger friend, the one who had been crying. The young woman looked up at us with red and puffy eyes, her unadorned cheeks were pink and lined with the traces of fresh tears.

"Why did you kill my husband?" Her voice was that of a little girl.

I looked back at Clyde, but then I realized she was looking at me. I just shook my head.

"What did he do to you?" All her energy had been spent. She tried to stand, but fell back to where she sat. The woman beside her gently stroked her hair and stared at us, moving her eyes from left to right and back, sizing us up.

"She's confused," Roger said.

"Ma'am, I didn't shoot your husband."

"Come on, let's get out of here," Roger said. "I'll come back and explain everything to her."

"Are you the one who killed Robert Earl?" she asked Clyde.

Clyde wouldn't look her in the eye. "Hey, it's too bad about your husband," Johnnie the Dime chimed in, "but it was self-defense."

"Self-defense? Was Robert Earl trying to hurt somebody?"

"He was trying to shoot *me*, okay?" Clyde pointed at his chest. "I told him to drop it, and he tried to blow me away."

"That's enough," Neal said.

"Hey, you're my lawyer. You gonna let people accuse me of murder and not say something?"

"Let's leave," Neal said.

"It was self-defense," Koscko said. "You're the lawyer, you better get used to saying it, by God."

The twin plateglass front doors leading into the station flew open so hard that they bounced back and closed behind the Reverend Billy Joe Newhart. He was tall and bronzed with a strong jawline, a dimpled chin, and high cheekbones. Had the wide shoulders and narrow waist of a natural athelete. He stopped three feet into the lobby and scanned the room, looking straight through me and Neal and Johnnie the Dime and Clyde until he spotted the two women on the couch. He closed his eyes, took a breath, and exhaled audibly before walking to them.

"Oh, Brother Billy Joe," Brenda whispered. "It's so awful."

"I came as soon as I heard," he said.

"It's that stolen money," she said. "That's what caused it."

Koscko cut his eyes toward Clyde, but Clyde just poked out his lip and shrugged. "You tellin' me your husband was stealing money from my casino? Is that what you're saying?"

"Oh, no!" she said. "Robert Earl wasn't stealing. He wouldn't do that."

"Hush, Brenda!" the older woman said. "Don't talk about that."

"Don't listen to that man," the reverend said. "Of course Robert Earl wasn't stealing. He was born again. Washed in the blood."

"Are you saying your husband was stealing from the business?" Koscko said. "You listening to this, Delmas?"

"She didn't say nothin' like that, mister!" the older woman said. "You quit tryin' to twist her words around."

"I ain't twisting nothin'. I heard her plain as day."

"Damn right," Clyde said.

"Forget these people. Let us pray," Newhart said as he reached for the hands of both of the women on the couch.

Brenda covered her ears with both hands and began rocking back and forth and humming "What a Friend We Have in Jesus."

"Sheriff," Johnnie said, "did you hear what she said?"

"Just get out of here," Roger said. "Just get the heck out of here right now."

"We need to pray for our deliverance, Brother Billy Joe." The bigger woman laid her arm across Brenda's narrow shoulders and drew her near. "I feel the presence of the devil himself in this place."

"Did she just say I was the devil?" Clyde said. "Is that what she's saying?"

"The Lord is my shepherd," Newhart said. "I shall not want . . ."

"I'll sue her. You hear me? I'll sue her for slander."

Brenda let out this painful wail and began crying with loud, almost convulsive gasps.

"That's it, by God! That's it!" Roger shouted. "One more word outta you, Clyde, and your ass is back in lockup for the night."

Johnnie grabbed Clyde by the elbow and pressed a finger to his lips to silence him.

"Yea, though I walk through the valley of the shadow of death, I shall fear no evil."

Koscko and Clyde walked to the door with Clyde looking back over his shoulder until they stepped through the door and out of sight. Roger stood where he was, but I could hear him breathing through his nose and he was shimmering with anger.

"Surely, goodness and mercy shall follow me all the days of my life. And I will dwell in the house of the Lord forever."

"Oh, my God, my God!" Brenda wailed. "Why have you forsaken me?"

"He hasn't forsaken you, sister," Newhart said as held her tiny hands. "God is with us right now."

Roger kept staring at the door and started flexing the fingers of his right hand into a fist. "Didn't you say the insurance company is reviewing the books at Jackpot Bay?"

"They're really more interested in security," I said, "but they'll take a look at the financial records."

"Y'all find anything funny in them books, you come tell me right away."

Brenda laid her head on the lap of the older woman and looked as if she were about to go to sleep. Newhart stood and stroked her temple a few times before he stepped toward us. "You filin' charges against that man who killed Brother Robert Earl?"

"It looks like self-defense," Roger said. "But we're still investigating."

Newhart frowned and tilted his head back. He is a tall man so that made him appear to be looking down at Roger. "I hear that Brother Robert Earl was saying that casino owed him some money."

Roger nodded. "He said it was seven hundred dollars."

"Did any of those people from that place have anything to say about that?"

"No sir," Roger said. "Not that I heard."

"Well, if that sorry bunch owes Sister Brenda and those two children one single penny, you just let me know." Reverend Newhart pressed his lips together and his eyes narrowed and the corner of his left eye began twitching ever so slightly. "I'll get the money for 'em, one way or th'other."

EIGHT

I don't know how Tara got to her hotel from the police station the night before. I didn't even know which hotel she was in or even which town it was in, could have been anywhere from here to Biloxi, and that's a lot of hotels. I had never asked her where she was staying before we took our detour into the casino, and she had been gone an hour when they finally got through questioning me at the sheriff's office. But she didn't wait around for me, and she's not the kind who would have any problem catching a ride.

It's cold and heartless work I have to do sometimes, and since Bayou Casualty sold out to what used to be Lippington Industries of Franklinburg, Pennsylvania, it's getting colder and more heartless by the day. Lippington used to be a candy company that started out sixty years ago as a family-run operation with this one candy bar, the ChocoBar, that is still a worldwide favorite. The Lippingtons became fairly rich and were mostly happy showing up at the factory every day and running the company until the third generation took over and Charles Anthony Lippington, III, got tired of the snow and the office and the Business After Hours meetings and decided to cash in his chips and spend the inheritance in Jamaica and St. Marten, fishing for marlin and knocking down rum drinks.

The group that bought out the Lippington family went public

and formed The Lippington Group and started buying up every company they could, with no common denominator other than the belief there is a quick buck to be made. They specialize in latching on to some company and sending in this asshole named Meat Axe Bob Dunbar, who sends out a flurry of pink slips, especially to anybody within a few years of vesting in the company's retirement plan, and then starts sucking the life out of what remains of the workforce. When they've bled it pale, they cash out and sell out to the next bottom feeder that comes along looking for salvage value. Things have changed a lot at Bayou Casualty since The Lippington Group came along. The only reason they've kept me around, and in fact increased my work, is because I'm on contract with them and don't represent any long-term obligation on their part. True parasites.

The company had called me early that morning and told me to fax them a copy of the personnel records of Robert Earl Bailey, so they could make an assesment of what his life was worth. In any wrongful-death action where our client's liability is clear, they have this new strategy to come up with a lump sum that most people consider to be fair. Then they cut it by a third and offer it to the family before the casket goes into the ground, about the time the funeral home is dropping a five-thousand-dollar funeral bill on them and before they have time to put a pencil to it and figure out how bad they're getting screwed. If our client's liability is iffy, as it was in this case, Bayou Casualty offers something less than half of what they estimate as a fair settlement. If the family of the deceased refuses, the company proceeds to lawyer-whip them and ties the case up in court for years.

This new strategy isn't written down anywhere, at least not word for word. They're too smart for that. But if you look at the letters from headquarters that come to the guys in the field, the pattern gets pretty clear. And I've been saving all my letters. Even installed a bug in my phone, which is perfectly legal in Mississippi.

So I keep close track of my dealings with the new and improved Bayou Casualty in case I ever need it. This may not fall into any private investigator's code of ethics, but in Mississippi there's no law governing private eyes, so where are they going to go to complain? I learned a lot in that bank up in Memphis, including some rules about covering my ass and what to do when swimming with the makos and great whites.

When I walked into the personnel director's office, Tara was already there in the conference room with two stacks of manila folders, one short and one tall, with a cup of steaming coffee in her hand and a cigarette smoldering in an ashtray. She was in a sculpted pair of jeans and an unbuttoned white blouse over a light blue crop top.

"What are you doing here?" The abruptness of her tone set me back some.

"I thought you'd hang around for a while last night."

"Don't like police stations."

"Did you get to your hotel without any problems?"

"Everything was fine." She reached for the ashtray. "Look, I don't mean to be rude, but I'm really busy here. Is there something you need?"

"I'm looking for the personnel file for Robert Earl Bailey. The company wanted to get some background on him."

She held the cigarette in her lips as she started flipping through the short stack of folders. She slid the Bailey file across the table toward me.

"Did I do something last night to make you angry?" I asked.

She looked puzzled. "No, not at all."

"You seemed a little more sociable last night."

She smiled. "Sometimes I have trouble shifting gears, y'know. I'm sorry if I'm being short with you, but when I get into a case I'm pretty focused."

"Well I'd hate to get you out of focus," I said. "I'll just make a copy of this file and let you get back to work."

She glanced at her watch. "Oh, why don't you stay for a while. It's time for a break anyway. Would you like a cup of coffee?"

"So what are you working on?" I asked as I sat and waited for the cup she was pouring for me.

"First step in any security audit is to go over the personnel files. You'd be amazed how much a simple NCIC check will turn up. I also look for garnishments, bankruptcies, judgments and liens, anything that points to an employee with money trouble. I target the guys who handle money or authorize the handling of money."

"Robert Earl Bailey's file was in your short stack. I assume you've looked at it already."

"Of course. That's the first thing I did when I got here this morning." She set the cup of coffee on the conference table in front of me, sat down beside it, and started rubbing the toe of her shoe along the side of my leg.

"When you shift gears," I said, "you shift gears."

She laughed. "I'm afraid I wouldn't make it here in the South. I don't play games. I found out early that you've got to go after what you love in life, and you can't let anything stand in your way."

"So what do you love in life?"

"I'm an action freak, and I can't stand to sit around. That's why I'm trying to get through with this as fast as I can. Bayou Casualty's paying me for a minimum of ten days' work here. If I can get my stuff done in four days, I still get paid for the ten. The problems in this place are so obvious that I can probably get it done in three. That puts me seven days ahead of the game."

"And then what?" I asked. "Do you go to the next job and rush through it and get seven more days ahead?"

"It doesn't work that way. When I leave here, I'll take my money and go shark fishing down in Louisiana. I only give a damn about money because it gives me the chance to have fun. My idea of heaven is hitting on a big score in the stock market or whatever and getting enough cash to where I can do nothing except run around the world climbing mountains and jumping out of planes and getting laid."

At one time, except for the part about jumping out of planes, I guess I saw the world in those same terms. Or at least I thought I did. But there's got to be a little more to it, at least for me. There's this business of other people—family, friends, wife, lovers, and now my eight-year-old up in Memphis—that has kept steering me away from that plan. Most of my fellow townspeople, who don't know the whole story and who listen to the gossip around town, look at the way I live and figure what Tara described is pretty much the approach to life that I take. I've had some of my married buddies tell me as much, usually after the introspection and envy that a few beers can stir up.

But I have to keep adding stuff to Tara's ideal lifestyle, or maybe I want what she said plus a few twists and variations. And maybe I can have that, have it all. Because nobody in the world is in a better position to pursue Life According to Tara Stocklin than I am right now. Who knows, maybe she herself might want more out of life than she's letting on. Tara's surely different from anyone I've been around in a long time, if ever. But different might not be all bad.

"So far I've found that Robert Earl Bailey was in a great place to rip the company off big time," she said, "and I don't doubt that he was doing just that. His job was to cut checks for deliveries coming into the place and sign off for them when they got here. If he wasn't around, the manager could sign for them. And guess who the manager was up until a few weeks ago."

"Clyde?"

"Exactly."

"These deliveries," I said, "are we talking about poker chips or what?"

"We're talking about the stuff you need for the thousands of patrons who come in. Everything from toilet tissue to salad dressing. A lot of it's perishable, mostly food and flowers. You could easily go through, like, six or eight thousand dollars' worth of food and a thousand dollars of fresh flowers in a day."

"In other words," I said, "the kind of stuff that has a shelf life of only a few days and is hard as hell to inventory. The kind of stuff you always buy more of than you use."

"He could have been taking delivery on phantom shipments, y'know, and paying for stuff that was never delivered. The casino orders a thousand dollars' worth of beef, and he writes out a dummy invoice to show that two thousand dollars' worth were delivered. Then he cuts a check for the higher amount and pockets the difference."

"I assume that would take some help."

"Of course it would." She drained the last of her coffee. "I'm getting a headache. Let's go take a look around this place."

Tara had a clipboard and a ballpoint pen, the kind with the retractable point, and she kept clicking it in and out as we walked. We approached the main entrance and through the big glass doors we saw a bus stopping at the curb, its yellow lights flashing. Clyde Dubardo stepped to the passenger door as it slid open.

"I'm going to step around the corner for a few minutes," she said. "I want you to stand here and count the number of people getting off that bus."

"Are you expecting this group?"

"The casino keeps up with every tour bus that's scheduled to come here." She looked at her watch and made a note of the time. "The bus company gets paid by the head for each patron they deliver to our front door."

"How much?"

"I don't want to stand here where Clyde can see me. Just count the heads and let me know when you're through. Oh, and get the number of that bus."

She stepped to the side and hid behind a wall that hid her from the view of anyone outside. Twenty-six persons emerged from the bus. When the last passenger got off, Clyde climbed inside and the driver shut the door behind him. I nodded to Tara and she signaled for me to come to where she was standing.

"Twenty-six passengers," I said. "Bus number 642-M."

"Is it still parked out there?" she asked as she wrote on the pad.

"Clyde's talking to the driver."

"Let's get away from this door," she said as she walked back toward the gaming area.

"So how much does the casino pay the bus company?"

"Ten bucks a head for every passenger delivered to the door. The greeter counts them as they get off the bus. Then he goes inside to the purchasing office and gets the cash to take to the driver. He goes back and pays the driver and gets him to sign for it."

"So the casino owes that driver two hundred and sixty bucks."

"Say, you're pretty good at math."

"But since you're hiding behind a wall while I'm counting the passengers, I assume there's a problem here."

"If the greeter reports thirty passengers instead of twenty-six," she said, "he can pocket the forty-dollar difference. Do that six or seven times a day and it adds up. If he doesn't get too greedy, nobody'll ever notice. Of course, some of these schemes get pretty elaborate, y'know, but that takes more work than somebody like Clyde is likely to do. Besides, if the IRS starts noticing that what the casino says it paid a bus company is a lot more than that company is reporting that it got, it sets off all kinds of alarms."

"And there's no way to monitor this?"

"The cheapest and easiest way to catch a bus scam is to do what we just did and go to purchasing and compare the numbers. But if you don't get it all on tape, it's only one person's word against another's. Knowing Clyde, he's probably raking some off the top, but this place has got bigger problems than that."

She made notes as we walked away from the mid-morning sunlight at the main entrance down the corridor toward the dimly lit gaming area. Outside it was a hazy June day, maybe eighty-five degrees and climbing, with a light breeze out of the west. The tide was on the rise and the gulls were active and loud. There was a strong smell of brine and seaweed from the nets of the boats that had come in with first light to unload their catch and wash their nets and sell to the people who drove their cars to the dock to buy the shrimp and load them into ice chests. But inside the Jackpot Bay Casino, it was dark and loud and smoky, could have just as well been the dead of winter in some cow town in Kansas.

"Have you been getting cooperation from everybody?" I asked. "That's part of what they want me to do. I'm supposed to see that management gives you what you need."

"I haven't heard a word out of Koscko or Clyde."

"That's a good thing, right?"

She nodded yes. "As far as Rulon goes, he's a pain in the ass. But I can take care of him myself if he gives me any trouble."

"I thought you two hit it off pretty well. I mean you were speaking French to each other and all."

"Like I said, he's a pain in the ass. Has to do things his way whether they make sense or not. And he doesn't know how to keep his mouth shut. That's dangerous."

"You want me to talk to him?"

"I can handle it." She looked up at the ceiling and frowned. "I can see they didn't listen to a word I said when I was here last time. Look up there at those cameras."

"You mean those black globes up on the ceiling? Looks like they got quite a few to me. Let's see . . . two, six, I count eight of them."

"There ought to be at least a dozen for this much floor space," she said. "There've got more blind spots out there than an eighteen-wheeler without any side mirrors."

"As long as it looks like they've got enough, does it really matter if they don't?" I asked. "Who could look up there and count the cameras and figure out that there wasn't enough surveillance?"

"A professional could. You don't put up cameras to catch some average jerk out for a day at the slots; you can usually catch guys like that the second they try to get cute. But a professional cheat, he'd know there weren't enough units spread around the minute he walked in here." She held up the clipboard and scribbled something as she glanced around at the cameras. "Do me a favor and keep an eye on that guy in the blue coat over by that last row of slots while I make a few notes."

"Doesn't he work here?"

"And that woman at the machine he's standing next to. See if she does anything."

"Am I supposed to be looking for something in particular?"

"Just keep an eye on them and don't be too obvious about it."

"But what am I supposed to see?"

She sighed. "Just do what I ask and don't ask me a bunch of questions. Okay? Watch them for ten minutes or so and remember what you see."

She pointed at the ceiling with her pen and appeared to be taking measurements by counting ceiling tiles. She caught me watching her, and glared at me, and pointed once more at the guy with the blue coat. She looked pissed, must have shifted those gears again. It was fairly easy to watch the guy without being noticed. He was so busy trying to make time with the woman sitting beside him that he never looked up. The place could have been on fire and he'd never know it.

"About what I figured," she said. "They got each camera covering about twice as much floor space as it should."

"Can I stop spying now?"

"What'd you see?"

"A guy in a navy blue coat hitting on some woman."

"Anything else?"

"Didn't look like he was getting anywhere."

She started writing on the pad again. "He's so busy watching her legs that she could have a partner walk out the door carrying one of the slots under his arm and he'd never know it."

"You think she's working with a team?"

"Probably not, but she damn sure could have been. This place is a crackerbox."

"So you think the casino's been losing money to professional cheats?"

"There must be a dozen ways money could be leaking out of this place. Sure, there could be pros coming in and working it over. The gaming world is a small one. Word about this cream puff will spread from Vegas to Bangkok in no time. And not to mention what the employees are probably doing. I mean look out there. You got any idea how much you could milk out of a slot machine with a monkey's paw in the ten minutes that floorwalker was trying to look down that girl's dress?"

"Let me guess," I said. "A whole lot?"

"And the way they handle money," she said. "Have you heard what they're doing with the money they take in from Snow Mountain?"

"I heard Johnnie the Dime say they wanted to be paid in cash."

"You ever heard of anything so crazy? And that fool agreed to it! I mean that concert might take in over two million in gate receipts alone. And that doesn't touch the band's share of concessions, T-shirt sales, album sales. Hell, there might be, like, four million dollars involved."

"But from what I hear, Koscko doesn't have any choice if he wants the concert."

"He's never even asked them to change their policy!" She reached into the front pocket of her jeans for a pack of cigarettes. We sat at a table just outside one of the three bars that are set off the main gaming area. "All that bullshit about being paid in cash came about thirty years ago when Kenny, Senior, was still around and the band was just starting. They got their first big gig, a solid week in Vegas with the old Cactus Casino. But they got snookered by Big Foot Bianco. You ever heard of him?"

"Wasn't he the mob guy who got killed in a car wreck?"

"He was in a Mustang convertible that got rear-ended and pushed under a cement truck that accidentally dropped its load on top of him. But that's another story. Big Foot owned the Cactus, and he was a greedy bastard even by Vegas standards. He convinced Kenny, Senior, to take a part of the profits rather than a set amount. Then he claimed he had to have some time to, like, total everything up before he cut the band a check. Two months later he said there were so many expenses that the week didn't turn a profit. In fact, Bianco claimed it had lost money."

"This Big Foot Bianco. He ever work in a bank in Memphis that you know of?"

"Huh?"

"Never mind. So that's why Snow Mountain insists on cash?"

"Kenny, Senior, was a country boy," she said. "He didn't know much about accounting, but he knew when he'd been screwed. After Bianco screwed him, he adopted a new policy. After any concert at a casino, all the gate receipts are converted into cash within twenty-four hours and sent by armored car to the band's headquarters in Nashville."

"And I assume Kenny, Junior, is following this same policy," I said.

Tara nodded. "His mother insists on it. She got religion soon after her husband died, and she thinks casinos are forces of evil."

"But if Junior's carrying on the family tradition, it sounds like Koscko's got no choice but to send the money to Nashville by armored car."

"Kenny, Senior, had dropped so much acid on those road tours that he tripped off most of his circuit breakers," she said. "But Junior's still got functioning brain cells, y'know. I could show him ten diferent ways that a couple of million in cash might not make it back to Nashville. We could set it up so his mother would never know the difference."

"So why don't you go talk to him?"

"I've already pointed this out to the brass in New Orleans. Now it's their call. They only pay me for advice on security. If they don't take that advice it's not my problem."

From behind us, I heard Rulon Hornbeck rattling off a list of orders and instructions to somebody. "All of this is going to have to go," he said. "This silver wallpaper has simply got to come down. It looks like some bad disco motif from 1972. Retro is one thing, but this is just plain tacky. And that picture! My, God! Looks like something from a TraveLodge." He was stepping along waving his hand at everything he found to be an affront to good taste, which was quite a list. The young man behind him was trying to spot all the deficiencies that Rulon was pointing out and struggling to write them all down as they walked along. He looked like he was about to cry.

"Oh, my stars! I hadn't even looked down at this carpet. It's glaringly hideous! It's got to come out."

"But Mr. Hornbeck," the young man said. "It would take thirty thousand dollars to replace it. Besides, Mr. Koscko picked out that carpet himself."

"Well, we can put it in his downtown office. But it is not, I repeat, NOT going to be the first thing one sees when coming in the door. Jackpot Bay Casino is no longer going after the trailer park crowd."

"Oh, goody, look who's coming," Tara said. "This ought to be fun."

Clyde Dubardo was coming from the opposite direction, strutting across the floor with a bleached blonde hanging on his arm. She had thick red lips and a pair of cantaloupe-sized breasts pressed into a form-fitting long white dress slit up the side almost to her hip. The blue-coated floor manager interrupted his attempt to pick up the girl he had been talking with and tried to look busy. Clyde led the blonde over to a crap table and handed her a roll of dollar chips. Rulon had spotted them and kept sneaking looks at them as he continued his rapid-fire list of instructions to his beleaguered assistant. Clyde got the blonde settled in at the table and snapped his fingers for a drink.

"I don't care if it IS thirty thousand dollars!" Rulon turned up the volume loud enough for Clyde and the rest of us to hear. "This carpet's got to be pulled up NOW!"

"But Mr. Koscko really likes this pattern."

"Well, it's hideous!"

Clyde craned his head toward Rulon and watched with a pronounced frown for a few minutes before he patted the blonde on her tightly packed tush and stepped toward Rulon and the assistant. He straightened his tie and hitched his pants as he walked.

"Aren't you supposed to be keeping those two apart?" Tara asked.

"I'm supposed to be keeping you and Johnnie the Dime from ripping each other's throats out. I couldn't care less if those two draw pistols and step off ten paces."

"What seems to be the problem here?" Clyde asked Rulon in his best Sylvester Stallone.

"I'm sure you have quite enough to do keeping the pit bosses in line," Rulon said. "What we're discussing is of no interest to you."

"What are you saying about this carpet? We had this stuff special made somewhere."

"Tijuana?" Rulon asked.

"Just take a flyin' jump up my ass," Clyde said. "It was Paprikastan or Tazbikastan or something like that. One of them 'Stan' countries over there. Them sum'bitches are the best in the world when it comes to carpets."

"Well, maybe you can take it to Bourbon Street and sell it. I'm sure your girlfriend over there at the craps table could sell it to the club where she obviously works. I understand they have to redo the runways at those strip joints every once in a while."

"You sho do have a purty mouth, sweetie," Clyde said. "And if you know what's good for ya, you'll keep it shut."

"Just stick to checking IDs and let me run the casino. I'll make sure the right people come through the doors."

"You mean like that British dude you been talking about?" Clyde said. "As far as I can tell, he's never laid down a single bet in here. I've never even seen the guy. I'm beginning to wonder if he even exists."

"Are you telling me you have friends who claim to know something about the British nobility?"

"I hear this guy has been in here a few times and he's already got a bunch of markers out. He's into this place for a big wad, and I think it's about time to call those markers in."

"Don't you dare!" Rulon said, his voice rising. "Don't you even think about it."

"Come to think of it, I wonder if he's laid down a single penny in hard cash. He might just be doing everything on credit."

"Now, you look here, Clyde," Rulon's voice had dropped a full octave, and there was a glint in his eye I had never seen before. "The earl will be here for another week. Gretchen La Pointe has already told me that and so has he. He settles up with us at the end of his stay. And as for not having any cash, that just shows how little you know. No earl or duke ever carries any cash. Over there, it's middle class to actually be holding money. It's a different world we're dealing with when we deal with those people, and it's a world you don't know anything about."

"I know a deadbeat when I see one."

"You press him for money right now and that insult will spread around the world." Rulon took a step toward Clyde. "You do something like that and you'll never get another high roller in here from Europe."

"Back off, Rulon. Don't get in my face."

"I'm warning you. Don't mess with the earl."

"Get out of my face, or I'm gonna whip your ass right here on the floor. I'm not gonna put up with some fag getting in my face."

"Look at those two, would you?" Tara was smiling.

"I think I'll put my money on Rulon," I said, "at least for the long haul. I mean he's got more brains. But then again, who knows? There might not be any long haul. Maybe he'll keep running his mouth and Clyde'll just kill him outright."

"I'd have to bet on Clyde," Tara said. "I know Rulon's smarter, but it's hard to overcome the fact that Clyde is Johnnie the Dime's nephew. Rulon screws up one time, and suddenly he's in the unemployment line."

"I don't give a shit *what* you say!" Clyde shouted. "People wanna come to a casino, not a damned art gallery! They like a lot of flashing lights and noise! And if you ain't got a Jeep or a four-by-four truck to give away, you're dead!"

They had gotten loud enough for everybody to hear them. Clyde's remark about the car giveaway brought clapping and whistles from several of the patrons at the tables and the slot machines.

"The thing about it is," Tara said, "Clyde's right. He knows this place'll never attract any high-rolling crowd. And his tastes are a hell of a lot closer to the bunch who'll come in here than Rulon's will ever be."

"But you've got to admit, Rulon's doing okay," I said. "After all, Gretchen La Pointe's supposed to be coming here and they've got Snow Mountain for a concert. That's big time. And one way or the other, he's actually got some British earl hanging around here."

"When Snow Mountain leaves after tomorrow night's concert, all that'll come to a halt and fast."

"This ain't the set for no James Bond movie," said Clyde, quieter now. "Ain't nobody in here wearin' no tuxedo."

"Mr. Koscko hired me to make decisions on how this place should be run," Rulon said. "Maybe you need to do what you know best, which is being a bouncer. Or at least I thought it was until last night. They still let you carry that big gun?"

"Up yours," Clyde said. "You ain't got a clue about what folks around here like."

"I trained in Monte Carlo, and I know what the high rollers like," Rulon said. "And I mean the real high rollers. Not somebody who cashes in his unemployment check and tries to double his money at the blackjack table."

Clyde pounded his fist into his hand before wheeling around

and stomping off toward the craps table, leaving Rulon standing there in the middle of the floor. Every employee on the floor was watching this spectacle, as were half of the patrons. Rulon put his hands on his hips and glared at him. The young man who had been following Rulon around sighed repeatedly as he stood by in silence and tapped his foot.

"Some management team," Tara said.

"Yeah, well, I've got to be going."

"Are you leaving me already?"

"I've got to get a handle on what's going on with Robert Earl's widow before some lawyer talks her into a lawsuit."

"Why don't you come back around lunchtime? I ought to be able to take a break by then."

"Can't do it," I said.

"How about dinner?"

"I'll be catching up on paperwork tonight."

"You do make it difficult for a working girl who needs a little companionship." She tapped the end of the cigarette against the bottom of the ashtray. "But you better not wait too long. I'm only going to be here a few days."

NINE

Back before Johnnie Koscko convinced himself that I was the guy at Bayou Casualty who was banging Tara Stocklin and keeping her on the payroll for the sole purpose of making his life miserable, he was feeling generous and gave me a pair of tickets to the VIP reception he was hosting for the Snow Mountain band in the casino's Jubilee Room two hours before their concert. Since that time, our relationship had slid all the way off the blacktop and down into the kudzu. Word had gotten back to me from our New Orleans headquarters that Johnnie the Dime was now trying to get me fired because he knew for a natural fact that Tara and I were over here in Bay St. Louis doing the wild thing on company time.

But that blowhard could think whatever he wanted to as far as I was concerned, I still had those VIP tickets in my hand, and I asked Tara if she wanted to go with me. I knew good and well that Koscko would see us together, and I knew that seeing us would confirm every one of his suspicions. I also knew Tara would read way too much into me asking her out. But what the hell. I was already guilty as far as Koscko was concerned. And if I was going to have to pay for a ticket to get into the fair, at least I ought to get to ride the merry-go-round.

Wherever Tara Stocklin came from out west was obviously a different universe than the manicured lawns and circular pea-gravel drives of east Memphis where my ex-wife Sandy grew up, and that suited me just fine. Sandy is the only child of T. W. "Buddy" Donovan, III, a big-time banker up there, and Sarah Nell, a former Queen of the Cotton Carnival who spends most of her time nowadays planning fund-raisers for the Memphis Symphony and arranging photo safaris for her Junior League friends to the grassland (make that veldt) of southern Africa, where they go up in hot-air balloons and take pictures of the running herds of wildebeest. Several years ago at one of the Donovan dinner parties up in Memphis, I made the mistake of calling the damn things antelopes. You'd have thought that I had broken wind or something.

With that group, you never knew where the land mines were. But I didn't figure I was in much danger of making a social faux pas around Tara. I couldn't think of anything I could do that she was likely to consider an embarrassment.

Johnnie the Dime had cordoned off the main restaurant. He had stuffed a couple of his no-neck bouncers into tight-fitting tuxedos and pressed them into service as security guards, and they were carefully and elegantly checking everyone's ticket as they entered. The place smelled of boiled shrimp and fried stuffed crabs, of roast beef and horseradish sauce.

One of the craps tables in the center of the room had been moved to make way for a shiny black grand piano, and the guy who usually played at the casino's piano bar was putting on a real good show. He mixed in a lot of Snow Mountain's big hits, hoping to catch the ear of the Kenny Folger, Jr., the band's leader known throughout the world as Kenny, Junior, but the band hadn't arrived yet.

Tara was in a long black dress with a long split up the side, backless all the way down to her waist. It clung to her sculpted body like Saran Wrap, clung so tight that it left no doubt that she was wearing nothing underneath. She had sharp muscle definition across her shoulders, but none of the bulk you can get with weights. Some few of us are just born with that body type. She had just discovered Rulon Hornbeck's crab puffs at the hors d'oeuvre table and wasn't even trying to resist them. Resisting just isn't her thing.

"So, what's this I hear about Satan and the Snow Mountain band?" she asked. "I heard on TV that Kenny, Junior, is supposed to be the Antichrist."

"Somehow I always pictured the Antichrist as being a little taller than that," I said.

"Have you tried one of these?" She held up a crab puff to feed it to me.

I didn't know most of the people in the crowd. But the few I did know, the ones from Bay St. Louis and surrounding area, were the right people. Ever since Sandy and I divorced and she went home to Memphis I haven't had anybody to tell me who the right people are. She had perfect pitch when it came to such things, except for the one time it failed her when she married me.

I have an especially hard time picking out the right people here in Bay St. Louis since I grew up with so many of them who weren't necessarily at the top of the social heap when we were in junior high but might be up there now. With Sandy out of the picture, the best way I have of telling who belongs where on the social spectrum is to go to a party at Neal and Kathy's house and see who shows up.

A lot of those folks I had seen at Neal's last campaign fund-raiser were now around the hors d'oeuvre table, so Johnnie the Dime's master plan to make Jackpot Bay Casino a class joint was off to a good start. Rulon Hornbeck was lit up, beaming, floating around the room, barely touching the floor, kissing women on the cheek and laughing with them and ordering the poor waiters around like he was Marie Antoinette, or worse, a wedding director.

Across the room Johnnie Koscko marched through the front

door looking for all the world like some kind of Hollywood mogul out of the 1950s. He had on a pair of black pants too tight around the waist, a pink shirt with a white ascot, and a cream-colored linen sports jacket with a blue silk hankie stuffed into the breast pocket. He was puffing on a cigar, a sour-smelling Churchill as big around as a broom handle. He had one of his beefy hands on the arm of Kenny Folger, Jr., whom he appeared to be dragging around the room introducing him to the various guests. Kenny grinned a sheepish grin, and appeared to be embarrassed. His eyes were dancing all around the room.

"So is Clyde going to get rung up on that shooting or not?" Tara asked. "I hear the DA might not press charges."

"Folks down here have always been big believers in self-defense. Ever since those attacks in Washington and New York, you start shooting up some public place and you can expect to draw heavy fire."

"So you think he shot that guy in self-defense?"

"Of course not. But what I think doesn't mean a thing."

"Johnnie the Dime sure doesn't look worried about it," she said.

"He's got him a new trophy."

"That Kenny, Junior, is a hunk," she said. "God, look at those eyes."

Kenny, Senior, died twenty some odd years ago near Steamboat Springs on a January night on a closed ski slope lighted only by a full moon. He slalomed into a bank of aspens and centered one of them, cracking his skull. The blood test later revealed near-lethal traces of a number of drugs. He left a widow and an infant son, Kenny, Junior. The wife took the baby back home to Arkansas and dropped out of sight.

The Snow Mountain Band had recorded three albums before Kenny, Senior, died, and one of them had gone platinum. Four singles had made the charts and one of them, a raunchy ballad named "Slippery Slopes," is still the unofficial anthem of the ski bum crowd throughout the world. They were one of the first crossover bands, a country/rock sound often compared to the Doobie Brothers and Creedence Clearwater Revival.

Kenny, Junior, grew up to look exactly like his father. Perhaps even more remarkable than their appearance is the similarity of their voices. With a blend of the band's old standards, perfect recreations of the originals, and a growing number of new ones written and sung by Kenny, Junior, Snow Mountain has become one of the hottest groups in the world. They're on the road nine months at a stretch, followed around by a entourage of followers with the derivative name of Snow Heads, a group with the sort of devotion usually seen only in religious cults.

Watching one of their concerts is like going back in time; it's as if the old man has returned from the dead. And that's where this recent trouble came in. "I'm the Man" is one of the weaker songs on Snow Mountain's latest CD. It has this one overly dramatic line that says "Take my hand, and I'll command the earth and sky and sea; There's nothing that can stop us, girl, if you'll believe in me."

Some Endtime preacher in a fundamentalist church out of Terre Haute saw Kenny, Junior, singing this line on MTV, looking and sounding for all the world like his long-dead father. And that's all it took. Next thing you knew the word was out that the Antichrist was here on Earth singing and dancing and pleading with the Bride of Christ to come over to his side so they can rule the world together. And the supermarket tabloids and the doomsday radio and TV preachers both rejoiced at their good fortune. It was a story that could bleed millions out of the circuit revival crowd.

Johnnie the Dime had his back to us so he didn't notice that he had pulled Kenny, Junior, so close to Tara and me. When he turned around we were face to face. He stiffened for a second when he saw Tara, but his smile returned quickly. Not even our presence was going to dampen his spirits.

"I'm surprised to see you two here."

I introduced Tara and myself to Kenny, Junior, since I knew Koscko wasn't about to do it.

"Is this your first time down here on the Coast?" I asked.

Kenny shook his head no. "When I was growin' up, me and Mama'd come down here in the summer. We'd pack our lunches and leave home at maybe four o'clock in the mornin' and get here around noon. We'd go straight to the beach before we even checked into the motel. Mama, she used to love to play Goofy Golf over in Biloxi. I went back over there this afternoon and played. I still ain't too good at it."

"Goofy Golf. Can ya believe it?" Johnnie the Dime patted the side of Kenny's face. "Just your All-American kid. Does this look like the face of the Antichrist to you? Come on, Kenny."

Kenny was saying that it was nice to meet us when he was pulled away in mid-sentence.

"Man," Tara said, "he's got a thicker Southern accent than you do."

"I didn't notice any accent."

Gretchen La Pointe was making her entrance, and Johnnie was making a beeline to her, pushing people to the side with one hand and pulling Kenny by the arm with the other. Gretchen paused to give everybody time to get a look at her. I don't even know if she does that intentionally anymore, it's become a reflex.

She was decked out in one of these flashy outfits she "picks up in Paris" every spring. Had on this turquoise long-sleeved net blouse that was embroidered with clusters of purple grapes and a floor-length velvet skirt a few shades darker than the blouse. Every woman in the place was taking mental notes. Turquoise was going to be a big color on the Coast for the next few months.

"So who's Johnnie the Dime trying to impress over there?" Tara asked.

"That's the queen bee. Gretchen La Pointe herself."

"She looks rich."

"The La Pointes were rich enough a hundred years ago to buy a summer place over here so they could get some breeze off the Gulf when it got too hot in New Orleans. We're talking old money."

"I thought you didn't hobnob with the moneyed set."

"I never said I don't like any rich people. I just can't stomach the pretentious ones."

"So I take it you consider her to be down to earth?"

"Gretchen's just as likely to jump up on that table and start doing a striptease as you'd be."

A young man, trim and blond, walked in behind Gretchen and caught up with her. He was decked out in a pair of white lightweight slacks, white buck shoes, a white knit shirt, open collar, and topped it all off with a light blue summer-weight blazer with a folded white handkerchief stuffed into the breast pocket. He had his hand planted in the lower-front pocket of the blazer the way most men would put their hand in the front pocket of their slacks. A pair of dark green Ray•Bans were suspended on a chain around his neck.

"So who's the guy with her?" Tara asked. "He looks familiar."

"You mean the *GQ* model? Never saw him before."

She scrutinized him as she chewed on a crab puff.

"I'd assume he's this earl we've been hearing about," I said.

She licked her lower lip, still looking at him. Then she smiled as she quietly snapped her fingers the way people do when an idea hits them. "So he's an earl, huh?"

"I'm sure you can meet him if you want to. I can get Gretchen to introduce you."

"Would you mind getting me a light screwdriver? I forgot to take my Vitamin C pill this morning."

She was across the room talking to the guy before I could get to the rear of the line at the bar. By the time I ordered her drink, she had steered him away from Gretchen off to the corner. Damn, the girl is fast.

"Is everything to your liking?" It was Rulon Hornbeck.

"Real nice, Rulon."

"Have you heard anything from the police?"

"About Clyde? You know as much about it as I do. By the way, where is he?"

Rulon waved at someone across the room. "He's parking cars. Buses actually. I do hope you're going to recommend that we not allow guns in the casino."

"You need to talk to Tara about that," I said. "Security is her show."

"I thought I saw you with her earlier."

I pointed to her across the room. "Is that the earl I've been hearing about?"

"You mean the one over there with your date? Yes, that's the Earl of Stropshire."

"Does he have a name?"

"David Stratton-Hume."

"And he's staying with Gretchen?"

"Miss La Pointe seems to be headed this way. I'll introduce you and you can ask her that question yourself."

Gretchen must have had another facelift since the last time I saw her. That, or a new nose job. Or maybe some injection of collagen or silicon or spackle. I have no problem with plastic surgery, but Gretchen's face was about to cross this line that I've drawn in my own mind. She was beginning to take on that Hollywood look, with just a touch too much flesh in the lips, the edges of the nose just a bit too sharp.

This inner voice that just annoys the hell out of me from time to time started whining in the background. That's it, Delmas, the voice said. Just sit back and expect the whole world to dance to your tune. Sit back smug and half broke and look down on somebody because they look a little different than what you'd like. You're getting old, Delmas, and starting to sound like every old fart sitting around the coffee shop out on the highway every morning.

What the hell, maybe that's where we're headed. Plastic surgery specifically designed to produce grotesque results. Twenty-first-century plumage for the Homo sapiens. Maybe we're going full circle to some earlier age and the next thing we know, we'll be sticking wooden disks into our women's lips and binding our baby daughters' feet in three-inch-long shoes. History is full of examples of adornments and tattoos and mutilations designed to achieve the ideal of feminine beauty in countless societies around the world. So what about it, Delmas? I mean, why does it bother you to see a pierced tongue but not a pierced earlobe? Is it because you didn't grow up around pierced tongues? Are you already so old that you're starting to calcify? Are you going to be stuck in the eighties the way those guys at the coffee shop are stuck in the forties and fifties?

Gretchen kissed me lightly on the lips. "Hello, handsome. Haven't seen you in a while."

"It has been a while, but you're still the best-looking woman on the Coast," I said. "You know Rulon Hornbeck, don't you?"

"Oh, yes, yes. Wonderful party, Rulon."

"Thank you, darling. But it's absolutely working me to death." He frowned at me as he backed away. "You'll have to excuse me. I see we've run out of crab puffs. Again."

Gretchen blew a kiss at him as he walked off. "You wouldn't have a light, would you?"

"I can find one for you," I said.

"Oh, forget it," she said. "So what are you doing here? I didn't think cocktail parties were your thing."

"I had some tickets and didn't want them to go to waste."

"If you don't have plans, why don't you join my group at the concert tonight?"

"Can I bring my date with me? She's the one over there talking to your date."

"Oh, yes," she said. "The earl. I'm still trying to remember where I met him."

"I thought he was staying at your place."

She spotted a matchbook on the table half hidden by a plate. "He called the other day and said he was passing through this area. I gather from what he said that I met him somewhere on the Riviera. I think the group was heavily into gin rickeys that week we were in Monaco."

"So you don't know him and he's staying with you?" Across the room, Tara was laughing loudly as she grasped the earl's forearm.

"Only at the guest house. I couldn't very well say I didn't remember him, now could I? I mean you just don't do that to an earl. Besides, he and Rulon Hornbeck know each other and Rulon told me all about him."

"Rulon?"

"They knew each other in Monaco. It's a rather cozy group over there." She handed me the matchbook. "Would you mind?"

I struck a match and held it up for her to light her cigarette. "So it really was Rulon who got the earl to come here."

"Jack, darling, that's no big accomplishment. The British aristocracy are as fine a set of moochers as you'll ever meet. And absolutely irresistible."

"So I can see."

"Don't worry about him flirting with your date. He doesn't mean anything by it." She reached over for an empty hors d'oeuvre plate to use as an ashtray. "But if he starts flirting with you, you need to take that very seriously indeed."

"Are you sure about that?"

"I suspect he and Rulon are an item, since they're trying so terribly hard not to appear to be. Would you be a dear and get me a drink?"

"I wonder if Tara has figured that out yet."

"You mean your date? Of course she has, dear." She took a light puff on her Virginia Slim. "I'm sure she picked up on David's proclivities in no more than a minute or two. No offense, but she looks like the type who can read sexual signals quite well. She certainly sends them out."

"Well, in that case I wonder what the hell she and the earl are talking about."

"Maybe she's interested in his collection of porcelains."

"Not hardly," I said.

TEN

The sun was low and yellow in the western sky, slowly sinking behind a gray bank of clouds over the Gulf's far horizon. In the calm of sunset, dry heat rose from the sand after having baked all day under a cloudless sky, and the Gulf was as still as a pond as orange-billed shearwaters raced just inches above the surface dipping into the water occasionally to pluck a silvery shad or menhaden.

The warm-up act, Clayton Broussard and the Red Bean Band, a zydeco group from somewhere over around New Iberia, was just getting into their grand finale, *Tante Na-Na*, and fifty Snow Heads who had laid down their blankets in front of the stage before noon were stumbling around in their swim trunks and Snow Mountain T-shirts trying to learn the Cajun two-step. Most of them were about a beer or a few tokes too late to take it up; the two-step can be tricky and very few folks around here know how to do it since we didn't grow up with it.

The city of Bay St. Louis had, despite the protests of some homeowners, blocked off three blocks of Beach Boulevard and routed traffic up through the neighborhoods. The turnout had been estimated at eighty to a hundred thousand, thick as the Canal Street crowd during a Rex Parade, and the best efforts of the six outmanned policemen the city could spare for such duty were not enough to keep it from spilling into the well-tended front yards of the big houses as the people who lived there watched through their windows, too cautious and scared to say anything about it.

There was not a hotel room to be had from Hattiesburg to Mobile to New Orleans. A lot of concert goers had been camping out for the past several days in state parks and RV campgrounds and on the sand bars of Red Creek and the Jourdan River. Some of the fans had come down from Kentucky, Illinois, Minnesota, and even Canada, and WXXV-TV out of Gulfport had a reporter with a cameraman in tow weaving through the throng trying to find who had come the greatest distance and was still sober enough to talk before the camera. WWL-TV out of New Orleans had sent their traffic copter over to take some footage, and it paced up and down the shoreline a few hundred yards out over the water, flying low over the hundred or so shallow-draft skiffs, sailboats, and runabouts anchored in close enough to catch the concert without the price of a ticket.

The heart of the Bay St. Louis historic district, Old Towne, is on a hurricane-proof bluff some twenty feet above the beach, and it was at the foot of this bluff that the stage had been erected for Snow Mountain. The street was covered with walkers and dancers, young and old, some sitting in lawn chairs on the front lawn of Saint Stanislaus School and some sitting on the seawall. The lightest hint of grilled chicken blended with the scents of coconut butter and bug repellent, and the grounds crew started lighting tiki lamps, hoping the black, oily smoke would discourage the mosquitoes. The beach below was completely covered in human beings, and from the street you could hardly see any open patches of white sand, most of it hidden by blankets on which hard-core Snow Heads had been lying all day.

The sun reddened as it touched the horizon and shrank to a pinpoint of light, which soon extinguished like a lighted match hitting the water. As it grew dark, around the streetlights the swirlings of summer bugs expanded into shimmering white halos. Along with the pleasant sounds of the accordions and fiddles of the zydeco band, was the smell of fried crawfish pies, chicken on a stick, beer, Polish sausage, and a mild undercurrent of marijuana.

Tara and I weaved through the dancing crowd, searching for the area that Neal had said he was going to set up. Neal, bless his heart, is the type who presses his Bermuda shorts before he attends something like this, but he's a great one to have around. He had planned the entire evening and was expecting some out-of-town guests. He had dutifully gone down his to-do list, checking off each item: blankets, lawn chairs, ice chest, towels, cell phone, and even a roll of disposable paper covers for the seat of the Porta-Potty. Those things are nightmares for women.

Sometimes when we go to football games together, Neal's attention to things such as starting times, rain gear, food, and where to park drives me a little crazy. But I'll admit my idea of planning ahead, which consists of sticking an extra twenty-dollar-bill and an ATM card in the pocket of my jeans and making sure I've got my ticket, sometimes meets with less-than-perfect results. My ex-wife Sandy could tell you all about that, and would be happy to do so. But for all his logistical expertise, not even Neal had planned on this many people.

He had told me the general area where he would set up, but when we descended into that mob, visibility was reduced to about twenty feet. Finally, by luck, we spotted my sister-in-law Kathy sitting cross legged on a blanket. As we approached she gave us the once-over. Tara had dressed for the occasion: a bikini, flip-flops, and an oversized T-shirt. I made the introductions and I could tell Kathy didn't like what she saw. But then I didn't expect her to.

Ever since Sandy left me—and, dammit, *she* was the one who left—the women of Bay St. Louis have been in not so secret conspiracy to get me remarried. Since I was the one who got dumped, they allowed me what they considered a respectable time to get over it, but that time has long since passed.

It's the usual alliance that forms in such instances, a group who may not have much to say to each other in normal times but band together for the common good when they detect the presence of that greatest of all dangers, the unmarried, unattached male. There's Mama's friends, who have daughters or nieces who have gone off for the past few years to the high-rises and traffic of New Orleans or Houston and have just about gotten that out of their systems, they of the ticking clocks who are ready to get back home and build the nest. And there's the group who are on the lookout for a husband themselves. They're the ones who have long since given up on being choosy, which allows me into the mix.

And finally, there's the most radical of the bunch, the Taliban element, the ones who know no bounds in their efforts to tie me down. I'm talking about any woman with a husband who is a friend of mine. Or with a husband who even knows me, friend or not. I'm not the kind of role model they want their man hanging around.

Some of them even come out and say the words. Settle down. Brings to mind visions of reclining on the ice floe just before they push you away from the bank. So they've got the entire program mapped out for me if I intend to stay in Bay St. Louis, and some wild woman from Las Vegas is not part of their master plan.

Now I'll admit that Kathy hasn't been bad lately about the matchmaker stuff, not since we had cleared the air with our little come-to-Jesus meeting. But that's only because she knows that the chances of Neal Delmas walking out of that law office and adopting my lifestyle are about the same as the chances of him shaving his head and wrapping up in a sheet and selling roses at some airport. She still wasn't too crazy about Tara.

But what choice did I have? If I *didn't* take Tara out after that display two days earlier back at the Jackpot Bay, and the word got out around town, I'd never live it down. That would be the kind of thing that could get some pretty bad rumors started about you up at the Broke Spoke.

"We'd just about given up on you," Kathy said.

"Looks like you're set up for a pretty good-sized crowd."

"One of your old friends is coming," she said. "In fact a couple of them are."

"Where's Neal?"

"He forgot something back at the house."

We sat and Tara slapped at a mosquito on her leg. She reached into her beach bag and handed me a bottle of liquid Off as she started pulling the T-shirt over her head.

"Josh Hallman called and said he's bringing a friend over from New Orleans," Kathy said.

"Damn mosquitoes," Tara said as she scratched the tiny red welt.

Josh Hallman is the best courtroom lawyer I have ever seen. He and my brother have known each other for several years, have tried cases together, and have a great deal of respect for one another. Once when I was in a particularly nasty jam in New Orleans, a charge of first-degree murder to be precise, Neal got Josh to represent me. Had it not been for him, I would probably be a resident of Angola Prison this very day. Josh is sometimes an insufferable egomaniac, bitchy, vain, and often pompous. He is, at the same time, kind, intelligent, and fiercely loyal to his friends. He is a small man, slightly built, but he's as brave as a New York fireman or cop when he's in a legal fight for some underdog.

"I guess everybody's a Snow Mountain fan, even Josh." I poured some of the clear oil onto my fingers and started rubbing it on Tara's bare back. She adjusted the top of her bikini. Kathy pretended to not be looking at the perfect curvature.

"You probably remember the friend he's bringing," Kathy said. "It's Gino Stafford."

"You're kidding!"

"Can you rub some of that on my legs while you're at it?"

"You mean Gino and Josh are together?" I asked.

"Wait a minute," Tara said. "Gino and Josh? Those are men's names. Isn't anybody straight in this town?"

Kathy looked down at my hand on Tara's back. "I haven't seen

Gino since the big news hit," she said. "I wonder if he's gotten over it yet."

In high school there was some real quiet talk about Gino Stafford. He was a big, strong guy and a hell of a tight end. But he was a loner and had this streak of melancholy and always seemed to want to be somewhere else. After we graduated he went for a while to some art school in Austin that nobody had ever heard of. Never finished, but never came back home either. So he ended up in the French Quarter, forty miles and a whole world away, a place filled with Gino Staffords from all over the country. Opened a restaurant on Burgundy Street featuring broiled seafood, and everybody says it's really good.

I'd see him in town every once in a while, typically holidays when he came back for a day, maybe two, to see the family. He has this friend from Vermont named George something who runs an antique store in Old Town and he'd spend some time there. Always in a new car, and always a convertible. Red Miata last time. Everything seemed fine. He'd run into old friends at the Sav-A-Center or at the gas pump of the 7-Eleven, and he'd always invite them to stop by the restaurant when they were over in New Orleans. The glaring absence of female company was something people in town silently noted, but just didn't talk about. Especially Mama and Daddy and their friends, a group that included Gino's parents. There was just enough distance and just enough evasiveness for everybody to be comfortable.

It was an arrangement that was holding up just fine until the e-mails started making their way around town. Even had pictures to download. Nothing racy, just scenes of Gino and some friends in one of the Crescent City's more well-known gay bars. Lots of hand holding and guys dancing together. Nothing that everybody didn't already know. But there had always been a curtain there before, and some horse's ass had pulled it back with no other motive than sheer meanness.

Any other time, it may have been an occasion of relief. But

whoever was sending out the poison pen e-mails did it a little too soon. Gino's father was dying with liver cancer and the e-mail blitz made him face up to something he would have avoided all the way to his grave. Mr. Stafford had known the score for years, at least that's what Mrs. Stafford later told Mama, but he didn't want to bring it up. Wanted to keep it inside not because of any pain it caused him, he just didn't want to put Gino through it. So Gino and his father were forced into what amounted to a tearful catharsis at the side of the hospital bed just a few days before death came. Maybe the e-mailer, despite his intentions, did them a favor.

But from what I hear, Gino didn't see it that way.

Through the crowd popped a smallish, trim, agile man in a white straw planter's hat with a yellow hatband, a Hawaiian shirt, and baggy shorts with a drawstring. He was pushing an igloo cooler mounted on wheels like an old-time ice-cream vendor, the kind you used to see years ago in Bienville Park over in Mobile. He waved at us and turned and looked behind him.

"Who's the little guy in the bright outfit?" Tara asked.

"That's the one and only Josh Hallman," I said.

"My God!" Josh said. "What a crowd! If they realized I was carrying a load of margaritas around in this ice chest, I would have been hijacked before I ever got past the seawall!"

"I sure didn't expect to see you here," I said. "Where's Gino?"

"He'll be along soon. We ran into Gretchen La Pointe and this gorgeous man who was with her, and Gino started talking to them."

Tara guided my hand to the lower rim of her bikini top and pressed my fingers against her chest. Kathy acted like she wasn't taking in what Tara was doing, but she wasn't fooling me. I kept on rubbing and tried to be nonchalant.

"I didn't realize you and Gino know each other," I said.

"We go back several years, ever since he moved to New Orleans." He reached into his pocket and pulled out a pack of cigarettes.

"Oh, God, can I please have one of those?" Tara said.

"Of course you can." He sat on the blanket beside her. "I don't believe we've met."

I introduced them. "This man who was with that Gretchen woman," she said, "was he British?"

"As a matter of fact he was." He lit her cigarette.

"How's Gino been getting along?" Kathy asked.

"Good days and bad days," Josh said. "He's been having such a rough time lately that he needed to get out among friends. I needed to come to this area anyway to look at some property. I've been holding out for years, but everybody's moving out of New Orleans. A lot of them are going to the north shore of Lake Pontchartrain, but I've thought I might want to go in this direction."

"You mean you'd actually leave the French Quarter?"

"I'd keep a place over there. I mean I'd hate to go, but the crime has gotten so bad. Besides, if that Saints football team is looking to move over here, I guess the whole city will be over here soon enough."

"There was no way on earth the Saints were coming here," I said. "They were just bluffing to get a new stadium built."

"Oh, there they come," Josh said.

"Gino looks good," Kathy said.

"That big one?" Tara asked as she slapped a mosquito at her ankle. "You can say that again."

"Honey," Josh said, "you might as well forget him and stick with Jack."

"I'm beginning to wonder about that," she said.

As they approached us, Gino, Gretchen La Pointe, David Stratton-Hume, and this home-grown social climber named Richie Leggett were laughing at something one of them had said. From up at the stage, a laser light show began and they paused to watch the green and blue lights swirling against the backdrop of the trees behind the houses across the street. Josh gazed at them with a slight smile. "It's so good to see Gino laugh again. These last few months have been hard on him, but I think he's about ready to get past it."

"You mean his father's death?" Kathy said.

"It was a whole series of things. First of all, Gino had been in a relationship that I knew from the start was no good for him. It ended when he got dumped in a nasty and very public scene in the foyer of his restaurant. Which reminds me, have you ever known Gino to be violent?"

"Never," I said. "He's gentle as a kitten."

"Well right after that scene at the restaurant, he disappeared. When he showed up three days later, he was drunk and belligerent. I'd never seen that side of him before. He came into Oscar's Lounge well after midnight with a three-day beard and couldn't walk a straight line. And he was carrying this truly wicked-looking pistol in his coat. We very carefully got him quite smashed, enough to where we could take the gun from him just before he passed out. I had to put him up for a few days in my guest house out by the pool."

"I've never known Gino to drink all that much," I said.

"That's what I'm saying. He never does. Which is a good thing because he is one mean drunk."

"Is he okay now?"

"Not completely. He stayed in bed for a few days, and just when he seemed to be getting better, those wretched e-mails started going out. I'm sure you know all about that."

"Josh," I said, "the fact that Gino Stafford is gay wasn't exactly news around here."

"Oh, I know that, and Gino knew it too. That's not the point. It was the effect it had on Gino's poor father. I mean, I know what was going on was hypocrisy. But after all, hypocrisy is the very basis of good manners."

"Do you know who outted him?" Kathy asked.

"There's no question in my mind, or in Gino's mind for that matter, but we don't have any direct proof. It was the pond scum he had broken up with a few weeks earlier."

The entourage made its way to us with Gretchen in the lead. Like Hemingway, she attracts a crowd of café dwellers wherever she goes. Refers to them simply as The Group. It is a protean bunch that hangs together for days at a time, sometimes weeks, and adds and loses members like skin cells, with the one constant being Gretchen. The membership is based on charm or wit or possession of some quality that Gretchen finds amusing or intriguing, but only after a tryout. But she must choose you, you can't apply. It's bad form and instant rejection to even try that.

"Oh, a welcome oasis!" Gretchen said as she reached for Josh's ice chest. "I trust everyone knows everyone else."

Josh pushed up from the blanket. "I don't believe I've actually been introduced to your new friend, Gretchen."

"Oh, of course you haven't," she said. "Everybody, I want you to meet David Stratton-Hume."

"Charmed," he said.

"David here's the Earl of Stropshire," Richie Leggett chimed in, "over in England."

"Stropshire?" Josh asked as he reached to shake hands. "Just where is that?"

"It's Wales, actually," the earl said. "And your name is?"

"Josh Hallman."

"Oh, David, I just adore Josh," Gretchen said, "even though I hate him because he's made such obscene amounts of money suing the tobacco companies that he's driven up the price of cigarettes to where I simply must stop smoking."

"Really," the earl said.

"I heard about that," Richie said. "Read about it in *Newsweek*."

"And who is this lovely creature?" Gretchen asked.

"I'm a smart-mouthed Yankee by the name of Tara Stocklin."

"So, lovely Tara Stocklin, the Yankee with the beautiful legs," Gretchen said, "just what do you do? The group must know all about you."

"Tara's a skydiver," the earl said. "She parachutes out of airplanes."

"Oh, I forgot," Gretchen said. "You two know each other."

David Stratton-Hume nodded and stared into Tara's eyes as he took her hand and kissed it. God, I wish I could do something like that with a straight face. "Yes," he said, "the lovely Tara was telling me about her perilous hobby last night. You know I too am a parachutist. It's the one good thing I got out of the Falklands campaign."

"Skydiving?" Gretchen said. "You jump out of perfectly good airplanes, my dear?"

"You ought to try it," Tara said with a wink. "It'll make you quiver in all the right spots."

"Well come with me to the ladies' room, darling. I want to hear all about this skydiving and this quivering. You come with us, dear Kathy."

"I've got to go back to the house and see what's keeping Neal."

"We'll wait here," the earl said, "and guard the margaritas."

"Yeah," Richie said, "y'all take your time. We need to talk about some investment opportunities down here."

"Oh, really, Rich." The earl stiffened a bit. "I'm sure there's plenty of time for that tomorrow."

Gretchen leveled a cool gaze at Richie that he was way too obtuse to pick up on. That remark might have just got him dropped from the group. Even I knew better than to talk money around the Gretchen La Pointe crowd. She cut her eyes toward the earl as she waited for Tara to join her.

"So, Mr. Hallman," David Stratton-Hume said, "your friend Gino tells me you're a barrister."

"I'd be closer to a solicitor if we had such distinctions over here."

"I run a restaurant," Gino said. "What do I know about lawyers?"

"So what brings you to the states?" Josh asked.

The earl began explaining where he had run into Gretchen, how he had been with this group she had put together in Monaco, how he just couldn't bear yet another summer in Nice and wanted to see the American South. Richie motioned me to the side and leaned close like he wanted to share a secret. "The real reason David came over here," he whispered, "is to find investors at thirty grand a pop for this group who plans to move into Havana and build a casino when Castro finally dies. Can you imagine what kinda gold rush that's gonna be?"

"He told you this?"

"He wants to keep it quiet. I told him he could trust me. I won't tell anybody who can't keep a secret."

"He came all the way from England to Bay St. Louis, Mississippi, to find investors?"

Richie snickered and shook his head. "He's got a couple of prospects in New Orleans and one in Mobile. He just dropped by here to see Gretchen. Had no idea there was any money here."

"Is there?"

"You'd be surprised," he said. "David sure was. He thought thirty thousand would be way out of our league down here."

"Well, it's way out of mine."

"You shoulda seen his face when I told him I could line up a dozen guys right here on the Coast who lose more than that at the golf course every year. He thought we barely could afford indoor plumbing in Mississippi."

"So that's the reason he's visiting Gretchen? He wants to line up investors?"

"Naw. He just came to be sociable, what with him being in the neighborhood, so to speak. But now that I've filled him in on how many high rollers we got down here, he'll probably stay a few days extra. But he ain't here for the money, he's just a good guy who wanted to see an old friend. Just like one of us'd do. He ain't stuffy a bit. Listen to this." He turned toward the earl. "Hey, Elvis! Great concert!"

Stratton-Hume looked over our way and smiled as he held an imaginary microphone to his lips. "Thank you," he said in a pretty good imitation of The King. "Thank you very much."

"If you didn't know better, you'd swear he was from Tupelo, wouldn't you?" Richie said. "You oughta hear him do Burt Reynolds in *Smokey and the Bandit*. He's good, son."

When the women returned, Gretchen and Tara were walking arm in arm and laughing at some joke one of them had told. They were both loud and earthy women and had hit it off well. I had worked up a thirst, so I stepped over to Neal's forty-gallon Coleman cooler for one of his Budweisers. Josh was sitting alone in his director's chair with his feet propped on the cooler.

"Wouldn't you rather have one of my famous margaritas?" Josh asked.

"Not yet," I said.

The rest of our bunch stood at Gretchen's insistence and went to get some glowing plastic loops that a local radio station was passing out from this golf cart they were driving through the crowd. They left Josh and me to take care of all the stuff spread out on our blanket.

"I think Gino's taken a liking to our friend the earl," he said, "or at least to those delicious blue eyes."

"I don't know about that, Josh. The guy looks pretty straight to me."

"I'm a lawyer and not a detective. But when you're, shall we say, different and grow up in a little Piney Woods town like Columbia, you become quite adept at picking up certain signals."

"And what signal is he sending out?" I asked.

"Charming, sophisticated, witty. Did I mention the eyes?"

The second warm-up band, a Bluegrass group that featured a steel guitar and an amplified zither, started their act with a medley of standards from the old Martha White Radio Show. The first song was the Jimmie Dickens song from the 1930s, "Old Cold Tater."

"Has he hit you up for any money?" I had to raise my voice some to overcome the music.

Josh stared at me over the rim of his glass and raised a questioning eyebrow as he sipped the green slushy drink.

"Don't you think it's unusual that a member of the British aristocracy would be trying to raise money for a business venture?" I asked.

Josh started laughing and got a little choked on the last vestiges of the swallow he had taken. "Oh, Jack, you really must get away from here more often."

"I can't hear you."

He leaned closer to me and cupped his hand to serve as a megaphone. "Many, many of the earls and dukes and other forms of British nobility make their living by giving guided tours of their manor house. It's not surprising one bit to find one who dirties his hands with base commerce. A good number of them are no better off financially than the people living along the beach here. In fact it's common for them to have jobs. A ton of them are stockbrokers."

"Are any of them lawyers?"

"That's too much work for a gentleman," he said. "If what you're saying about him trying to scour up a few investors for some venture is true, it wouldn't surprise me a bit." The music stopped and he caught himself shouting. "God, they're loud."

"So you don't see anything unusual about an earl scouring the countryside for investors?" I asked.

"Not as a general proposition. But I'll admit I had David pegged more as a playboy than a rainmaker. I'll say this, he's not quite like any of the nobility I've ever been around before."

"How's that?"

They finished the first number and things quieted as the lead singer introduced each of the band members to the crowd.

"I can't put my finger on it," Josh said. "He's certainly an engaging sort of fellow. But when we were introduced, I talked to him maybe five minutes and during that time, he dropped the names of Princess Di, Dodi al-Fayed, Sara Ferguson, whom he called Fergie, and for good measure he threw in King Juan Carlos and Queen Sophia of Spain. He confided to me that the royal family is mortified that Fergie is doing American TV commercials, and he even mentioned that Carlos and Sophia were pleased with the Majesty of Spain exhibit here in Mississippi, though they found the place too hot for their liking."

"So the weather was too hot for them," I said. "Maybe that's why the Spanish pulled out of Mexico."

"He threw in the names of a few Parisian fashion designers, and he asked me where I bought these shorts I'm wearing."

"Celebrities, clothes, I guess that's the kind of stuff those folks talk about," I said. "Maybe he doesn't know much about bass fishing or deer hunting."

"No, Jack, that's what I mean. Those are most certainly *not* the kind of things those folks talk about. At least not that I've ever heard."

"So how many dukes, earls, and what-not do you know?"

"I admit it, not many. But David's certainly got more personality than any of them I've been around before."

"You wouldn't be stereotyping now would you, counselor?"

"If you're trying to put me on the defensive, you'll have to come up with something stronger that that." He pointed toward the group as they made their way back toward us. "Besides, I find stereotyping to come in handy every once in a while."

"We need two for the road," Gretchen said. She had slipped up on us. "Go cups, please."

"Where are y'all going?" I asked.

Tara stepped in front of me and reached out to put her hands on either side of my neck. Then she ground her pelvis against me a few times, which was kind of a thrill. She smelled of tequila. "Gretchen wants us to go meet the band."

"But the concert's supposed to start any minute."

"Which is exactly why we need to hurry," Gretchen said.

"Do you want to come with us?" Tara asked.

"I'm really not into the rock band groupie scene. I'll just wait here."

"How about you, Josh?" Gretchen asked. "The earl says he's up for it."

"Somebody's got to stay and watch the margaritas," he said as he held one out for whoever wanted it.

"Good point," Tara said. "Damn good point."

"You realize that those stage mangers won't let you backstage for free," Josh said.

She let go of my neck and grabbed the top of her bikini. "Hey, no problem." She yanked the top down and her nicely rounded C-cups plopped out. Josh's jaw dropped and Gretchen howled with delight. Her breasts were as tanned as the rest of her and on the inside of the left one there was a dime-sized tattoo of a red rose. She held the top down for maybe two full seconds before she slipped the covering back into place. "You think those would get us past security?"

"Oh, let's *hurry* over there!" Gretchen said as she reached underneath her T-shirt to unsnap her bra and join in the fun. "I just love your new friend, Jack."

"Let's get our drinks first," Tara said.

"David!" Gretchen shouted. "Come with us!"

Gretchen grabbed Tara by the arm and pulled her away, nearly causing her to spill the drink that she snatched out of Josh's hand. The earl stood and brushed the sand from the back of his legs and hurried to catch up with them. Gretchen has always loved anything that would give them something to talk about at the yacht club, and it was clear she couldn't wait to parade Tara around just to see what would come next. I also suspected the Jose Cuervo was kicking in. Josh, who had been stunned into silence, began smiling as he watched them disappear into the herd of Snow Heads that surrounded us.

"You really think you can handle that?" Josh asked.

"If I ever get the chance," I said.

"So tell me once again why the lovely Tara has come to town."

"Bayou Casualty brought her in to do a security analysis on Jackpot Bay."

"You mean as in preventing people from being shot on the gaming floor?"

That was not something I wanted to hear from Josh Hallman. I didn't need the hassle of facing one of the best trial lawyers in the country in a lawsuit, especially one where I may have to take the stand. "You know good and well I can't talk about that," I said.

He sipped his drink and nodded. "Before you go into a shell, let me say that I've got too much going on with all this tobacco litigation to take on any wrongful-death case right now. But you can rest assured somebody'll do it. I'd suggest a settlement as soon as possible."

"For the record, I never said the words 'wrongful death.' "

"Just tell those cheap bastards you work for that I know about the case, and they'll come out ahead if they don't try to lowball a grieving widow."

"I'll be surprised if they pay anything," I said. "They don't pay off when the insured gets killed while he's committing a felony."

"Where's the felony?"

"He fired a gun in a crowded room and threatened Clyde in front of no telling how many witnesses."

"He took deliberate aim at a piece of mechanical equipment and shot it," Josh said. "From everything I hear it was a perfect, well-controlled shot. As I see it that's merely vandalism."

"Isn't there a law against reckless endangerment?"

"Now don't start practicing law. You had your chance to go to law school and found it far too tame for your tastes."

"I don't believe this."

"A crime is an act that violates some statute that has been passed by the Mississippi legislature and signed into law. There must be criminal intent on the part of the accused. And it takes a Mississippi jury to determine whether each and every provision of such an act has been violated. Short of such a finding, there is no crime."

"So you're saying that Robert Earl didn't do anything wrong?"

"I'm saying there is great doubt as to whether it can be proven that he committed a felony."

"I don't know that Bayou Casualty will buy your line of reasoning," I said.

"One thing I didn't mention about criminal law is that a case must be proven beyond a reasonable doubt. Civil law, on the other hand, allows a jury much more leeway. For example, consider the case of Clyde Dubardo. He's an employee of Jackpot Bay Casino and is on the job when he kills Robert Earl Bailey. If a jury finds he didn't act in a reasonable manner, they can hold the company he works for liable for any damage he caused."

"I see where you're going," I said. "And I'll be sure to pass this along to them."

Josh took a sip of his drink. "Look at poor Gino," he said. "I don't think he's having much fun."

Gino was sitting on the edge of the blanket, where Richie the bond salesman had him trapped. It's a terrible fate. As I took a step toward them, I glanced toward the street and happened to catch the fierce, unblinking eyes of the Reverend Billy Joe Newhart.

He stood beside a set of concrete steps on the incline of the seawall as it rose out of the stand looking at us across the top of the crowd with the glower of a pissed-off Puritan at a witch trial.

There was no doubt he caught Tara's little flashing episode, and obviously hadn't gotten as big a kick out of it as we had.

"I wonder what he's doing here," I said.

"Who?" Josh asked.

"Nobody you know. Let's sit for a while."

Richie had been bending Gino's ear about the Cuban casino investment the earl had asked him to keep quiet about and you could see the boredom in Gino's eyes. Josh plopped down right between them and handed Gino a Diet Coke. Richie never missed a beat and he tried to talk around Josh, who rocked back and forth as a sort of moving screen to shield Gino from the incessant chatter. With all the social skills of a cow, Richie bobbed and weaved and kept trying to hammer home the sales pitch, but Josh blocked him every time he shifted positions. He didn't seem to realize that Josh was messing with him. Gino took a sip of the canned soda and sighed. He glanced at me with a little smile in his eyes, clearly relieved and amused by Josh's antics.

"Are you ready to meet the Lord?" the woman asked, and all four of us looked up at her. She had appeared out of the crowd without warning. She pushed a pamphlet toward me, which I reached for out of reflex. "What will happen to you if the rapture comes tonight?"

"I do declare," Josh whispered, "I haven't seen anything like this in years."

"Would you meet Him in the air," she asked, "or would you be left behind?"

"How about something to drink?" Josh asked the woman.

"The spirit of evil is strong in this place."

Her hair was brown but had a lot of gray in it. It was piled high in a tight bun. No makeup. She wore a gray cotton blouse, long-sleeved even in the sweltering summer night, and a pair of cheap sandals with white cotton socks. The dress was ankle length. She was a big strapping woman with a clear, grim, contralto voice. "Tonight the devil's own music will be played here. They say it's Lucifer's son who's up on that stage, but it's not. It's the same one who was here before. He's come back, recovered from his head wound just like it says in The Book."

"Oh, for goodness sake," Josh said. "Do you want a drink or not?"

Richie took one of her tracts, and she offered one to Gino, who simply shook his head. The woman turned and, without another word to us, plodded away on her solemn and solitary task with the look and the gait of a soldier walking toward the front lines.

"What in the world was that all about?" Josh asked.

I explained to him the rumors that had been circulating on the Internet and around the town of Bay St. Louis, about the uncanny resemblance both in voice and appearance of Kenny, Junior, to his deceased father.

"Let me guess," Josh said, "if you play their music backwards there's a satanic message."

"So you've heard the rumors?"

"I've heard the same rumor about every big-time recording group since the Beatles came over from Liverpool."

"Well, this week all those rumors are focused right here in Bay St. Louis," I said. "There's a tent revivalist named Newhart who's been hammering the casinos for weeks, and this concert has turned up the burner."

"Back when we were in high school," Gino said, "there was one evangelist who'd come into town every year about a week before the county fair and hold a five-day-long community revival."

"You mean the trumpet player?" I asked. "Wore a red brocaded vest?"

"They'd call an assembly in the gym and he'd speak and try to get us to come to the services. Then that night he'd get an army of kids from the church to swarm the local hangout and ask all the kids there if they knew Jesus. Didn't matter that the strongest stuff we were drinking was milkshakes, this guy talked like any kid hanging out in a parking lot was going straight to hell and that Bay St. Louis was the only town in the South that let such evil go on."

"I think that same guy used to come to Columbia," Josh said.

"He'd preach this same sermon every year," Gino said. "Even had a title. 'Burning Rubber on the Road to Hell!' "

"Oh, God yes!" Josh said. "Now I'm sure it was him!"

"There's no telling how many people's heads he screwed up," Gino said.

The zydeco band finished their show and most of the crowd clapped and cheered. While the stage crew hustled to rearrange the speakers for the Snow Mountain band, a local FM station deejay grabbed the mike and started talking too fast and too loud and telling everybody the show would be on in fifteen minutes and that it was being taped live for an album.

"I represented a revival preacher who had a TV ministry out of Baton Rouge," Josh said. "He had a yacht out on Lake Pontchartrain, a mansion in Mandeville, and he and his wife had matching baby blue Mercedes. The Feds came after him on an income tax–evasion charge."

"I heard about that guy," I said. "As I recall, he got off without jail time."

"Of course he did. As I said, I represented him. But counting the fines, it cost him a half million."

"So, what's he doing now?"

"Same thing he's always done. When I told him the fine was four hundred grand, he never so much as blinked. Had it in my office in cash within three hours."

"Well, I don't know if Newhart is raking in that much yet," I said. "But I understand he did pay cash for this warehouse he's converting into a church."

By this time the sky was getting dark over Cat Island, and the white slice of the waxing moon glowed brighter, but there was too much light from the street and the buildings along the boulevard for us to see any stars. The stage stood dark and empty now that the equipment of the zydeco band was gone, and flanking the platform on both sides were tall stacks of speakers for Snow Mountain's impending show. The soft sand pressed against me as I lay on my side and scraped gently against my elbow as I propped myself up.

"Is anyone hungry?" Josh asked. "I stocked up at the concession stand and put it in that warmer so we wouldn't have to get up during the concert. Those crawfish pies just smell like heaven."

Gino bit into one. "Oh yeah, this is great. I wonder who has the concessions."

"The casino's handling all of it," I said. "This new manager has really put a lot of emphasis on the food."

"Let me have one of those," Josh said.

"Has anybody seen my date?" I asked. "I'm beginning to get worried about her."

"She's been drinking margaritas and walking around with Gretchen La Pointe," Josh said. "What could possibly go wrong?"

Richie slapped at his ankles. "Are the mosquitoes bothering you?"

"Oh . . . my . . . God!" Josh said, each word spoken like a a separate sentence.

"What's the problem?" I asked.

Josh leaned over and whispered something in Gino's ear and pointed in the direction of the stage. Gino's eyes widened and he lost his color as he reached for Josh's hand. I rolled over and looked to where Josh had pointed. It was Rulon Hornbeck strolling through the crowd wearing a lightweight linen suit, ivory, with a coral knit shirt, a pair of soft leather loafers, and no socks. A guy I didn't know was walking beside him carrying a shoulder bag. They were passing out one-page flyers printed on light green paper.

"It can't be him," Gino said.

"Is something wrong?" I asked.

"Over there," Josh indicated with his head. "Do you know that person?"

"The one in the white suit? That's Rulon Hornbeck. He's with the Jackpot Bay Casino."

"Oh, shit," Josh said. "So it is."

"So how do you two know Rulon?"

"What does he do with the casino?"

"He's the new manager I was telling you about, the one I was saying had such good food."

Gino glared at the half-eaten crawfish pie he was holding as if it had a roach in it. He threw it to the ground. "I think I'm going to be sick."

By this time Rulon was nearly on top of us. When he saw Josh, he was startled for a second, but almost immediately he recovered and pressed his lips together with an expression of disgust. Josh returned the poisoned look. The guy walking with Rulon grabbed his arm and pulled him away from us.

"What the hell's going on?" I asked.

Gino had started sweating and looked as if he could vomit. He propped his elbows on his knees and rested his head in his hands. Josh stood and squared off toward Rulon, but the guy with the shoulder bag grasped Rulon's chin and turned his face away from us. The guy started shaking his head and wagging his finger under Rulon's nose as he talked to him in low tones. As Josh stood there staring them down, Rulon and his companion merged into the crowd and disappeared without looking back, headed toward the concrete steps where the Reverend Newhart had been standing just a few minutes earlier.

"What was all that about?" I asked.

"He's gone," Josh said.

Gino looked up, pale and breathing hard through his mouth. Josh knelt beside him and started fanning him with one of the flyers Rulon had dropped to the ground. He scooped a pair of ice cubes from the cooler and rubbed them on the back of Gino's neck. At first I thought it was nothing but dramatics, but Gino turned his eyes to the sky and I could see some real pain there.

"Are you going to be okay?" Josh asked.

"That woman handing out those pamphlets was right," Gino said in a small, weak voice. "The devil really does have a presence here tonight."

ELEVEN

We never saw Tara, Gretchen, or David again that night after they walked away from us to see if they could get backstage. I stayed with Josh and Gino until the first intermission, but they didn't even seem to know I was there as Josh tried to talk to Gino and get him calmed down. That chance encounter was the first time Gino had seen Rulon since their breakup a few months earlier, and it undid a lot of the emotional healing that had taken place. He didn't even know Rulon was over here in Bay St. Louis, thought he had gone back to this guy in Europe he had been living with before he came back to the States.

Gino started slugging back margaritas over Josh's objections and his despondency was slowly shifting into anger. Josh was right, Gino was a mean drunk. I tried to wait for Tara, but the situation was real uncomfortable for me and I sure as hell didn't have any words of wisdom to help out in Gino's situation. I mean, that's not the kind of thing I encounter in Bay St. Louis a whole lot. So I left the first chance I got and made my way through the crowd to my camp house a couple of miles down the beach. Called Tara's room a few times later that night, but she never answered.

The next day I went to the casino to check on the status of the life insurance policy that Robert Earl Bailey had with the company, needed to see if there was any grace period that kept it in effect after he got fired. I needed some good news to take to the family if I had any hope of staving off the lawsuit. I stepped back to the business office, and Tara was right there, seated in front of a computer screen, poring over the casino's disbursements from the past three months.

"Where in the world did you disappear to last night?" I asked. "I stayed until intermission and you never came back. I figured you had left me, so I went home."

"It's a long story," she said.

"Would the story have anything to do with margaritas?"

"You're not mad at me, are you?"

"Oh, no," I said. "I just love getting dumped halfway through a date."

"We came back, but they said you had just left. I didn't know where you live. You should have stayed."

"Gino wasn't exactly in a party mood," I said. "I stayed around as long as I could stand it."

"We heard all about that. We didn't stay very long either." She moved the mouse to the Close File button. "But I wish you had gone to Gretchen's place. We could have had some real three-way fun in that huge hot tub."

"You, me, and Gretchen?"

"Gretchen's still back there partying with the band as far as I know. I was talking about you, me, and the Earl of Stropshire."

Now all of this was getting real confusing to me right about then. Was the guy gay or was he straight? Looked straight to me, but then I've never been too good at picking up the signals, as Josh put it. So maybe he and Tara really did end up in the Jacuzzi. She might have been telling me the truth, but then again I had the feeling that she was not above exaggerating about some of her sexual exploits.

"So you ended up in a hot tub with David?"

She ran her finger down the bridge of my nose. "Only because I couldn't find you, honey."

I had this twinge of jealousy. Jealous of some British guy I hardly knew who probably didn't even care for women anyhow. Now how stupid was that? Tara Stocklin couldn't care less if she were in the hot tub with me or David Stratton-Hume or any guy who happened to be there. But, dammit, it should have been me.

"I've got to get Robert Earl Bailey's insurance records," I said.

"Those are at the downtown office. If you go down there, I wish you'd tell the personnel director I need to set up interviews with everybody who works in the finance department."

"Have you tried telling Rulon to set up your interviews?" I asked.

"Twice. But he's stonewalling me, and I'm not about to wait around for him to get off his ass. I'd be here another month."

"So how many more days are you planning to be here?"

She turned back to the screen and called up another file. "Maybe two more days. I thought it would take longer, but this morning I got some good news. Now that the concert's over, Johnnie the Dime and his Neanderthal nephew are leaving town for a few days. With those two gone, I ought to be able to wrap my work up twice as fast."

"I thought they'd at least hang around long enough to count the money."

"Koscko doesn't like to get into the details of running the business," she said. "He thinks the owner needs to show up for opening night, y'know, and that's about it. He's leaving any minute now, and he's supposed to be out on some boat for a few days with a couple of bimbos from over in Biloxi. And I hear that Clyde's headed over to Gulf Shores as soon as Uncle Johnnie gets out of town."

"You seem to know a lot about their personal lives," I said.

"Talk to some of the employees around here and you'll find out, like, eveything that's going on. Hell, they know every move that Clyde and Johnnie make."

I ran into Rulon in the lobby as I was headed to the front door on my way to the downtown office. He was red with anger and kept biting off bits of his thumbnail and spitting them out. Clyde had just smarted off to him in front of one of the blackjack dealers and it had just flown all over him, and he was going to try to catch Johnnie the Dime before he got out of town and tell him all about it.

I had gotten an earful the night before about how vindictive the man is, and I was beginning to believe it, judging from the way he just wouldn't let the business with Clyde drop.

"That knuckle dragger is going to ruin everything we've accomplished this weekend," he said. "Nephew or not, he's got to go."

"Ms. Stocklin needs to set up interviews with some of the employees as part of her security audit."

"Well, why didn't she just say so?"

"If we go to the downtown office, would it be possible to take care of it today?"

"I was just on my way down there," he said. "I need to talk with Mr. Koscko before he goes out of town."

"And I need to ask you a few questions about Robert Earl Bailey."

"Such as?"

"Did he and Clyde have any problems getting along?" I asked.

"Everybody has problems getting along with Clyde."

"You really hate the guy, don't you?"

"He's the one who keeps attacking *me*," Rulon said. "I'm just trying run a casino."

"What do you know about the seven hundred dollars that Robert Earl was saying Clyde owed him?"

"Could have been anything. Probably a loan, maybe a bet."

"Do you know of any unusual purchases that Robert Earl made for the casino?"

"I'm sure it was all routine," he said. "I'll double check, but I doubt that I'll find anything other than normal transactions. You're welcome to look at the records."

We stepped through the front doors into the wet heat. I slipped on my sunglasses as we walked across the gleaming surface of the concrete wharf that had been built to dock the casino barge and serve as its promenade deck and grand entranceway. Rulon pulled out a pack of cigarettes and cupped his hand against the wind to light one of them.

"I saw you at the concert last night with Josh Hallman," he said.

"He's an old friend."

"And Gino Stafford? Is he an old friend, too?"

"Yeah," I said. "We were in high school together."

He took a deep draw on the cigarette and blew it straight up into the incoming wind. "Then I'm sure you heard just how horrible I am. How conniving and vindictive. Well, don't believe it for a minute. Gino is a mean and abusive monster. I had to get away from him, or he might have killed me. I'll bet Josh didn't tell you about that side of him, did he?"

"He didn't tell me much of anything," I said.

"I don't care if you believe me or not," Rulon said. "It wasn't my fault."

My past few years as a private investigator have taught me that in a divorce there are always three sides. His side, her side, and the truth. I guess Gino's breakup with Rulon was as close to a divorce as you get when you're on that side of the street. Usually, I'd trust the word and the judgment of Josh Hallman.

But Josh has a weakness. When it comes to matters of friendship or affairs of the heart, Josh tends to put the claws out. After all, I heard him defend me once in a court of law and he made me out to be one hell of a lot better guy than I really am, and it sounded as if he believed what he was saying. But even factoring in the emotional bias, I still believed Josh and Gino's side of the story rather than Rulon's.

"You think I'm lying, don't you?" Rulon asked.

"I'm trying to head off a wrongful-death lawsuit. Nothing more."

"Gino's a real son of a bitch."

"Come on, Rulon. Let it drop."

"Well I just want you to know that I didn't have anyhting to do with those e-mails. That was the local Gay Pride Association. They take it on themselves to out anybody they think is a little too discreet about their preferences."

Rulon had called the valet to bring his car around to the front. We stood leaning against the railing overlooking the Gulf some ten feet above the water that splashed against the pilings, sometimes sending salt spray all the way to our feet. There was a constant chirping of seagulls. Two steel-hulled shrimp boats were headed out of the channel that ran by the casino, the throb of their big diesels carrying on the breeze.

"So what else do you want to know about Robert Earl Bailey?" he asked.

"Do you know if he was having any personal problems?"

"Not that I know of."

"Was he having any problems in his marriage?" I asked.

"Why do you need to know about that?"

"I'm trying to find out why a man comes into a casino with a pair of loaded guns," I said. "Also trying to figure out if there was any motive other than self-defense for Clyde to shoot the guy."

"Such as?"

"Such as money, such as an affair, such as blackmail. The usual stuff."

"How about Clyde just acting like a cowboy?" he asked. "How about him just having to prove he was a big man? I mean, Clyde's nothing but a thug and he looks the part. He'll attract every trashy element within a five-hundred-mile radius. And he's given the antigambling crowd something they can score some points with. Just look over there if you don't believe me."

Along the seawall at the edge of the parking lot there must have been forty Pentecostals with hand-painted signs that they held up every time a car drove into the place. Despite the heat the women were all wearing the ankle-length dresses and long-sleeved white blouses that I had seen Robert Earl's widow wearing the day before at the police station. There were some hats, mostly straw and wide-brimmed, but more umbrellas and a lot of cardboard funeral home fans.

The men all wore black slacks and black shoes and plaid, short-sleeved shirts of cotton broadcloth so thin you could see the A-shirts, those undershirts that look like tank tops, the kind with the thin straps that the kids call wife-beaters. But one of the men, a broad-shouldered guy with thick black hair, was wearing a white, long-sleeved shirt with a tie. Looked like Reverend Newhart, but he was too far away for me to tell.

"They were here before the shooting," I said. "I don't see where you can blame Clyde for them being here."

"A little of that is a good thing, but he's about to screw it up. Five or six at a time would come here before the shooting, which was fine. But just look at that crowd now."

"I hear what you're saying, Rulon. But you might as well get used to it. Koscko isn't about to send Clyde packing."

"He'll ship Clyde off if he ever becomes aware of how much money it's costing to keep him around." He took a final drag and flipped the cigarette into the water. "Here's my car now. You're welcome to ride to the office with me."

I would have just taken my truck, but a kid in a blue knit shirt with a Jackpot Bay logo embroidered on the pocket drove up in this BMW Z3 two-seater convertible, Dakar yellow with a black top, and hopped out and held the door open as we walked toward him. I've always wanted to ride in one of those to see what forty thousand dollars' worth of car feels like. The seats were firm and the car was tight and smelled like it had just rolled off the assembly line. Rulon insisted that we put the top down, even as bright and hot as it was.

"At first, I offered to run these protestors off," he said. "But then I realized what an absolute bonanza it's been for the free publicity. Once the stink about that shooting dies down, it'll be a good thing again. That preacher is on the radio every day and they're even putting up billboards on the highway, for Christ's sake. Thanks to the Right Reverend Billy Joe Newhart everybody along the Coast and in at least three states has heard of this casino. We couldn't have bought that much press for a million bucks. I even hear that *60 Minutes II* is thinking of doing a special on it. Wouldn't that be wonderful?"

"I wouldn't play around with these folks too much," I said. "Not everybody in this state thinks casinos are a good thing. You get north of Interstate 10, and these church groups can do you some damage, especially in the legislature. You wouldn't believe the letters my brother's been getting about that plan to teach gaming courses at the community college."

"Jack, dear boy, the people who sympathize with those protestors aren't coming to the casino anyway. And the people who do come to casinos don't give a rip what a bunch of peanut-brittle-selling, snake-handling footwashers have to say. If we can keep Clyde from killing any more people on the gaming floor, we'll be fine. Besides, I can keep this bunch from getting out of hand."

We slowed to idle speed as we approached the grouping of protestors. They stayed on the outside of the seawall, on public property, since Johnny Koscko had already made threats about having trespassers arrested. Three of the women were holding up umbrellas for shade and this pudgy man about to pop the lower buttons on his shirt was sitting on the concrete railing, his sparse and slick hair glistening in the sun. There were several signs, most of them hand-printed in Marks-A-Lot on flimsy white poster board. The only sign I could read was held by a stout, grim-faced woman who thrust it at us like she wanted to jam it into our face. "WOULD YOU TAKE JESUS WITH YOU INTO THIS PLACE?"

And sure enough, from out of nowhere came this camera from WXXV-TV. Here I was, the brother of a state senator, low-ridin' in a convertible with a casino manager who had recently broken up with a gay lover, a gay lover well known to the whole city of Bay St. Louis, Mississippi.

The rumor had spread that the casino manager had taken up with some other man. And everybody from Mama's bridge club to the *Monday Night Football* crowd at the Fire Dog Saloon had been wondering just who this other man might be. Hot damn, like I needed to get thrown into the middle of that rumor mill. I slouched in the seat and felt my cheeks heating up. I tilted my head so far forward that my chin touched my chest, and I put my hand up to the side of my face.

Someone must have recognized Rulon because everybody started yelling at us and waving their signs above their heads and playing up to the camera. Why the hell did he have to put that top down anyway? And amidst all the flipping and flapping and chanting, the Reverend Billy Joe Newhart stepped up on the seawall railing and towered above the crowd, his shirt glowing white in the sunlight, making his bronze face and raven hair appear to be even darker. He held his arms out like Charlton Heston parting the Red Sea.

Newhart's got big features, a square jaw, deep-set eyes, beetling brow, and hands that could palm a basketball. He's always got the blue traces of a heavy beard even right after he shaves. He's a handsome man in a rugged sort of way, and he can assume this piercing look, a blend of anger and indignation, that darkens when he gears up to take on the forces of sin.

By the time he got to the top of that seawall, he was getting worked up pretty good. But before he said anything, before he looked down and saw us, the stormy look vanished. The sharp lines at the corners of his eyes melted away when he recognized Rulon. He glanced around as if nervous, and dropped his arms to his side.

"Nice crowd, preacher!" Rulon shouted.

"Don't start anything," I said. "Not in front of those TV cameras."

"Oh, the Right Reverend and I, we're big buddies." He stopped the car.

"Leave him alone," I said.

"We're buddies!" he shouted. "Isn't that right, Joe Don?"

Newhart didn't respond, and uncertainty, if not outright fear, passed across those steelly eyes. He turned his head and started telling a group of teenagers, all wearing T-shirts with Christian slogans, to back up and stand behind a line that someone had drawn with white chalk.

"It's mighty hot out here, Joe Don!" Rulon yelled. "Maybe later on, you and I can go out and get a beer for old times' sake!"

The big preacher never turned around, but started leading the protestors in singing "Faith of Our Fathers." I couldn't tell if the TV camera was getting any shots of me, but I was growing self-conscious as I was twisting around in order to avoid showing my face. God, if I showed up on the five o'clock report Neal would chew my ass out but good. Not to mention what the boys up at the Broke Spoke would do if they happened to turn off ESPN and flip to the local news and see me in the car with Rulon. Not too likely that would happen, but with my luck not impossible.

"Why don't we get the hell out of here?" I said.

"You don't enjoy their singing?"

"Let's move, dammit!"

"See you later, Joe Don," Rulon hollered in a mocking singsong. He stepped on the gas and the tires squeaked as we took off.

"Do you know that preacher?" I asked.

"I assume everybody around here knows him."

"His name is Billy Joe Newhart. Why did you call him Joe Don?"

"Oh, did I say that? I must have been confused." Rulon wiped his lips with his fingers. "Billy Joe, Joe Don. All those cracker double-names sound so much alike."

TWELVE

One thing I really hate about my work is when I have to go to the home of somebody who just died unexpectedly, somebody insured by the company, and ask them the jillion different questions that the paper pushers and make-work guys at headquarters insist that they must have an answer for before they'll cut a check. Maybe if some of those desk jockeys had to actually sit across the table from someone whose child, or wife, or father just got pulled off the respirator, actually had to look into their eyes while going through some checklist of stupid questions, they wouldn't come up with so many of them. But then again, they might. Especially now that The Lippington Group has taken over.

Long before any of us were born, banks and insurance companies and other institutions that deal with great sums of money figured out how to play the float. Over the years they've gotten so good at using other people's money for a few days at a time, and it's become so routine, that there are no more moral compunctions about squeezing an extra two weeks' worth of short-term interest out of the money that should be in the hands of some dead guy's widow. It's such a long-standing practice that the question never even comes up anymore. So they pay me fifty bucks an hour to go ask a bunch of questions and put off the day they have to hand over the cash. Of course, they don't admit that's what they're doing, don't even say that to me.

But then I can't get too damn self-righteous about it. After all, I don't turn down their money. But I do at least try to speed up the payments to the injured parties. Never have much success at it, and I guess I never will, but it makes me feel better to think I'm trying.

The good news for the Bailey family was that the life insurance policy on Robert Earl, the one the company has on all regular employees, was paid up to the end of the month and still in force when Clyde shot him. There was an exclusion for deaths during the commission of a criminal act, but it was just vague enough to be dangerous in a courtroom and the company didn't want to chance it, especially when I told them of Josh Hallman's interest in the matter. In fact, they seemed real anxious to try to call the death an accident, and a primary benefit of three times annual salary plus an accidental death benefit came to just over two hundred thousand dollars. And since my orders were to try to head off any thoughts that young widow might have about a wrongful-death lawsuit, I could get that check cut and delivered pretty damn fast.

The trailer was a big one, a double-wide with a brick skirt along the bottom and a front deck of knotty pine stained to look like redwood. It was set in the shade of a copse of water oaks and hickory trees in what looked to be the site of an old homeplace. Pink wild roses set out by some long-dead and long-forgotten farmwife a hundred years ago climbed along a rusted barbed-wire fence. At one end of the trailer was a round bank of blue hydrangeas, and at the other end was a split and gnarled tree with its limbs bending under the weight of hundreds of yellow-green pears, clustered like grapes, so many that the people in the trailer had long since gathered all they could use or even give away. There were pears rotting on the ground and turning brown, sending off a sweet fragrance. A low swarm of tiny bees hovered a foot off the ground, feasting on the mushy fruit and setting up a soft buzzing.

Behind the trailer sat two outbuildings of gray, weathered planks with roofs of corrugated tin, brown and rough and worn thin with age. One was an old chicken coop, still in use, and the other a cow pen, so long abandoned that weeds and honeysuckle had taken over. The chicken coop was fenced in and a number of brown yard walkers were clucking and pecking on the bare, gray earth at some cracked corn that someone had recently thrown out.

When I shut the door of my truck behind me, a spotted mongerel dog came around the corner, mostly hound, judging from ears and tail and the sound of the bark. Hounds don't generally bite, it's those yappy little lap dogs you've got to watch. The dog barked with its head held high, as if baying at the sky, not a serious bark, more like an alert or maybe even a greeting. Before I got halfway to the steps, the woman I had seen at the sheriff's office two nights earlier was standing in the front door drying a plate with a threadbare aqua dish towel.

"Lightnin'! Shut up that barkin' and get on back around there!" The dog promptly shut up and obeyed. "Something I can do for you?"

"I'm Jack Delmas with Bayou Casualty Insurance Company. I got this address from Sheriff Partridge."

She kept rubbing the plate as she looked me up and down. "Insurance?"

"I'm trying to get some information about Robert Earl Bailey."

"You're too late to ask him anything. He got killed th'other night," she said. "Say, didn't I see you down to the sheriff's office?"

"I was there."

"Well, Brenda, she already told all she knows, told it all that night."

"I just need to ask her a few more questions."

"Robert Earl's dead, mister. There's no use stirring all that up again, not right now. We haven't even had the funeral yet."

"When would be a good time for me to come back?"

Her mouth tightened and this righteous flame flared up in her eyes. "Now, mister, we done heard all about the camera that Robert Earl shot up. Brenda, she ain't hardly got enough money right now to bury him proper. We're gonna take up a love offering at the church to pay for whatever damage Robert Earl done, but y'all oughta at least have the decency to wait until he's in the ground before you start tryin' to get your money outta his widow."

"Whoa," I said. "Slow down. I'm not here to get any money from her or anybody else. I'm trying to give some money to her. I need to get some information before we can process his life insurance policy."

"So you talkin' about *life* insurance?" she asked. "She never said nothing about no life insurance."

"He had the employee policy that the company had taken out on him."

"But he got fired from that place 'fore he got killed."

"The policy's still good," I said. "I can get the money to his widow faster if I can just get a little more information. That's all I'm looking for."

"Well, in that case, come on in," she said. "You'll have to excuse the place. I was just trying to straighten it up for Brenda so's she wouldn't have the funeral company comin' into no messy house."

I sat in a wooden rocking chair near the door. She sat across from me on a couch, a wood frame model with square pillows covered with a brown-and-yellow-plaid material loosely woven from coarse wool. On the shelves beside the TV set were framed pictures and a brass table clock with a second hand that wasn't moving. The windows were open and there was a box fan in one of them, pulling in a breeze that made the sheers inside the drapes billow and roll. I could smell the sweet pickles and the deviled eggs from the next room. Can't have a funeral around here without deviled eggs.

"I don't know much about Robert Earl's business, but I know some," she said. "His widow, Brenda, she's my first cousin once't removed. Her daddy and me, we was first cousins."

"I just need to confirm a few things," I said. "First of all, Robert Earl and your cousin were legally married, right?"

She nodded.

"And did they have any children?"

She pointed to a picture on top of the TV set. "Had two young 'uns, a girl and a boy. Got another one on the way."

"Do you know how old Robert Earl was?"

"Thirty-two. I remember he's fifteen years younger'n me."

"Was he having any trouble at home?"

Her mouth drew tight as she closed her eyes and shook her head. "Never had no trouble at all until he went to work for that casino," she said. "Me and Brenda, we kept telling him to just walk away and leave it behind him. We prayed every day he'd get out of that place. Then one day, God answered our prayers and he come in just out of the blue and said he was gonna quit. Just like that. One of the deacons at the church said he could take him on at his auto repair shop he's got up around Picayune. Robert Earl, he was real good with engines."

"So did he quit right away?"

"Not right then. Not soon enough." She got a faraway look in her eyes as she stared out the window. "When the devil gets his clutches in you, he don't turn you a-loose all that easy."

"What about the seven hundred dollars Robert Earl was saying that Clyde owed him?"

She glanced down at the floor. Her breathing picked up some, and she started drumming her fingers on the wooden arm of the couch. "Don't know nothin' about that." But her eyes said she did.

"According to the casino's records," I said, "Robert Earl got paid everything he had coming to him."

"Is that so? Well, you might oughta ask that Clyde fella about that."

She wasn't one who could hide her emotions, not even a little. So I decided to try running a bluff to see how she'd react. "I hate to bring this up," I said, "but Clyde says that Robert Earl was stealing money."

"Like *hell* he . . ." She almost lifted off the couch. "I mean, that's a lie!"

"Clyde tells me he found the seven hundred in cash in Robert Earl's desk and knew it was stolen. Says he planned to take it to the head bookkeeper."

"Lies! Lies!"

"Well, I'm going to have to find out how much money was stolen," I said, "so we can take it out of the life insurance money. If you or your cousin Brenda don't know, I guess I'll have to ask Clyde."

"Mister, you think you gonna get a straight answer outta him?"

"I'm not getting a straight answer now."

She kept her head down and closed her eyes as her lips moved in a silent prayer. I rocked and watched the flapping of the sheers at the windows and waited until she got ready to talk. When she looked back up, she was close to spilling tears. "I don't guess it can hurt him none now. Not as much as keeping quiet would."

I nodded and bit lightly on my lower lip, and generally tried to look sympathetic.

"It started out little," she said, "and it wasn't Robert Earl's idea. I know that don't matter none, but I'm just sayin' he didn't think it up. That Clyde, he come to Robert Earl to get him to write up some dummy invoices to show that the casino was gettin' a lot more stuff delivered to them than they actually was. And Robert Earl, he'd cut a check for the full amount."

"What kind of stuff was getting delivered?"

"Food mostly. Some flowers, but mostly food. Clyde, he'd order way too much. But there wasn't much way to keep track of it. They buy lots of food at those casinos, and most of it don't last long enough to count what's there after a day or two."

One of the great joys in life is not just knowing the real scoop, it's letting somebody else know that you know it. It's a phenomenon that shows up a lot when it's time for college football recruiting or when there's a fresh divorce in town. I had planted the idea that somebody had better come forward quickly and tell Robert Earl's side of the story or Clyde was going to win by default. That was all it took. She had been given the green light to spill her guts, and once she got started doing just that I had trouble keeping up with her.

When the last baby had come, there was this kidney problem that required an operation. Twenty-six thousand dollars and no insurance to cover it. They got some help from the church, but those folks are poor themselves, and that's more money than any bake sales or car washes were ever going to take in. They even put out Mason jars with the baby's picture at the check-out counters of some convenience stores, but that was taking in maybe twenty bucks a day, mostly in nickels and pennies.

So they were about to lose the double-wide when all of a sudden Robert Earl started bringing home this extra money. Claimed he was doing tune-ups and ring jobs on the side, but he wasn't much of a liar and Brenda got the truth out of him within a week. Turns out that the casino manager Clyde Dubardo had come to Robert Earl with this scheme to fix up fake purchase orders and cut checks for stuff that never existed. Clyde had set up a phony food brokerage house and was depositing checks that Robert Earl would write for thousands of dollars. Clyde would give Robert Earl cash money for his part in the scheme, and this came to anywhere from five hundred to a thousand a week.

"I believe Robert Earl was gonna stop foolin' around with all that stealing once he got the hospital bills paid off," she said. "I guess it warn't quite so bad takin' money from a casino as it woulda been if he was stealin' from a real business or somethin'."

"How close was he to paying off the hospital?"

"He got 'em paid down pretty good, about cut the bills in half. But then he got fired."

"How could he possibly get fired?" I asked. "Sounds like Robert

Earl had so much dirt on Clyde that he'd be safe. Besides, didn't Clyde need him to keep up the phony invoice scheme?"

"Sure he did. But that came to a stop when they got that new manager."

"Rulon Hornbeck?"

"The devil's right-hand man," she said. "Rulon figured out what was going on and he took over the scheme himself. Cut Clyde slam out of it, at least out of the part where you get any money."

"But if Rulon wanted to keep the scheme going, he'd still need Robert Earl. He'd still need the guy who cut the checks."

"Let me tell you how greedy that Rulon is. He tried to make Clyde Dubardo keep on paying Robert Earl out of his own pocket. Threatened to go tell that Koscko man everything if Clyde didn't keep paying. Can you believe the snake was that greedy? But when Robert Earl goes to Clyde to get his money, just like always, Clyde tells him to go fly a kite. It just really made Robert Earl mad, so he and Clyde have words and Clyde fires him. I believe Robert Earl wanted to get out of that cesspool anyhow, but he wasn't about to let Clyde keep that last bit of money he was owed. Robert Earl, he could be stubborn."

"I can't believe Rulon wouldn't try to get Robert Earl to stay," I said. "Not if you're talking about thousands of dollars a week."

"Oh, he did try. Tried hard. Even drove out here in that shiny yellow convertible one day to get Robert Earl to come back. I saw him when he drove up. He had this other man with him."

"Who was the other man?"

She curled the corner of her lip. "You know anything about that Rulon?"

I nodded.

"Well let's just say they was birds of a feather," she said. "You understand what I'm saying? They was practically holdin' hands out there in that car. It's a sin, pure and simple."

"Who was this other guy?"

"Don't know, and not givin' you a short answer, don't care," she said. "All I know is he was some fancy pants with a foreign accent."

"Was it a British accent?"

"Ain't never been to Britain, so I couldn't tell you. But let me put it this way, he warn't from around here."

"What did he look like?"

"I didn't look all that good." She waved her hand to dismiss the subject. "But listen to me, I need to ask you about that money."

"You mean the insurance proceeds?"

"I mean the seven hundred dollars what Clyde Dubardo owed to Robert Earl. You reckon you could get somebody from the casino to pay that money to Brenda?"

"I don't think so."

"I'm just trying to hold down on any trouble, mister. Brenda, she'd just as soon never take another shiny penny from that place. But our preacher, he knows the whole story and he says even if it's dirty money, it's wrong for that Rulon to keep it."

"So what does Reverend Newhart plan to do about it?" I asked.

She clasped her hands together and closed her eyes as if in prayer. "Brother Billy Joe's a good man," she said, "but his weakness is his temper. I say that seven hundred dollars ain't nothing but bait. And sure as the world the devil's gonna try to use it to lure Brother Billy Joe into a trap."

THIRTEEN

Jack, we've got a problem." Even though we had a bad cell phone connection I could hear the urgency in Tara's voice. "I need to find Rulon Hornbeck ASAP."

"So why are you calling me? You probably need to call the casino."

"I'm sitting in the damn casino! Nobody here's seen him since Snow Mountain checked out of town."

"I don't keep up with Rulon," I said. "Have you asked Johnnie Koscko?"

"Where are you right now? Are you in your truck?"

"I'm at home. I just finished up the paperwork so I can get paid, and I'm taking the rest of the day off. If you're not too busy, maybe you'd like to come over later on and grill some steaks. I could get a bottle of wine and some cheese."

"Yeah, yeah. Look, we can play around at your place some other time, but right now, I've got to find Rulon Hornbeck. This is important."

"Tara, honey, I don't want to sound like a bureaucrat, but it's not my job to deal with Rulon or with Jackpot Bay's money problems. For the past two days, they've had me trying to head off a lawsuit, which I think I might have done. The only thing I was supposed to do at the casino in the first place was to keep you and Koscko from fighting long enough for you to complete that security audit. I was hoping maybe you were calling to tell me that you and Johnnie the Dime had kissed and made up."

"I'd rather French kiss a pig. I'm sorry to be such a terrible bother, but Koscko's out of town so I couldn't ask him."

"Where did he go?"

"I told you yesterday! He's on somebody's yacht off the coast of Destin with a couple of paid bimbos."

"How about Clyde? Have you tried him?"

"Johnnie wasn't five minutes past the city limits before Clyde skipped town too."

"I've got some personal things I need to take care of today," I said. "I need to pay my power bill before they cut my lights off. Isn't there somebody over there besides Rulon to do whatever it is that you need?"

"Jack, shut up and get your ass back on the clock and get over here fast. We've got a hell of a lot bigger problem than paying off some holy roller to keep her from taking Bayou Casualty to court."

I stepped into the storeroom that Tara had been using as her makeshift office. The air was saturated with cigarette smoke and there was the biting smell of scorched coffee. She was furiously puffing on the stub of a Marlboro and tapping a number onto the keypad of the phone in front of her. She looked up when I came in and slammed the receiver down.

"I don't know where the hell it went to," she said as she mashed out the cigarette into an already full ashtray, "but there was one-point-three million in cash money that was supposed to show up at Nashville that never got there."

"Never got there?" I plopped into the chair in front of her desk. "Did somebody hijack the armored car or something?"

"Hell, no! Somebody made a switch somewhere. All those big canvas money bags that everybody thought were stuffed with dollars were filled up with nothing but a bunch of cut-up newspapers when they opened them in Nashville." She lit another cigarette, took a deep drag, and blew a plume of smoke toward the ceiling. "I told that ignorant-assed Koscko the whole scheme was a disaster waiting to happen."

"Have you called the cops?"

"Of course not! Do I look like an idiot? The whole frigging idea is to keep the damn cops out of this. The business manager for Snow Mountain called from Nashville and wanted to know where the money is. He was some kind of pissed off, like this shit is my fault or something. It's been all I can do to keep him from calling in the FBI. I'm thinking maybe, just maybe, it's some kind of a switch that Rulon thought up. Maybe that first truck was a decoy or something. I get the impression that he's sneaky enough to think up almost anything. But now I can't find the skinny bastard, and I can't hold off that guy in Nashville much longer. God, the way they handle money around this place, they're going to lose their license as sure as shit. And your company's going to lose a client."

"So that's why you're not calling the cops? You're afraid it's going to make Bayou Casualty lose money? I'm impressed by your loyalty."

"Loyalty, hell! They sent me over here to tighten up security and review the way money is handled. And now over a million in cash is missing. My reputation is at stake here."

"But it's not your fault. You're just an adviser."

"If it happens on my watch, there are a lot of people who'll blame me regardless of whose fault it is."

"In that case, what we need to do is find the money fast," I said. "And we're losing time by not calling the cops."

"I gotta talk to Rulon before we call the cops. Once we call them in, my reputation takes a hit." She pinched the bridge of her nose. "It'll be in the newspapers the next edition that comes out. What pisses me off is that I had sent an e-mail to New Orleans and told them they better not go along with this, but I never got an answer."

"Do you have a copy of the e-mail?"

"I'm getting one."

"When did you find out about all of this?"

"I was here when the phone call came in from Nashville about thirty minutes ago. This dumb-ass bean counter down in accounting took the call, and he nearly shit in his pants. He tried to find every swingin' dick in management before he finally gave up and came to me."

"Exactly what did he say?" I asked.

"What did *who* say, dammit?"

"It's not going to help for you to raise your voice," I said. "The guy from Nashville, what did he say? Take a few deep breaths and calm down and tell me step by step what he said to you."

"Don't patronize me. I'll scream my head off if I feel like it."

"Humor me, okay. I can't take it all in if you don't slow down."

She shot me the bird, puffed on the cigarette, and flicked the ashes on the floor. "He said the armored car came to the office in Nashville, just the way it was supposed to." She started talking about as slowly as I do. "They got out and had this shipping invoice all filled out and ready for him to sign. But about the time he was writing his name, one of the clerks who was there with him opened one of the bags, and there was nothing in there except for bundles of newspaper the same size as stacks of bills. They checked all the bags and it was the same story with every one of them. Am I going too fast?"

"You mean it wasn't even going to a bank up there? It was somebody's office?"

"The whole thing is one giant screwup," she said. "The guy in Nashville said he'd wait for a while before doing anything so I could have some time to find out what happened. But he didn't sound like he'd hold off too long."

"So as of now," I said, "where are the guards from the truck?"

"They're sitting there in the Snow Mountain office waiting to hear back from me."

"So the guy in Nashville thinks they're legit?"

"No, not at all," she said sweetly. "He thinks they're the criminal masterminds who pulled off this switch. They just decided to hang around and drink coffee with him."

"Were there any cops here at the casino when they loaded the money?" I asked.

"They were outside in their squad cars. At least that's what the guy from accounting tells me. The cash was bagged in the accounting office, and the only people there were Clyde, Rulon, and some auditor the Snow Mountain band sent down."

"The auditor for Snow Mountain, did you catch his name?"

She shook her head no. "I'm sure Rulon knows who he is. We can ask the bean counter, but I doubt that he'll remember. He was plenty damn nervous."

"Were they standing at the curb when they put the bags into the armored car?"

"As far as I know."

"Well if the cops were sitting there, where could anybody have made the switch?"

"Hell, I don't know. It could have been some place on the road."

"Did anybody check out the drivers?" I asked. "Any time there's a theft involving an armored car, you've got to check for an inside job."

"I know, I know. But that comes later. Right now we need to find Rulon's skinny white ass in a hurry."

"How long has it been since you talked to Nashville?"

"Why don't you call him and try to buy some time?" she asked. "Tell him the whole thing is part of a security plan."

"Why me? Why don't you call?"

"I warned Bayou Casualty that the whole thing was a stupid idea, and I'm not about to get dragged into it now. Besides, you've got that mushmouth drawl just like he does. Hell, talk to him about cooking grits, or coon hunting, or shotguns, or whatever you crackers talk about. Make him think everything's under control."

"Gee, Tara, I don't know. With all your charm, it might be better if you called him."

"If I could visit him in person, I could damn sure keep him distracted for a few hours. But I can't do it over the phone." She punched in the number and handed me the receiver. "You talk to him. And find out where that auditor is."

When I phoned the guy at the Snow Mountain office, he was a horse's ass at first. Kept yelling about how the shipment from Gulfport was our responsibility and how we'd better find the damn money within the next two hours. But I reminded him several times that the whole stupid plan was their idea to begin with, and I doubted that any insurance company in the world was going to fork over a million and a third, or any amount at all, once they found out what had happened. Suddenly he became interested in hearing me out. Halfway through our conversation, a secretary stuck her head in and told Tara that she had Koscko on the line in the main office, so Tara left the room. I noticed the trace of a smirk as she walked past me. She was going to enjoy sharing this bit of news with Johnnie the Dime.

"So let's give this a little time before we do anything," I said to the man in Nashville. "I'm sure everything's all right. I just need to talk to the casino manager down here before we call any cops."

"I've got a call in to Kenny, Junior," he said. "They're on the road setting up for their next trip, and he doesn't return phone calls too quick. Might not hear from him until tomorrow. But when he calls back, I can't just act like nothing's happened."

"You need to talk to that auditor you sent down here," I said. "Maybe he could give you some idea of what's going on."

There was a pause at the other end of the line. "What auditor are you talking about?"

FOURTEEN

"As soon as you get all this Mickey Mouse stuff out of your system," Neal said, "we can start working on a plan to get the money back."

"I'll Mickey Mouse you!" Koscko shouted. Clyde took one menacing step toward Neal, but Neal backed him off with a hard glare. "I've already told ya how I'm gonna handle this."

"You're not going to break anybody's face," Neal said. "This isn't Las Vegas back in the fifties, this is simply a case of some money that's unaccounted for."

"And the weasel who took it."

"We don't know that it was embezzlement," Neal said.

"Oh, no! That cash just got up and walked outta here! And there just happened to be some clown there who gets his rocks off by dressing up like an auditor. Some perverts dress up in women's underwear, this one likes to wear auditor costumes."

Koscko still had on the Bermuda shorts and blue tropical print shirt he was wearing on the boat four hours earlier when he called in and talked to Tara. He had been sipping mimosas earlier in the day and was even louder and more florid than usual. He had taken a private plane back to Bay St. Louis.

"Okay, it could have been a robbery," Neal said. "Or it could be nothing more than a mistake. For all we know Rulon Hornbeck used his head and arranged for the money to be sent to Nashville some other way."

"There was only two people on the face of the earth that knew the whole plan," Koscko said. "Me and that queer son of a bitch who worked for me up until yesterday. He didn't change no plan. He stole that damn money, plain and simple."

"You better hope he didn't," Neal said. "If it was the armored car company who lost it, Jackpot Bay might be off the hook. But if it was one of your employees who pulled a switch, that's a different story."

"So what about you?" Koscko said to me. "You think you can break away from screwin' that Tara broad long enough to help us out here?"

"I'm just trying to find Rulon Hornbeck," I said, "and I'm trying to do it before the cops get called in tomorrow morning."

"Cops! We don't need no stinkin' cops! I'll take care of this myself."

"Listen, Mr. Koscko," I said, "I don't work for you. I work for Bayou Casualty Insurance Company out of New Orleans, Louisiana. Bayou Casualty, in case you've forgotten, carries your liability insurance. That money that's missing isn't your money, it belongs to the Snow Mountain Band. I'm going to call their manager back and try to convince him that they don't need publicity like this any more than you do. But my bosses over at Bayou Casualty don't want to have to answer to stockholders about why a million-plus dollars turned up missing and they didn't call in the cops first thing. The trail's getting colder every minute we piss away up here listening to you two talk about how you plan to whack Rulon Hornbeck."

"I'll find him," Clyde said. "No problem."

"Yeah, that sounds good," Johnnie the Dime said. "And when you do, you beat that damn money out of him."

"But I'm gonna hafta borrow one of your guns, Uncle Johnnie."

"Where the hell is yours?"

"The cops still got it."

"Delmas," Johnnie said to Neal, "what am I payin' you for? When you gonna get that gun back?"

"About the only way you or Clyde could possibly make things any worse is to be hunting down somebody with a gun," Neal said. "You won't be needing it."

Johnnie glared at Neal and put his hand to his stomach. "I figure ten grand ought to smoke him out." He pointed at me. "I'm puttin' the word out. They can call me or they can call you. But I ain't puttin' up with no shakedowns. Not a penny more, y'hear me? What's your cell phone number?"

From out on the street below us came the voice of the Reverend Billy Joe Newhart, amplified through a bull horn. "FATHER, BLESS US THIS DAY AS WE SEEK TO DRIVE THE DEVIL OUT OF OUR TOWN."

"Oh, Sweet Mother of God." Johnnie put his hand to his temple. "Not today."

"WE PRAY THAT YOU WILL SPARE BAY ST. LOUIS AND NOT SEND DOWN ON US YOUR HORRIBLE WRATH LIKE YOU DID BACK WHEN THE DEVIL TOOK OVER SODOM AND GOMMORAH!"

"I know you'll go to hell if you whack a priest," Johnnie the Dime said. "I wonder if that same rule covers redneck tent preachers."

"A-MEN!!" the crowd shouted.

"You want I should go find a priest and ask him about it, Uncle Johnnie?"

"No, I don't want you to go find no priest! I want you to go find Rulon!"

"WE PRAY, O LORD, FOR THE SOUL OF BROTHER ROBERT EARL, WHO GOT CAUGHT IN THE DEVIL'S TRAP, THAT TRAP WE CALL A CASINO! WE PRAY FOR HIS WIDOW AND HIS TWO BABIES, NOW LEFT WITHOUT AN EARTHLY FATHER . . ."

"Jesus! Would you shut them windows?" Johnnie opened his

desk drawer and pulled out the brown plastic prescription bottle. "I'd just as soon sit hear and sweat without no air conditioning as to listen to all that."

"That preacher's still talking about the shooting," Neal said. "When we get all this straightened out, we need to get together to discuss whether we should settle with the widow."

"You talkin' about that guy who shot up my casino? You outta your friggin' mind?"

"Yeah," Clyde chimed in. "It was a good thing I had my gun that day."

"WE PRAY FOR ALL THE POOR SOULS WHO GET CAUGHT IN THE TRAP . . ."

"We'll talk about it later," Neal said. "Let's just get out of here and look for Rulon. We either find him before tomorrow morning or we call the sheriff's office."

Bayou Casualty had offered me a hell of a deal if I'd find their money. I had already worked the number of days we had agreed to for that month, and I was turning down good jobs because I had been baby-sitting and trying to keep Tara and Johnnie the Dime and Clyde and Rulon from getting into some kind of marathon pissing contest. I was about tired of it, and I told them so. Told them I was finished with baby-sitting Tara and Johnnie the Dime, and their best bet was to let the cops find their stolen money.

But they countered and said if I found the cash from the Snow Mountain heist they'd give me fifteen thousand bucks over and above my monthly guarantee. I wasn't eligible for the ten grand that Koscko was offering, because I was a Bayou Casualty employee. But I'd get fifteen from the company if I recovered the cash. They didn't care if I caught the person who stole it, just wanted the cash. It was a long shot at best, but it was enough to get me back into the search.

I had warned Johnnie—and threatened that dumb-ass Clyde—

about mentioning all that missing money to anybody. I had already talked to Bayou Casualty headquarters about that very thing. A big reward would get Rulon Hornbeck brought in if he was still anywhere within a hundred miles of the Coast. But if you let it be known out on the street that he may be holding a million-plus bucks in cash, they wouldn't bother with trying to collect any reward. We'd never see Rulon or the money again.

The prospect of Rulon being dragged up in some shrimp net was of no more concern to Johnnie Koscko or Clyde Dubardo than the fate of some jellyfish that washes up on the beach. And I've been around Bayou Casualty long enough to know that the men on the board of directors, that faceless few who nobody ever sees eyeball to eyeball, share about that same degree of concern for the Rulon Hornbecks of the world. But they have a great deal of concern indeed for big chunks of money, and would hate to lose anywhere close to a million and change. So that meant there was at least a chance the amount of the missing money could be kept secret for a day or two.

I called an old Army buddy who is a lieutenant with the New Orleans Police Department. No sign of Rulon over there. Then I hit some of the usual spots, beginning with Froggie's north of town. I drove over to the Cadillac Club in Gulfport and made a quick swing up Highway 49 all the way to a few of the honky-tonks up around Lyman. Bars might not be the best place to start, but I couldn't go to the Hancock County cops just yet, and Rulon didn't have any family or friends I could go to. There was no way to keep the lid on any longer than a few hours, and once the cops got involved they'd muscle me out. So I figured the best use of the limited time was to set out a few trot-lines among the barflies and hustlers who are familiar with the cheap hotels and flophouses where a man on the run is likely to show up.

By ten o'clock I was worn out. I went back to my house and poured myself three fingers of Old Charter and topped it off with Coke and sat out on the deck to listen to the waves for a while before I hit the sack. I hadn't been listening to the waves much lately. Hadn't done any sailing either. There was a lot I had been missing out on the past few months since I signed on for what I thought was going to be semi-steady work with Bayou Casualty.

At first, I hadn't paid much attention to Tara's remark about the company trying to get more business with the casinos. She had said that the day I picked her up at the airport, said they didn't care whether the mob was involved or not. I didn't figure she knew what she was talking about then, but maybe she knew more than I thought. Bayou Casualty sure was cutting Johnnie the Dime a hell of a lot of slack, and there had to be a reason.

Why would they hang so long with a small-timer like him, especially after he ran Tara off the first time and just flat refused to install the security measures she recommended. That had already cost the casino, and probably the company, half a million bucks from cheating or embezzlement or just plain bad management. So maybe Tara was right, maybe they were making a deal with the devil to get in with some of the casinos, and Johnnie the Dime was their foot in the door. Was that a sign of what I had to look forward to if I stayed with Bayou Casualty?

One thing was for sure, if Rulon didn't show up by morning, I was going to the cops. I get along fine with most of the cops here on the Coast, and that's not something many private investigators can say. And I wasn't about to screw that up for Johnnie Koscko and his nephew or even for Bayou Casualty. They don't pay me that much, and the fifteen grand finder's fee was a long shot at best. Besides, if I didn't act fairly soon, the DA might want to know what took me so long. Obstruction of justice can be a real bitch to defend because the lines are so fuzzy.

But I was way too tired to think about such things, and I almost fell asleep there on the deck. The breeze was warm and on the water near the horizon a storm was building up sending out an occasional soft rumble of distant thunder. The wind chimes above the door tinkled and the there was a pleasant odor of smoke from a bonfire and weenie roast some group was having upwind on the beach. I had just gotten under the sheets and cradled my head into my pillow, lulled to the edge of sleep by the quiet whirring of the ceiling fan when the phone rang.

"I tried to reach you earlier," Tara said. "I've looked over the files on Rulon."

"Anything interesting?"

"You sound like you're asleep. We can talk about it tomorrow."

"How about the earl?" I asked. "What did he have to say?"

"He's not at Gretchen's guest house. Looks like he's moved out."

I yawned, and she heard me.

"I'll let you get back to sleep," she said. "Oh, one more thing. When I went to the personnel office, the woman I talked to said somebody had been there the day before trying to get a home address for Rulon."

"Anybody we know?"

"Somebody you've known for years," she said. "It's Gino Stafford."

FIFTEEN

"Here it is." Tara tossed the folder onto her desk. "Rulon's address, social security number, unlisted phone number, next of kin. Even got references. I guarantee you they're fake."

"This woman in personnel, did she say why Gino Stafford was looking for Rulon?"

"Gino claimed he had some furniture over in New Orleans that belonged to Rulon, and he wanted to get it out of his place."

"Did she tell him where Rulon lived?" I asked.

Tara shook her head no. "He got mad when she wouldn't give out the address and told her he'd dump the damn stuff at the front door of the casino. Got loud and cussed at her some. She called Security, but he left before they got there. She said Gino had been drinking. Smelled it on his breath."

I made a mental note to call Josh Hallman and see if he could rein Gino in, or at least get him off the sauce for a few days. Gino's a good guy, and he didn't need to be screwing up here in his old hometown.

"I've been needing to tell you something," I said, "but with all the commotion about the money being stolen I haven't had the chance. You were right. Clyde was getting Robert Earl Bailey to write out phony purchase orders."

"Just like I figured," she said. "I've already called the wholesale grocery and did a quick check of their records. They weren't sending half the food over here that the casino records said they had ordered. Clyde was ordering enough steak to feed all the troops in Afghanistan."

"It wasn't just Clyde. Rulon took over the scam when he became manager."

"How do you know that?"

"Got a statement from Robert Earl's cousin." I picked up the file on Rulon and thumbed through the pile of paper inside it. "Well, I'll be. Did you notice where it says Rulon went to high school?"

"Tomball, Texas. I remember you said that radio preacher is from there. Hard to forget a name like that."

"So that's the connection," I said. "Rulon told me they were buddies."

"Buddies?" she asked. "Hornbeck and a preacher were buddies?"

Rulon's full name was Rulon James Hornbeck and he had been born in Tomball, Texas. He had an associate's degree from Tomball Community College. There were several gaps in the work history, with a collection of minimum-wage jobs when he left high school and some time spent at a college or two, but no four-year degree. He left the States and went overseas where he landed a job as a blackjack dealer in Monte Carlo. That was ten years ago. He stayed there for six years, eventually working his way up to floor manager. Then he landed in New Orleans at the Harrah's Casino at the foot of Canal Street. His current address was an apartment here in town.

"Couldn't find anything about Billy Joe Newhart," she said. "I called the high school out there to see what records they had, y'know, on Rulon and on Newhart. Not much on Rulon and nothing on the preacher."

"Tomball's a pretty good-sized town," I said. "Maybe there was another high school."

"Well, you can call and find out," she said, "because it's all yours now. I've got things I want to do, and that doesn't include playing detective. This investigation stuff's not all it's cracked up to be."

It kind of hurt my feelings, not to mention my pride, to think that Tara was going to just up and leave. She was right, of course. They had hired her as a security expert for a one-shot evaluation, and she was under no obligation to stay around to search for Rulon or the money.

From the start, she had been upfront about how she felt about me. A quick round of bedroom olympics, with nothing more, would have suited her just fine. But since that hadn't worked out and she was through with the job, no use hanging around. She'd just move on to the next place, and get laid with no more effort, and even less commitment, than it would take to book a rental car. She had told me that she lived for thrills. Now that she had some money and the time to spend it, she was restless.

Maybe I figured I was so irresistible she'd think I was worth the wait. Of course, I also figure my ex-wife is going to leave that millionaire radiologist up in Memphis she's engaged to and come back to me, and that hasn't happened either. I've been getting my share of such reality checks lately.

"So when are you going to turn in your report?" I asked.

"I'll take it straight to New Orleans as soon as I can get the last details typed in. I mean, like, in an hour or two."

"At least fill me in on Rulon before you leave," I said.

"I spoke to the principal of Tomball High," she said. "He grew up there and he remembered Rulon well. Said Rulon was always in trouble. Little stuff like skipping school, drinking beer. Your standard high-school punk."

"Has this principal seen him lately?"

"Not in years," she said. "Rulon was an only child. His father died young and he was raised by his mother. She never remarried. She died years ago."

"Aside from skipping school and such, did he ever get in any trouble with the cops?"

"The closest he came was this car wreck when some of the guys were coming back to town from some beer joint late one night. He wasn't driving. In fact, he was passed out on the back seat when it happened. Two people in the other car got killed. It was a big deal at the time. The principal's wife works at the local newspaper and he got her to fax the story to me. It's right there in the file."

The wreck was on a two-lane state highway on a straight stretch of flat land. The big Pontiac Bonneville Rulon was riding in had crossed the line and hit the Pinto head-on. The couple in the Pinto was a local hardware store owner and his wife, both in their sixties. The smaller car had exploded and the autopsies showed smoke in the lungs of both. They had burned to death.

A charge of vehicular manslaughter was filed against the driver of the Bonneville. The other three passengers, all underage, were charged with possession of alchohol with public drunkenness thrown in for good measure. No names were given except for the driver, who was charged as an adult. The sender of the fax had written on the cover sheet "Rulon Hornbeck was one of the underage drinkers." The driver plead guilty and, because of his age, was let off with a suspended sentence. But because the charge was a felony, his name was the only one made public.

The name was Joe Don Newsome.

SIXTEEN

Shortly before he died, Shorty Evans made a deal with the local concrete contractor to overhaul the engines in three Ford F-350 concrete mixers in exchange for four inches of fresh concrete on the parking lot at his auto parts place out on the highway close to the interstate about three miles north of Bay St. Louis. Back then, the casinos had only recently come to town. Bay St. Louis is the first stop in Mississippi for all those folks coming in from New Orleans and all points west, and Shorty had figured that somehow he was going to make a killing out at that interchange. Figured all those folks would stop at his place to get their spark plugs and radiator hoses since they were passing right by there. Lord knows why he thought folks coming into town to play the slots would be needing auto parts, but somehow he got that idea in his head.

So Shorty built himself a new sheet metal building, and after he swapped out for the new parking lot he was on his way, if not to making a killing in the auto parts business at least in opening a Stuckey's if the auto parts thing fell through. A Stuckey's on an interstate cloverleaf is like money in the bank and not a bad fall-back position for a business to have.

But then one night in December a wicked front moved in all the way from Canada, and it got so cold that there was ice on the Jour-dan River for the first time since back when I was in college. The blower on the central heating unit in Shorty's house went out, so he turned on the eyes of the gas stove. Just long enough to warm the place up, his wife would say later. She got out of the burning house, but only because a neighbor who had been outside wrapping his pipes saw the fire. He broke through the back door to haul Shorty's wife out, still in her nightclothes. Hauled Shorty out too, but he was already unconscious from all the smoke he had inhaled. He didn't pull through. An ice storm this far south is a damn serious thing.

So Shorty's place sat there empty for a full year. The bankers who had foreclosed on it after he died got dollar signs in their eyes just like everybody else gets when they own a patch of dirt anywhere close to a casino. They set the asking price so high that nobody could touch it.

Soon the windows got broken out by hitchhikers passing through, and weeds started growing in the cracks and seams of the concrete, and the property didn't look so good anymore, especially after the plans for the big theme park out on the interstate, the one that had caused everybody in the Chamber of Commerce to start drooling, didn't come through. The bank was glad to have the Reverend Billy Joe Newhart blow into town and take it off their hands, but even then they almost ran him off by trying to stick to their asking price a little too long. When they closed the deal the loan officers sat around at the Rotary Club snickering about how they had unloaded that dog on some radio evangelist.

Newhart and the members of his growing congregation were doing the work on the building themselves. They first transformed it into a no-frills meeting hall and lately had been putting a steeple above the front door and adding a vestibule so the place would look more like a house of God and less like an auto parts house. The reverend was often out there in blue jeans and a denim workshirt, and on his radio appearances, just before railing against the casinos, he would invite anybody who could swing a hammer to come join him to build this new temple.

I had a feeling Newhart might know where to look for Rulon, so

I drove up to Shorty's old place. As I turned into that nice concrete parking lot, I saw the preacher and three other men, all dressed in denim workshirts. They had put up a sign right below the new steeple, a professionally painted billboard as wide as the new vestibule. In fact, it extended out past the corners. It featured a portrait of Jesus under the name the church had adopted, "The Narow Path Independent Bible Church of Charismatic Believers."

With the whine of an electric saw, the ping of hammers, and the pine fragrance of fresh cut lumber, I could have closed my eyes and thought I was fourteen again and helping out at my daddy's boatyard. These guys looked like they knew what they were doing, even down to their faded-out carpenter jeans, steel-toed shoes, and canvas nail pouches. Newhart was at the tin water bucket holding a plastic Hardees cup under the spigot.

"How you today, brother?" he said.

"You got the place looking good, Reverend."

"It's not me, my friend. It's these men here. They're the ones doing the Lord's work today."

"I'd like to talk with you when you get a second."

He pulled a bandana out of his back pocket and wiped the sweat off his forehead and out of his eyes. "You care for some water?"

An electric saw ripping through a two-by-six drowned out my response, so I just shook my head and he motioned for me to follow him toward a water oak at the edge of the concrete. "What can I do for you today?" He sat on the grass in the shade and motioned for me to do the same. He turned up the glass and drained it. "You know, every time I drink some of this cool water, I'm reminded of the story of Lazarus and the rich man. You know that story, brother?"

"Isn't he the one who was raised from the dead?"

"Different Lazarus. But it's good that you know that. You must read the scriptures."

"Sometimes."

"No, I'm talking about the beggar Lazarus, not the one who was friends with Jesus. The scriptures tell us that there was a certain rich man, which was clothed in purple and fine linen, and fared sumptuously every day. And there was a certain beggar named Lazarus, which was laid at his gate full of sores, and desiring to be fed with the crumbs which fell from the rich man's table." His dark eyes narrowed as he stared into mine.

I had seen it before, the otherworldly cast in the eyes of the true believers, the earnest tone, the urgency. Billy Joe Newhart had slipped into his evangelist voice, telling once more the old, old story interspersed with Bible passages that he knew by heart.

"Now think about that, my friend," he said as he reached to shake my hand. "I apologize for not introducing myself earlier. I'm Billy Joe Newhart. I'm the pastor here."

"I'm Jack Delmas, Reverend."

"You sure you don't want some water, friend? There's plenty of it here. And it's free to all who need it. Not like what happened to that rich man."

"Rich man?"

"The one who wouldn't share his wealth with poor Lazarus. You remember what happened to him, don't you. When he died, he went to hell, my friend. And hell is hot, hot, hot. We think it's hot here today, but this is like a snowy mountain top compared to the fires of hell. And in hell the rich man lifted up his eyes, being in torment, and he seeth Abraham afar off and Lazarus resting in his bosom. Lazarus, he who had been last, was now first in the Kingdom of Heaven. And he cried and said, Father Abraham have mercy on me and send Lazarus that he may dip the tip of his finger in water, and cool my tongue; for I am tormented in this flame."

I nodded. "Maybe I will take some of that water."

"But Abraham said, and this is the important part, Abraham

said, son, remember that thou in thy lifetime receivedst thy good things, and likewise Lazarus evil things; but now he is comforted and thou art tormented. And that's the message we proclaim right here every Sunday, friend. The allure of sin and greed is a false allure that satisfies our wordly desires but leaves us in the pits of hell when we leave this world. All the poker chips in the world can't buy you a drop of water on your tongue when you send yourself, and notice I say send your own self, to hell because you have hoarded the things of this world and refused to share with your brothers and sisters. Greed, greed and pride, they're the worst sins of all."

"Yeah, I think you could make a case for that."

"Do you have a spiritual home, my friend? Because we'd sure love to have you join our fellowship right here this Sunday morning."

"Reverend, I appreciate that, but I've been going to the same church in Bay St. Louis my whole life."

"Most all our members came from some other church. The churches today have gotten away from the Bible and there's a hunger in the people they aren't filling."

"I really need to talk some business with you." I held out my busines card. "I know you're busy trying to get that steeple built, so I won't take much of your time."

He took my card and studied it. There was a light of recognition. "Are you related to the senator?"

"He's my brother."

"And what's this company you're working for?" He pulled a pair of horn rims out of his front pants pocket.

"Bayou Casualty Insurance."

"The Lord is our insurance, friend. The only insurance we need here at the Narrow Path Church."

"I'm not selling. I'm an investigator. I'm here to ask you about Rulon Hornbeck."

He snatched the glasses away from his face. "I knew I'd seen you somewhere. You and Hornbeck. You were in the car with him the other day. What are you doing here?"

"I'm not connected with Rulon Hornbeck, Reverend. I'm with an insurance company out of New Orleans."

"Are you telling me it wasn't you in that car the other day?"

I held my hand up to try to calm him. "The company insures Jackpot Bay Casino. I was only catching a ride with him to the company office downtown."

Newhart pushed himself up and grabbed the bandana. He had started sweating and his eyes were angry. The yellow flecks in his brown eyes seemed to glow. "Why are you here?"

"Rulon Hornbeck is missing."

"What am I supposed to know about that? Why would I have a clue where he is?"

"Aren't you from Tomball, Texas?"

His face fell a bit and his eyes, which had been so intense, widened. "Lots of folks are. Just because we're from the same town don't mean we know each other."

"So you're saying Rulon Hornbeck is from Tomball, too."

"You just said he was."

I shook my head. "I only asked if you were from there. Didn't say anything about where Hornbeck came from."

The big man raised his hand about to point his finger at my face. But as he started to speak, he stopped and licked his bottom lip. He held the cup below the spigot and his hand trembled. "You're pretty slick, I'll give you that," he said in a quiet voice. "I don't know what your game is, but you won't get nothing outta me."

"You knew him from back home, didn't you?"

He focused on some spot far away and downed the glass of water in quick gulps. The hammering picked up as all three of the carpenters began tacking up a sheet of plywood. A fly buzzed around his face and he waved it away. "You're too late. I've already told the deacons about my life back in Tomball. That's the chairman of the deacons up on that ladder. They forgave me, friend, just like the Lord did the day I got saved. Old sins were washed away."

"He's been blackmailing you, hasn't he?"

He reached down for a couple of acorns that he cupped in his hand. "So you know about the accident, I suppose."

"I know your real name is Joe Don Newsome," I said, "and I know Rulon was in the car. It's not hard to figure out what's been happening."

"I never was trying to hide it, at least not for the past ten years or so. But when I first started my ministry, back before I learned to trust in the forgiveness of fellow believers, I used a different name, and it's stuck with me. Rulon, he came to me soon after those billboards went up. Told me I was making plenty of money nowadays and he wanted a cut to keep quiet. He'd call and tell me where to meet him and how much to bring."

"How much did he hit you for?"

"Maybe two thousand in the past three months. That much money could've laid the carpet for this new church." He looked down and shook his head before tossing one of the acorns into the woods. "At first I was weak and gave in. But I prayed about it, and it came to me clear as could be. It wasn't just me he was stealing from, he was stealing from this church, the very church that God called me to lead. It came to me as clear as a vision that I needed to go to the deacons and tell them the truth. We're told in First John, 'If we confess our sins, He is faithful and just to forgive us our sins, and to cleanse us from all unrighteousness.' So neither Rulon Hornbeck or you have any power over me or this church now. We've both been set free."

"I'm not trying to get anything out of you, Brother Newhart. I just need to find Rulon."

"I don't have any idea where he is, my friend. And not to give you a short answer, I don't care. I don't know why there's evil in the world, but Rulon, he was one of the devil's own. And in the scriptures God's children are called on to resist evil. It's a command."

"Nobody's seen or heard from him for three days," I said.

"Rulon, he come from a good family over in Tomball." The voice that had been so strong, so intense when he was telling the Bible story was now almost soft. "His mama, she was just as fine as they come. But somehow he just went wrong and chose to follow the ways of this world. If things change, maybe I'll see Rulon in the next life. I'm not the one to judge."

"Does he know you're not planning to give him any more money?"

He dropped the remaining acorns and stared at the ground as he slapped his hands together to knock the dirt off. "Like I said, I'm free of him and so is our church. Now and forever."

SEVENTEEN

A couple of years ago, they filmed a movie over in Pascagoula and I picked up a few days' work as a location scout. If they needed an abandoned shack in a swamp or a rusty tugboat or some secluded, moss-covered courtyard, I'd find it for them. They paid two hundred a day plus a thirty-dollar meal allowance. I got to know this guy on the set who was the continuity editor. His job was to see that when filming was interrupted, the sets were exactly the same when filming resumed.

If the actress was four feet from the left wall when they stopped shooting for the day, he made sure she was four feet from the left wall when it started the next day. He made sure the lighting stayed the same, saw to it that if an actor wore a red tie one day he had that same red one on when they resumed the scene the next day, and checked to see that if a glass on a table had in inch of dark liquid in it one day, it had that same inch of dark liquid the next.

Continuity editing on a movie set is one hell of a complex assignment. But once you train your eye for it and reduce the number of variables you look for, it gets a lot easier. Football coaches watching game films are continuity editors, although they've probably never heard the term. They watch a tape for eighty or ninety plays to see if their offensive guard, who all of a sudden is getting rocked back on his heels for a game or two, has started setting his feet closer together by a few inches. Same way with golf instructors, who know that an extra six inches on the backswing can make a difference of twenty yards on the drive.

Compared to what a continuity editor for a movie is called on to do, looking at surveillance films is a stroll on the beach. I wanted to see if Jackpot Bay's cheap-ass dome cameras had picked up any hint of how that money was stolen, and the lighting and camera angles and quality of the image didn't mean a thing to me. Neal was letting me use the big-screen TV in his conference room to go over the videotape recorded by the casino's security cameras when the money from the Snow Mountain concert was transferred to the armored car.

The casino had hired a dozen moonlighting bank tellers, local people, to run the concessions for the concert. They sold Snow Mountain T-shirts, caps, posters, cassettes, and CDs out of half a dozen five-by-fifteen plywood stands that were scattered around the beach. There were another dozen stands that handled nothing but food. The moonlighters had counted the money with the same concentration, speed, and teamwork they used on Fridays when the paychecks came in. They separated the bills into stacks and wrapped them with paper bands. They matched the receipts with the cash left in the drawers and the unsold merchandise left on the shelves.

When the concert ended, Rulon and Clyde made their way to each of the stands in a canopied golf cart, flanked front and rear by two other carts staffed by armed off-duty sheriff's deputies. The whole load of money bags was taken to the casino and carried with ceremony and drawn guns to the cashier's office for bagging and tagging and loading into the truck from Armadillo Couriers. The film I was reviewing covered the eighteen minutes from the time they put the money bags into the cashier's office until the guards took it to the armored car.

The cameras covered four areas: the rear parking lot outside the casino, a back door that opened to this rear parking lot, the hall outside the cashier's office, and the inside of that same office. The quality of the tape was awful. All four cameras fed into a single monitor. The tape showed a seven-second glimpse of an area and then rolled over to the next area for seven seconds. The tape was black-and-white, obviously worn out. And what I was watching wasn't even the original, the cops had already taken that. There was so much snow it was nearly impossible to make out faces. To make matters worse, the picture had a jerky motion because it had been slowed down too much. Good video is set at a speed of thirty frames per second, but if you set the camera to record at a slower speed you won't use up the tape so fast. This tape must have been set at five or six frames per second.

From the angle of the dappled sunlight streaming through the big windows of the conference room, I figured it was getting on toward late afternoon. The onions on the hamburger I ate for lunch were blowing up in my gut and I felt like I needed to brush my teeth. The sibilance of the cool air blowing across the vents of the air conditioner combined with the painful monotony of watching the same grainy tapes for the third time and made it hard to keep my eyes open. The only thing keeping me awake was the pain of the gas expanding in my stomach. I was rewinding the tape yet again when Neal stuck his head into the room.

"Have you figured it out yet?" he asked.

"Maybe," I said. "I've got one more angle I want to check out."

He pulled a chair out from the table. "Just what do you hope to see?"

"It took eighteen minutes from the time they pulled up to the rear door in the golf carts until they tagged the bags and transferred them to the armored car." I punched the play button. "Those three carts you see are pulling up to one of the rear entrances of the casino."

"Is that Rulon and Clyde in that middle cart?"

"Yeah. Now watch the bags. They've got six canvas bags in their cart, which is the money from the six concession stands."

"Are you sure there's cash in there?" he asked.

"I'm not sure, but there were always a lot of people around when they were gathering those bags. It would've been mighty hard to pull a switch when you've got three security guards hanging around. Keep your eyes on those bags."

The security guards hopped out of their carts and carried the bags into the building. Of course, we could only see seven seconds' worth of action before the picture changed. They walked down the hall to the cashier's office with Rulon leading the way and Clyde bringing up the rear. Once they got into the office, a man in a dark suit was waiting for them. He was seated at an angle where the camera only caught an occasional profile, but usually all we saw was the back of his head. The flurry of white specks on the screen and the jerkiness of the slow-moving film made the whole thing about as clear as a sonogram.

"Who's that man in the suit?" Neal asked.

"I assume he's the guy who claimed to be an auditor for Snow Mountain."

"Do they have any clearer shots than this?"

"Koscko's such a tightwad he wouldn't buy new tapes," I said, "especially for the cameras that weren't covering the gaming tables. You can barely see the bank bags, and if I didn't already know that I was watching Clyde and Rulon, I'd never recognize them."

"So why are we sitting here straining our eyes?"

"Just keep your eyes on those bags."

They set the six bags on the desk and the guards stepped out into the hall, closing the door behind them. Clyde sat beside the auditor while Rulon reached into the desk drawer and pulled out a handful of what appeared to be tags, a lot like the baggage tags they use in airports. He reached into the first bag and pulled out a sheet of paper that he flattened out on the desktop. He ran his finger along the sheet and then started writing something on one of the tags. The film switched to the hallway out side where the guards were standing around smoking cigarettes.

"Rulon's tagging the bags," I said. "He writes down what's inside each one of them, and then he seals it with one of those plastic strips."

"Looks like twist ties for garbage bags."

"That's about what they are. But they've got an adhesive that seals them about like one of those armbands they use at rock concerts. You can tell if that seal's been broken."

It took Rulon a little over nine minutes to fill out the tags on the six bags and seal them. Eight of those minutes were spent writing on the tags. The sealing process took maybe three seconds per bag. Clyde and the auditor just sat and watched. Rulon set the bags in a row on the edge of the desk. I put the film on pause.

"I want you to pay attention to these next frames. You see that big cardboard box over in the corner? It's no more than six inches away from the wall. Remember that. But I want you to watch those bags. Notice exactly how close to the edge of the desk they are. Try to estimate how many inches they're apart from each other."

"Gotcha."

"You notice the time in the lower corner of the screen? It was one-fifty-five A.M. The tape automatically rewinds at two A.M. That's when they take out the old tape, put it in a drawer, and pop in a new one. Same routine they follow every day. You with me so far?"

"I'm with you."

"Now here's where things get interesting," I said. "Look at the camera at the rear door the next time it comes up."

"Who's that woman?" Neal asked.

"She's come to see Clyde."

The woman knocked on the door and the guards let her in. She stepped to the cashier's office and stood in the hall as one of the guards stuck his head in to call Clyde and Rulon out. This happened at one-fifty-nine. They walked out into the hall and left the auditor sitting in the office. When Rulon stepped out, he pulled the door shut behind him. The last scene showed the woman waving her arms around, apparently shouting at Rulon and Clyde. The screen went blank.

"What happened?" Neal asked.

"The tape ran out." I stepped to the video player and pushed the eject button. "It takes two minutes and thirty seconds for one of these tapes to rewind. I've tested it three times."

"So is that where they switched the bags?"

"It would fit. Rulon would know the exact time the camera would be down. Say he hires that woman as a decoy to come pull Clyde out of the room at straight-up two o'clock. He knows there's at least a three-minute window."

"So who's the phony auditor?"

"I've watched this tape ten times." I shoved the next tape into the slot and punched the play button. "I even stopped the frame every time there was a chance to get a shot of the guy's face. And I still wouldn't recognize him if he walked in that door."

The next film picked up the action at two-o-four A.M. The woman was being escorted to the back door by the security guards and Clyde was gesturing with his hand as he followed them down the hall. The new film was a shade lighter, but had these horizontal lines across the screen and appeared to be dragging. The scene cut to the cashier's office. The auditor was still seated in the same chair. Nothing appeared to have changed. I hit the pause button.

"The only thing I can figure is that they had a second set of bags already tagged and ready to go. They could have put them in that cardboard box in the corner and made the switch when Clyde was out in the hall fussing with that woman. But look at the box. It hasn't moved at all. And as far as I can tell, those bank bags on the desk are exactly where they were when Clyde and Rulon left the room."

Neal stood and walked to the monitor. "That bag on the end

hasn't been moved. But to make sure, you might want to take a still shot of the bags before and after they switched out the tapes."

"I'll do it tomorrow," I said. "My eyes are about to cross."

"Does anything else happen?"

I shook my head as I hit the play button. "They all stand up and call the guards in and walk out with the bags. The last thing on the tape is a shot of them walking up the hall to take the money to the armored car out front."

The three men on camera stood as the guards stepped into the room and grabbed the bags. The guards walked out first, and Rulon fell in close behind them. The auditor turned and just before he took a step toward the door he did something that seemed familiar.

"Look at this," I said as I hit the rewind button on the remote control. "Watch what the auditor does when he walks toward the door."

"I don't see him doing anything unusual."

"Watch his right hand," I said.

"He's sticking it in the front pocket of his jacket. So what does that mean?"

"I may not know how they switched out those money bags," I said. "But I might just know who that auditor is."

EIGHTEEN

"So what's this I hear about a few tons of money getting stolen and nobody reportin' it?" Roger didn't even look up as he studied the report. "Y'all forget where my office is or something?"

"I tried to get them to call you earlier," I said. "But they wanted to hold off until they knew for sure it was stolen. They thought maybe it was going to show up."

"Yeah, sure. Johnnie Koscko's already tried to sell me that line of bullshit. One million, three hundred thousand dollars gets switched with a load of damn confetti, and nobody assumes anything's wrong. Don't want to jump the gun or nothin'."

"It was his call," I said. "His or Snow Mountain's."

He sucked on his teeth and looked at me over his reading glasses. "If you know anything about all this, you tell me now. You hear me? We've been friends too long for you to try to sandbag me."

"I don't work for Jackpot Bay Casino, Roger. You need to ask them about that money, not me."

"Come on, man. I know you've been all over the coast looking for Rulon Hornbeck."

"He was the one in charge of the money. We were hoping maybe he had set up a decoy shipment."

"What's this 'we' business? I thought you didn't work for them."

I was just about to step into some deep fecal matter, so I bit down on my bottom lip to shut myself up. This was exactly the kind of situation I was going to get into again and again if I kept trying to play cop for Bayou Casualty. Roger hadn't been sheriff all that long, but he was already developing that withering, accusing glare of the hardbitten cop.

"Hey, no cross-examinations. Okay?" I said. "As I recall the last time I called in a missing-person report, y'all said the person had to be missing for twenty-four hours."

"That rule's just for people. Money's different. Money don't just go off on a drunk and come back home two days later."

"It was just a few hours, Roger. It didn't make any difference."

"Looks like we'll never know that for sure," he said. "You and the casino that you don't work for can call off the search. They found Rulon Hornbeck's body this morning in a motel room over in Gulfport."

"His body?" I asked.

"Don't tell me you're surprised. You had to see that coming, didn't you?"

"Not really."

"If we had been searching for Rulon a day earlier like we should have been, he might be alive now."

"Would you give me a break on the reporting business?" I said. "It took a long time before we knew for sure he was missing. Why don't you just let it drop, and tell me how you found his body"

He put his tongue to the bottom of his front teeth and made a sucking sound. "We got a call from one of the maids."

"It was a maid? The manager didn't make the call?"

"It was one of those no-frills joints on 49 South near the airport. If there was a manager on duty, he was probably over at the Krispy Kreme or something."

"So how did he die?"

"He got shot in the head. One shot, well-placed." He pointed at the right side of his skull an inch above the ear. "Of course we didn't find any gun."

"And the money?"

"It wasn't there. Hard to believe, isn't it?" Roger scribbled on a notepad and tapped his pen on the desk. "You got anything you want to tell me? You find out anything when you were pokin' around earlier today?"

"Have you seen the surveillance tape from the casino?"

"It's so damn fuzzy you can't see much."

"Have you talked to Clyde about what's on it?" I asked.

"We haven't been able to catch up with Clyde yet. You see Mr. Koscko before I do, you tell him to get his nephew in here quick. When Clyde gets hard to find it starts looking real suspicious."

"Mister Koscko? So he's 'Mister' now?"

"He's a law-abiding citizen who's gonna be paying a hell of a lot of property tax when that new hotel gets built. They don't pay me for my personal opinions."

I've known Roger long enough to believe he was telling the truth, his feelings about Johnnie the Dime were strictly professional. Besides, I was working for Koscko myself, so I guess he was Mister to me too. "If you're looking to question Clyde," I said, "there's another guy you might want to talk to."

"We're already questioning the drivers of that armored car."

I shook my head. "That auditor guy did something on the surveillance tape that reminded me of a guy who had been staying in Gretchen La Pointe's guest house."

"Wait a minute. You kept a copy of that tape?"

"Is that a problem?"

He shrugged. "So why do you think it might be this guy who was at Gretchen's?"

"Because the guy on the tape did his hand like this in the front pocket of his jacket." I demonstrated the move. "I mean I couldn't see the face of the the guy on the tape. But that's an unusual gesture, and one time I noticed Gretchen's house guest doing that same thing."

"What's this guy's name?"

"David Stratton-Hume. The guy's actually got a title. He's the Earl of Stropshire."

"Any aliases?"

"I don't know of any," I said. "But you need to ask Clyde if that Snow Mountain auditor had a British accent. Maybe get a description."

"Don't give Clyde too much credit for any powers of observation. Spell Stropshire for me."

"I guess it's spelled the way it sounds."

"Who else have you talked to?" he asked.

"This preacher who's been leading all those demonstrations against the casino."

Roger hooked his glasses into his shirt pocket, put his feet on his desk, and laced his fingers behind his head. "Why'd you go talk to Newhart?"

I told Roger about us checking Rulon's personnel file and making the Tomball connection. Told him how Tara had got on the phone and talked with the guy at the high school over there. Told him about the newspaper story and offered to give him a copy. I explained that I had remembered that Rulon called the preacher by the name Joe Don, and how I guessed correctly that Rulon had been trying to shake him down.

"So where's this Tara?" he asked.

"As far as I know, she's wrapped everything up and left town. She mentioned something about going down to Cocodrie or Empire to do a little shark fishing out by the oil rigs."

He frowned and looked at me funny. "Shark fishing?"

"Or maybe skydiving."

"Is this the same woman I've heard you been screwin'?"

"Where'd you hear that?"

"You grew up here," he said. "You know how stuff like that gets spread around."

"It spreads by rumor, which is exactly what that story is."

"Yeah, right."

"Besides, she left town before we ever got together."

"So you think she needs to come back to town?" he asked. "Maybe as a material witness?"

I debated with myself, but only for a second. Tara could have stayed if she wanted to, and it would be a cheap trick to have the cops drag her back to town just so I could get another shot at her. "She doesn't know anything more about it than what you'll read in the newspaper story they faxed to her from Texas. You can find her later if you need to."

"Suit yourself," he said. "So tell me what Reverend Newhart had to say about getting blackmailed."

"Said he had paid Rulon off a few times, but he wasn't going to pay any more. He came clean with the deacons and they figured it was so far in the past it didn't matter."

"Anything else?"

"He said if the casino owed Robert Earl's widow that seven hundred dollars, he was going to get it one way or the other."

"So you think Newhart could have killed Rulon?" Roger asked.

"I've heard he's got a bad temper," I said. "But, no, I don't think he did."

Roger yawned and stretched his arms upward. "I'll put out a BOLO for that British dude."

"BOLO?"

"It means 'be on the lookout.' I'll put some notices up around town, but since we don't have a photograph I wouldn't get my hopes up. We can put out a description, but that's about it."

"You might ought to try the airports," I said.

"Gee, I woulda never thought of that. How about the preacher. Where can I find him?"

"I don't think Reverend Newhart did it, Roger."

"You say he's known to have a bad temper, and now you tell me that he's been blackmailed by a guy who shows up dead. Don't you think I ought to at least ask him what the hell he's been up to for the past day or so?"

NINETEEN

Johnnie the Dime kept me waiting in the anteroom outside his office, but I could still hear snatches of the shouted phone conversation through the closed door. The secretary, a thin and pleasant sort with highlighted blond hair, would give me embarrased smiles when the conversation in the next room would get loud. She must have needed the job pretty bad. She offered me coffee, and I declined three different times as she kept a steady eye on the tiny yellow light which indicated that Koscko was on the phone.

"Is he always like this?" I asked as a roar echoed against the door to Johnnie's office.

She shook her head. "He's been under a lot of pressure."

"Do you think he'll be on the phone much longer?"

"He's talking to Las Vegas. Sometimes those calls last for an hour."

The instant the light indicated he had hung up the phone, she let out a sigh and called into his office to announce I was there.

"So whatcha need, Delmas?" He propped his elbows on his desktop. "I'm kinda in a hurry here."

"The sheriff wants to talk with Clyde. I told him I'd pass the word along."

"He's already given his statement. He don't know nothin' about that heist."

"It's about Rulon's murder."

He frowned and his eyes went flat. "I ain't seen Clyde since yesterday."

"Don't mess with these people, Mr. Koscko. They want to talk with your nephew real soon."

"Didn't they arrest that preacher?"

"Questioned and released, or so I hear." I sat in the armchair in front of the desk. "I imagine they want to know where Clyde was about the time Rulon Hornbeck died."

"So why ain't they come here theirselves to find him? They expect us to guess that they wanna talk with him?" He ran his tongue along the inside of his cheek and put his hand up to cover a silent belch. "Damn red beans give me gas every time."

"He doesn't need to dodge the sheriff, Mr. Koscko. Makes him look suspicious."

Johnnie popped a couple of pink tablets into his mouth and started chewing them. "You take pills, Delmas?"

"Just vitamins."

He pulled a square, shallow plastic box out of the top drawer of the desk and set it before him. It was divided into seven little compartments, each marked with a day of the week. He also set out two brown bottles with prescription labels pasted on them. "I had angioplasty done on me last year. That's when they take this Roto Rooter and run it through the arteries in ya heart. The doc, he says I gotta cut down on stress."

"You ought to try walking," I said.

"I been thinkin' about one of them treadmills."

"That'll work."

He sank back in his chair. "I keep thinkin' maybe I oughta just cash in all my chips and retire. I could get a condo right there on the golf course, maybe run over to Evangeline Downs every once in a while and watch the ponies run. Maybe I could get me a part-time job with one of these casinos as a consultant. I mean, hell, I know this stuff backwards and forwards."

He looked tired, and his eyes had shrunk back some. He stared at a spot in space a few feet in front of him like a daydreamer. If I hadn't been there, he would have probably started talking to himself.

"I need to be going," I said. "Tell Clyde about the sheriff."

"We're waiting for the lawyer before we go talk to any cops," he said. "He's flying in from Vegas this afternoon."

"A Las Vegas lawyer? Don't you think that might be a little overkill?"

"Best in the business," he said. "Soon as he gets here we'll go talk to the sheriff. Now look, this ain't nothin' against your brother. But this guy comin' in, he's the best there is when you get charged with a crime."

I shrugged. "I didn't know Clyde had been charged with anything."

"I bet you don't think it looks good to have an out-of-town lawyer. Bet you think it makes him look guilty."

"I'd say it's a little unusual."

He burped softly and pushed against his belly with his fist. "People like us, we already look guilty to the cops no matter what we do. I'd have me a lawyer if they called me in, and Clyde needs one with him a lot more than I do. They'd twist him around so bad, they'd be charging him with shit that went down before he was even born. Clyde don't watch his temper too good sometimes."

I leaned forward to get out of my chair. "Before he goes to the sheriff's office, I'd like to talk to him myself."

"Clyde's been kind of a screwup, I know that. But he's the reason I want to hang on to this place. He's the closest thing I got to a son, and I want to be able to give it all to him one day. I know I ride his ass pretty hard, but it's payin' off. He's growin' up."

"Yeah, maybe so," I said. "Look, I've got to be going."

"Let me tell you what he did. He come in here the other day and told me what's been happening with all the money around here."

I sat back down.

"Yeah, he figured it out," he said. "Clyde started lookin' over the books and he found out that Rulon and that Robert Earl was teaming up and stealin' me blind."

"Just how did he say they were doing this stealing?"

"Fake invoices. That Robert Earl character, he'd write 'em up and Rulon'd sign for stuff that never got delivered. They'd pocket the difference."

"And Clyde figured all this out?"

"So y'all didn't need to hire any Las Vegas security expert after all." He cocked his head to study my reaction. "Everybody talks like Clyde's stupid or something. He's got plenty of sense."

Suddenly, Johnnie the Dime Koscko didn't look so much like a tough guy. In his eyes there was the same pleading look that parents of an ugly baby have when they desperately fish for someone to tell them how cute it is. The thought flashed through my mind of bringing up the seven hundred dollars and asking why it sure seemed that Clyde was in on that, but instead I just gave him a knowing smile and a slight nod.

Didn't have the heart to bring Johnnie the Dime back down to solid ground. Probably couldn't do it if I tried. Since the two other principals in the dummy inventory ripoff were now dead, there was no way he was going to believe any story other than that of his one and only heir, no way he was going to deny his blood kin. They'd find a way around whatever findings were in Tara's report. And when enough time passed, Johnnie would get to where he believed Clyde's story himself.

"Like I said, I'd like to ask him a few questions before he talks with the sheriff."

"Why you think they just let that holy roller preacher walk?" he asked.

"I don't think they've got enough evidence to hold him."

"Well, if the preacher didn't do it, I can tell 'em who they need to talk to," he said. "They need to find Rulon's boyfriend who lives over in New Orleans, the one he dumped."

"Why do you think Gino Stafford had anything to do with it?"

"Rulon spread a buncha stuff over here about the guy. Jerked him right outta the closet. I hear that Gino threatened to kill the son of a bitch. I wish he had."

"You seem mighty interested in finding out who killed Rulon," I said.

"I know how this stuff works. They pull in everybody for questioning and they decide which one they gonna pin with the murder. And Clyde's probably their easiest target." He drew in a deep breath and puffed his cheeks as he blew it out as he locked his eyes in on mine. "I can make it worth your time to find the right guy."

"Mr. Koscko, I'm not accusing anybody of anything, but can't you see why the cops might think Clyde's a possible suspect? He's been known to use a gun."

"That was self-defense, dammit."

"And when y'all found out that Rulon was missing along with the money, he offered to hunt Rulon down for you. He did that in front of witnesses."

He started shaking his head. "That was just talk, nothin' but talk. You think if I wanted Clyde to kill the guy, I'd say it out in the open? He knows I wasn't serious."

"Well, I still say you don't need to waste any time getting him to go talk with the sheriff."

"Why ain't the sheriff out lookin' for Rulon's blow buddy? Tell me why that Gino Stafford character ain't gettin' called in."

"I guess they've got to have more evidence than some quarrel that happened months ago."

"Hey, I seen it a hundred times out in Las Vegas." He grimaced and put his hand to his chest as he flinched from an acid reflux. "Some of them sugar cubes can be mean as a damn rattlesnake when they get pissed off about something. And hell ain't got no fury like a homo who's done got dumped."

I had already planned to drive over to New Orleans to see if Josh had any idea where the earl might have gone. Stratton-Hume had been working on Josh and Gino as possible investors in that Havana casino deal, and I had the feeling they had all three been seeing a lot of each other. Now that I had seen the video from the bank, I had this strong hunch that the earl, or whatever he was, had been in on the heist and would know where the loot was stashed. He was surely long gone, and I doubted he would have told Gino or Josh anything that would help me to find him. But you never know what he might have let slip.

I had to admit that Gino had plenty of reason to kill Rulon, but it just didn't fit, just couldn't picture it. But killer or not, he still knew Rulon better than anyone in the area, and it couldn't hurt to ask him a few questions.

On the way out of town, I went by the hotel where Tara had been staying to see if maybe she was still in town. They said she was still paid up for two more days and hadn't checked out, so I left her a message to call me. I've got this buddy in Biloxi who owns a charter fishing boat, and if she really wanted to fish for shark we could head out early the next morning. We could drop her report in the mail, leave the cell phones behind, and spend a little quiet time together out on the water. Relax and see what happens.

I took old Highway 90 toward New Orleans. It's a slow, back-road route through the swamps where the Pearl River splits and flows into the Mississippi Sound, low country too close to salt water for trees to grow. The reeds and bullrushes are thick and flat as carpet on both sides of the road and just below eye level as you drive along. The cars are few, lots of Jeeps and pickups, and slow moving. When the wind blows from the south, there is the aroma of the ocean, salt spray and decaying seaweed and the rotten egg smell of black marsh mud at low tide.

It's a good ride to take all your thoughts and stir them around, to turn off the radio and the air conditioner and let the windows down until the ingredients simmer and bubble and, with occasional stirring, blend together. And before I reached the Riggolets, that's just what happened.

I had been assuming that the murder of Rulon Hornbeck was directly connected with the theft of a million three hundred thousand from the take at the Snow Mountain concert. But what if that wasn't the case?

What if he died because he knew all about the phony invoice rip-off that Clyde had started? Rulon knew enough to blackmail Clyde for the rest of his life, or at least keep Clyde under his thumb. And he had already shown that he would launch a poison pen e-mail campaign for nothing more than pure meanness. So if he ever went back to Europe, what would keep him from screwing with Clyde by sending an e-mail to Uncle Johnnie?

Say Clyde's getting blackmailed just like Billy Joe Newhart, so he trails Rulon to the motel and pops a slug into his head. Then, with both Robert Earl and Rulon out of the way, he struts into Uncle Johnnie's office and says he solved the mystery of the leaking money. Not only does he get out of the mess he had started with those fake invoices, but he comes across to his uncle as a hero to boot.

But if that was the plan, there was still one other person who could mess things up for Clyde, one other person he'd have to take care of to make sure his secret stayed safe. Johnnie Koscko would never sit still long enough to listen to any accusations against Clyde from Robert Earl Bailey's widow, the widow's first cousin once removed, or the Reverend Billy Joe Newhart. And even if he did hear them out, the best they had to offer was some secondhand story that Robert Earl had been telling them. And if they weren't able to lay a hand on Clyde, that left only one person who had both the knowledge and the documentation to present a believable case to Johnnie the Dime that his nephew had been ripping him off.

And that was Tara Stocklin.

TWENTY

Josh Hallman's office is on Tulane Avenue not far from the Orleans Parish Courthouse. It's a converted two-story warehouse built shortly after World War I that served as the original company headquarters and distribution center for the Purity Sugar Company. Josh restored the building and was in the running for an award from the Crescent City Historic Preservation League, but he lost out when he rejected their color guidelines and painted the wooden moldings around the windows a distinctly nonhistoric pale yellow and replaced the original solid wood front doors with a pair of doors made of polished red oak surrounding a beveled, leaded-glass design created by his friend, the French Quarter artist Jontille. The doors featured slim ribbons of purple and green glass to represent stylized stalks of sugar cane swaying in a tropical wind, way too contemporary for the Preservation League. But Josh says he has better taste than whoever built the place ninety years ago and the building needed some color, and he was keeping the new doors, award or no award.

I had earlier stopped by Bayou Casualty's main office over on Poydras Street to see if Tara had been by there. My gut told me that I needed to let her know about my concern about her being the only one who can document Clyde's role in the fake invoice rip-off. But they hadn't heard from her and hadn't been able to get her on the phone for two days. They were surprised to learn that she was through with the job, and wanted me to see if I could find her for them so they could get her report and final bill.

At Josh's office, I was met at the receptionist's desk in the foyer by a soft-spoken kid with a sparse goatee and a sterling silver stud stuck through his lower lip. The last time I had been there the receptionist had been a handsome and pleasant young man named Kirk. I remembered that he could mix one hell of a fine gin-and-tonic. This new guy had a Yankee accent and sighed and fidgeted in an ongoing exhibition of boredom. I told him I knew the way to Josh's upstairs office and could get there by myself. When I walked in, Josh was leaning forward in his chair clipping his fingernails over the waste basket.

"What happened to Kirk?" I asked.

"He fell in love and moved to Key West." He extended his arm and spread his fingers as he regarded his nails "A real shame. I haven't had a decent martini since he left. But Timmy can make the best cappuccino in the city."

"I've been trying to find David Stratton-Hume."

"Oh, really? Am I to assume you think his lordship had something to do with the theft of all that money?"

"I don't think he was a lord," I said, "and it's just a hunch."

"Apparently you're not the only one who had that particular hunch. The sheriff of Hancock County has practically put out a dragnet for him."

"I talked with Roger earlier today, and he didn't even seem to know the guy."

"You're the one who talked to him? So you're the reason the good sheriff suddenly developed an interest in David?"

"I need to find that money, and I think our British friend may be able to help me."

"Just what makes you think that?" he asked.

"Wait a minute. By any chance are you representing Stratton-Hume?"

Josh reached into the side drawer of his desk and pulled out a long skinny cigarette. "They've got his description out at all the airports and bus stations. The cops in patrol cars are watching for him, and the television stations are running stories about how he's being pursued."

"So, are you representing him or not?"

"He hasn't called me for that, at least not yet. So far the only thing he can be charged with is impersonating a British earl." He lit the cigarette and smiled. "And on that count I'm afraid he is very guilty indeed."

"If he's a fake, he's pretty good at it."

"How good would you have to be to get away with impersonating an English aristocrat in Bay St. Louis?"

"So what makes you think he's *not* for real?" I asked.

"For one thing, the way he dresses."

"Every time I've seen him," I said, "he's dressed like he's on his way to the polo match or the yacht races."

"Exactly. He dresses the same way *you'd* be decked out if you were going to such an event. But the British upper class dresses as if they buy their clothes at the Salvation Army Thrift Store, and the bargain table at that. It's almost considered middle class to dress well."

"I can't believe that," I said. "As much money as they've got."

"I'm telling you, those people inherit the clothes they wear. And all that talk about Prince Andrew and Fergie and Dodi al-Fayed? That came straight out of the London tabloids. The upper crust doesn't talk about those things, at least not around commoners."

"How do you know all this?"

"I've been there," he said. "I've had occasion to be with a number of the right people in London."

"Maybe this one's different."

"I thought the same thing at first. But then he did one thing that no real duke or earl would do even if you held a gun to their head."

"You mean he told a joke that was actually funny?"

"Jack, the man said the word 'pardon.' "

"He said what?"

"Pardon."

I clutched my chest. "Why that sorry, no-good son of a bitch!"

"I'm serious. The upper classes seem to think that asking for a pardon in any form is something only the lower classes need to do. But whatever the reason, among the British aristocracy 'pardon' is much worse than the F word."

"Well, in that case we need to go catch that mother-pardoner and get his ass off the streets."

He drew his lips into a tight line, clearly irritated. Took a short puff from the cigarette and blew it straight out. I tried my best not to laugh, but he was just so damn serious that it struck me as funny and trying to hold back was about like stifling a hiccup.

"I fear David's here to run a scam," Josh said. "I tried to check him out, but I couldn't find anyone who was familiar with the Earl of Stropshire. They have so many aristocrats over there that nobody could say whether or not David's for real."

"So if he's not the Earl of Stropshire, who is he?"

"He's a charming, handsome man who's having a wonderful time acting out his fantasy and getting other people to pick up the tab."

"But I think this fantasy involved stealing over a million dollars from the Jackpot Bay Casino," I said, "and I'd like to get that money back."

Josh stubbed out his cigarette in a brass tray. "Would you care for some cappuccino? I can have Timmy bring one in."

"You heard me, counselor."

"I suppose you have evidence of his involvement?" Josh asked.

"You're talking like you're his lawyer."

"If I represented him," Josh said, "I wouldn't be telling any of this to you or anybody else. What evidence do you have that David stole that money?"

"I noticed something on the bank's video surveillance tape. I think David was playing the part of the Snow Mountain auditor. I also think that he's the guy Rulon was living with over in Monaco."

If Josh was surprised, it didn't show. "And that's what you told the sheriff?"

"Just the part about him being in on the heist. I didn't say a word about his relationship with Rulon. I thought I'd run that by you and Gino first to see if you knew anything about it."

His eyes narrowed for a moment. "Please leave Gino out of it. He's vulnerable right now."

"I need to talk to Gino about Rulon. He may be able to give me a whole list of people who'd like to see Rulon dead."

"He doesn't know that those two were involved with each other over in Europe. It'd kill him if he found out."

"He's going to learn about that soon enough when the cops talk to him."

Josh started nibbling on one of the fingernails he had just trimmed. "As you recall, I thought something was fishy the first time we met David at that concert on the beach. So I tried to check him out through this friend who travels to Europe each spring to buy antiques. He knows someone who's a bureau chief at Scotland Yard."

"Did you send them a photograph?"

"Didn't have one. But the contact at Scotland Yard said he knew of a case that involved someone passing himself off as a nobleman, and the description fit David. He suspected that David's real name is Dennis Strayhorn. It seems that Strayhorn was the son of a landscaper who tended the grounds at a number of the estates that have started receiving tourists to make ends meet. It would be an effective way to learn what you need to know to assume an identity."

"Does this Strayhorn have a criminal record?"

"Nothing to speak of. Certainly he's not wanted for anything right now. He's a small-time operator who was banned from one casino in the Bahamas for counting cards, but that was under the name Strayhorn. He usually tags along with rich Americans and passes himself off as aristocracy. It's a fantasy they seem to enjoy as much as he does."

"Maybe he decided to step up into the big leagues this time."

"I'm afraid he wouldn't be very good at it," he said. "This Strayhorn was described to me as more of a sponge than a thief. Not that he'd be above stealing if something safe and easy came his way, but there's too much risk in knocking off an armored truck."

Timmy walked in with two cappuccinos that Josh must have called for somehow without my noticing it. The sun had moved to an angle where it was streaming through the French doors that opened out to a little balcony creating a harsh, white glare. Josh got up and walked toward them and grasped the cord to close the curtains. "David once told me about the repugnance the British upper class has for sheer curtains. They call it netting and for some reason consider it a sure sign of the working class. He said in England there are two classes, the Haves and the Have Nets." He pulled the cord and drew the curtains tight. "He certainly played a convincing role as a nobleman."

I took one sip of the cappuccino to be polite. It was way too steamy outside to be drinking what amounted to hot chocolate. "You seem to like this guy. But don't let it cloud your judgment. He may be more than a two-bit con man. Our friend David Stratton-Hume might be a lead suspect in Rulon's murder."

"That's absurd!"

"Let's just say he and Rulon were former lovers and ran into each other here in Bay St. Louis. Could have been by accident, could have been planned. But they realize that the Snow Mountain group is going to leave a ton of cash hanging out for the taking, and they grab it. And once they get the cash, his lordship decides that there's no reason to share. So he shoots Rulon and makes off with all the money."

"David is a charming liar and impostor," Josh said. "He's not a killer."

"David's not a killer, and Gino's not a killer. Nobody's a killer. But somehow Rulon Hornbeck is dead." I set the cup of cappuccino on his desk and leaned toward him. "All I want to know is where to find David Stratton-Hume or Dennis Strayhorn or whoever the hell he is. And I'll track down Gino and question him about it if I have to."

"Listen, dammit! I've probably seen David more recently than Gino has. In fact, I saw him over here the day before that armored truck was robbed. We met for drinks at LeMoyne Landing over by the Riverwalk. I planned to warn him he'd beter not try to sell any of those phony bonds. But he brought someone with him, and it wasn't comfortable to bring the subject up." He finished off his cappuccino and set the cup on the desk. "In fact, the person he brought with him was that Tara woman you had a date with at that beach concert."

As Mama always says, well if that just don't beat all.

"Maybe I'm reading this all wrong," I said. "This David Stratton-Hume or Dennis Strayhorn or whoever the hell he is, is he gay or straight?"

"Maybe either, maybe both. It's possible the same could be said about Tara."

"Bullshit!"

"Jack, she's not your type. Whether you admit it or not, you're looking for a woman who wants to share the quiet life with you in your cabin on the beach. You'd grow tired of Tara's antics, and I'm afraid you would very quickily bore her to tears."

"I am not boring."

"He may dabble in both worlds," Josh said. "I've never asked. And when was the last time you jumped out of an airplane?"

"I wasn't talking about getting married to her. I was just looking for some fun."

"I know it would be a blow to your ego to think that some woman with such a magnificent set of legs might actually prefer the company of a more cosmopolitan man. But if you think about it, could you ever see yourself moving to St. Tropez or Milan? Hell, you couldn't even handle Memphis. No matter what their sexual preferences are, Tara and David have a lot more in common than you and she ever will."

"Did you hear that from her? Or is that something you're assuming?"

"Believe it or not, we didn't talk about you," he said. "We talked about Rulon and Gino as much as anything. I told him about the poison pen e-mails concerning Gino that Rulon sent. He seemed to be genuinely shocked that Rulon would do such a thing. He said he wanted to get to the bottom of it."

"How about Tara? What did she think about the e-mails?"

"She said he ought to let the whole thing drop. Said Gino's a big boy now. Tara's sort of tough, I gather."

"So do you think David might know where she is?" I asked.

"Is she missing?"

"She was supposed to turn in her final report to Bayou Casualty and take some time off. Nobody's seen her for a couple of days."

"There are hundreds of things she could do on the Coast. Have you checked out that skydiving outfit over in Pascagoula that she went to the last time she was here?"

"I'd feel better if I could talk with David or Dennis or whoever he is and ask him where she might be. And I think Gino may know where I can find him."

"Please leave Gino out of this."

"Have you told him that the earl is a fake?"

"I don't know what good it would do to tell him that. He's had all the deceit he can handle for a while."

"You're welcome to come with me," I said, "but I'm going to find him today. Aside from the fact that a man is dead, we've got well over a million in cash missing, and the company I work for may find itself on the hook for it. I don't want to hurt his feelings any more than you do, but I'm going to find out what he knows about Stratton-Hume."

Before we left Josh's office to begin our search for Gino, I called back home to get the latest news from Neal. Turns out I wasn't the only person searching for Clyde Dubardo. The sheriff's office had just called a few minutes before I did, and they were looking for him too.

Tara was still not answering the phone at her hotel room. I called Neal once more and asked him to phone Pascagoula and check with the skydiving school. I was told words to the effect that he didn't have time to do all the work that he was getting paid for, much less track down every one of my whims.

Josh got Timmy the receptionist to drive us up Canal Street in his red Miata, top down of course, and drop us off at the street car stop where St. Charles peels off from Canal back uptown toward Lee Circle and the Garden District. We walked across Canal with a herd of twenty pedestrians and entered the Vieux Carré at Royal Street with Josh talking out loud the whole time about how ridiculous it was to even think that Dennis a.k.a. David could be involved in a big-time robbery much less the killing of Rulon. Before we got to Iberville, the first cross street, the street urchins raced toward us, shoeshine kits in hand.

"Shoeshine, mister?"

"I'm wearing buckskins," Josh said with a dismissive wave, never slowing down.

"I bet I can tell you where you got them shoes," the oldest one said. He was twelve years old at the most.

I played along. "I bet you can't."

"Betcha a dollar."

It's a ritual that goes back at least twenty years, I've been watching it that long. The black kids who stream out of the projects on the other side of Rampart Street, the upper boundary of the Quarter, shine kits in hand, kits they never use and have no intention of using to hit up the tourists for a buck or two with their time-worn routine. They start when they're maybe six years old and by the time they're ten they've got as much street smarts as I do. Some of them work their way up to sidewalk tap dancer, performing for Hurricane-guzzling tourists for tips thrown into an open guitar case set by the curb. They perform seven days a week, school in session or not.

"Okay." I held up the dollar, walking all the time. "Tell me where I got my shoes."

"You got 'em on yo' feet in the City of N'Awlins in the State of Luziana. That'll be one dollar, please."

I handed him the dollar and a second kid, younger and clearly the understudy, chimed in with his pitch. "I betch I can . . ."

"Run along now," Josh said. "We're not tourists."

"I betcha I can . . ."

"You heard me," Josh said. "Now scram."

The leader of the group had spotted a new target, a couple coming toward us from Canal Street, tourists complete with Bermuda shorts and a camera around the man's neck. Easy marks. He pulled the younger kid away in mid-sentence and the whole bunch raced toward this new pair of suckers.

"You shouldn't be giving them any money," Josh said.

"It's only a dollar."

"You're not doing them any favors. If they didn't make those dollars they might go back to school." He stepped on a piece of used chewing gum and stopped to scrape the bottom of his shoe on the curb. "I'll go to court to defend the worst murderer in the world," he said, "unless it turns out that he had spit gum onto the sidewalk."

Royal Street had a lot of window-shoppers creeping along and stopping every forty feet or so. Josh stayed a stride or two ahead of me, stepping out into the street when we needed to pass a slow group. He was clearly irritated with me for wanting to find Gino. Sometimes Josh lets his personal feelings cloud his judgment, and the very passion he brings into a court case, his greatest strength, can just as easily become his weakness. We got to W. S. Sillers & Sons, an antique dealership near Brennan's, and he stopped in front of their window.

"They've started buying junk," he said. "Just look at some of that trash."

"Looks okay to me."

"Then it's a good thing you don't spend your money on antiques."

Josh had told me the story about how he had started as an in-house salesman at Sillers & Sons right out of college. It took him less than two years to work his way up to buyer and soon he was going to Europe for three weeks each spring, primarily to search for porcelains and commemorative wares. Sillers handles some domestic merchandise now, but back then it all came from France and England.

Those were the years before that night when he tried to come to the aid of a drunken friend on Bourbon Street. For his efforts he got maced and billy-clubbed by a beat cop who yelled the whole time about queers who dared to talk back to him. He landed in central lockup for two hellacious nights, two nights that lit the fire that drove him to enroll in the Tulane Law School. And for years that same beat cop paid dearly every time he found Josh on the other side in a courtroom. I wondered if he was thinking of those days as he looked at the display.

"You miss it, don't you?"

He smiled and nodded. "We need to hurry. Need to get there before the offices close and the crowd comes in."

He started walking even faster, and I fell behind when he cut around a group of Japanese tourists who were standing in front of

Brennan's snapping photographs. By the time I caught up with him, he had turned down Rue St. Louis toward the river.

"I thought Gino's restaurant was on Burgundy," I said as I caught him in front of the cathedral at Jackson Square. "Don't we need to go farther up toward Rampart?"

"He hasn't been going to the restaurant lately. I doubt that he'll be there."

"Does he live around here?"

"Watch out!" He pointed to the sidewalk right in front of my feet. "You'd think the drunks would at least have the class to crawl to the gutter to throw up."

On the far side of the square, a block or two beyond the Pontalba, the crowds thinned. "I don't recognize these places," I said. "Have they always been here?"

"This part of the Quarter may have changed some since the last time you saw it."

We came to a cross street and Josh never broke stride as he held up his hand in the manner of a traffic cop and walked in front of this Ford Explorer that was moving way too fast. I paused out of reflex and then scooted ahead to catch up with him once the thing came to a stop. I haven't developed the nerve it takes to walk fast through the Quarter. Two blocks later we reached a place called Scores.

It was a corner bar near Esplanade with a recessed door and Boston ferns hanging from metal arms above the windows. There was a framed menu mounted beside the front door and illuminated by a gaslight. The windows were smoked glass, dark enough to block a clear view of the interior. I could discern images of people moving and the fuzzy, flickering iridescence of six or eight TV screens on the walls.

"Gino hangs out here a lot," Josh said.

"What are all those TV sets for?" I asked.

"It's a sports bar."

"You're shittin' me."

He pushed the door open and stepped inside, leaving me standing at the entranceway. I glanced all around and didn't see anybody I knew, so I scooted inside right behind him. To the right was a bar with a copper surface that ran the length of the wall. The bar stools had backs and armrests, the tables had round tops the size of manhole covers and white tablecloths. Around the walls a foot below the ceiling was a display of pennants of all the teams of the NFL and below each pennant was mounted a miniature team helmet and a pompom with the team colors. Each display was lighted by a tiny spotlight. I saw Josh at the bar talking to the bartender, who kept looking up at the steeplechase race on the TV above him.

"Rance says he hasn't seen Gino today," Josh said.

"You may want to try one of the biker bars," Rance said.

"What's that supposed to mean?" Josh asked.

"You must not have seen him lately." He started drawing a beer into a stem glass. "Can I get you something?"

"Do y'all have Dixie longnecks?" I asked.

He curled his lip. "The only *domestic* beer we carry is Anchor Steam."

"Knock it off, Jack." Josh said without looking at me. "So when was the last time you saw him in here?"

"What did I do wrong?"

"Let me take care of the customers for a minute," Rance said over his shoulder as he stepped to the far end of the bar. "If you're interested in trying something different, sir, we have a special on Lobkowicz Trend."

"What the hell is that?" I asked Josh.

"It's a blond beer from Poland. You wouldn't like it."

I looked to see what was on the various screens. "So Gino's been a bad boy?"

"If you use that term in here, you might get more attention than you want."

"Didn't you say this was a sports bar?"

"There are sports other than football."

"A surfing championship?" I asked.

"They award trophies, don't they?"

"Judging from these TV screens, body-building is a lot more popular than I would have guessed."

"Quit complaining. You were the one who wanted to hunt for Gino," he said. "I can leave you here and let you ask around on your own."

"Don't even kid around about doing that."

"You seem to have stirred some interest at the table over by the bumper pool table. You could go ask that cute one swirling the brandy snifter if he's seen Gino. He'd be glad to talk to you."

"Why don't we wait and see what this bartender knows," I said.

"I'll get you a beer and you sit right here and keep your mouth shut while I do the talking. No more snide remarks."

I glanced at the table by the bumper pool table. Big mistake, three guys and one of them was looking at me. I turned back around real fast. "Oh, shit! Those guys over there, they don't think I'm . . . uh . . ."

"Think you're what?"

"You know."

"Are you afraid they might get the wrong idea just because you come into this place with me and sit at the bar watching body-building championships?"

"Can we hurry this along?"

"Jack, you're the one who insisted on finding Gino."

"What kind of beer are you drinking?" The guy who had been watching me was on the stool beside me. Slipped right in without me realizing it.

"Uh, I'm just looking," I said.

"Well I'm sure glad to hear that." He smiled and raised his eyebrows.

"Forget it," Josh said, "I'm buying for him."

"I haven't seen you in here before," the guy said. "Are you new in town?"

"He's with me," Josh said as he patted the back of my hand. "Can we have a little privacy?"

Rance stepped back toward us. The guy stayed on the stool beside me and kept smiling at me as he sipped his brandy. I kept cutting my eyes toward Josh to bail me out, but he had started talking with Rance and was paying me no mind. The guy reached over and stuck a paper napkin in my shirt pocket. "Call me," he whispered as he stood and walked back toward the table by the bumper pool table.

"So do you think he'll be coming in tonight?" Josh said to the bartender.

"I couldn't care less if he ever comes back," Rance said as he set a beer in a squat stem glass on the bar in front of me. "I've seen enough of him lately."

"So what has he done to make you so angry?" Josh asked Rance.

"He gets drunk and then he gets mean. He tries to hurt people."

I quaffed about half the beer before I noticed there was a damn lemon slice floating in it.

"You know he's not usually like that," Josh said.

"I haven't seen him for a few days," Rance said. "The last time he came in, he was with this man with the most wonderful British accent."

"Blue eyes?" Josh asked.

"Oh, yes," he said. "They sat where you're sitting now. I got a good look at the eyes."

"You say they were together?" I asked.

"Gino got here first and started drinking stingers. He was on his third by the time the other guy got here. They started talking and he got loud almost immediately. I thought he was going to cause trouble at first but the British gentleman calmed him down."

"Do you remember that guy's name?" I asked. "Was it David?"

"That's it. How do you like that beer?"

I nodded as I set the glass down. "Do you remember what they were talking about?"

"I really wasn't paying much attention."

Josh reached into his pocket and slipped a crumpled twenty-dollar bill on the bar. He set my glass on top of it. "Try to remember."

"It seems that David knew Rulon." Rance picked up the glass and the twenty with the same hand. "He and Gino started arguing, and I heard Rulon's name a lot."

"Arguing?" Josh asked.

"Maybe not exactly arguing. Gino was saying what a son of a bitch Rulon was, loud enough for everybody in the bar to hear. The same stuff we've all heard him say a million times. The other guy, that David, was saying that Rulon wasn't all that bad. He knew about the e-mails and was trying to tell Gino that Rulon didn't send them."

"Did they say anything about what Rulon was doing in Bay St. Louis?" I asked.

Rance's eyes went past us and he held back what he was about to say. He turned without a word and stepped toward the sink with the glass as he eased the twenty into his pocket.

"You want to know what I've been doing," Gino said from somewhere behind us and off to the side, "why don't you ask me?"

He hadn't shaved that morning, and maybe not the morning before. He wore a black cap with a Harley Davidson logo and a gray T-shirt under a leather vest. A pair of yellow wrap-around sunglasses had been set on the bill of the cap and he had a big silver loop in his left earlobe. His eyes were puffy and had a bleary cast to them, more pink than red, and he had tracks pressed into the side of his face that looked as if he had been sleeping on somebody's couch.

"My God!" Josh said. "Just look at you!"

"So what're you doing over here, Jack?" he asked. "The folks back home need some more stuff to gossip about?"

"Don't you start anything," Josh said, all but wagging his finger.

"Jack is trying to find David Stratton-Hume and we think you might know where he is."

"I just need to ask him a few questions."

"I'd suggest you tell Jack what you know," Josh said, "or you can just forget about me trying to keep bailing your ass out of trouble."

Gino rolled his eyes like some belligerent teenager and plopped down on the stool beside me. Smelled like bourbon, and not just on his breath. He had the odor that comes from a long binge, when that scent of the booze hangs around like a gas that seeps through the pores of the skin. "I didn't know you were into the gay bar scene, Jack."

"Give me a break, Gino."

"Why don't you let Rance tell you?" Gino said. "He seems to listen to every word I say in here."

"If I don't find David soon," I said, "the cops are going to be asking you about him."

"I haven't seen him since he came in here that last time." He pulled out his wallet and laid it on the bar. "Don't imagine I'll be seeing him again."

"The usual?" Rance said.

"I'll sit here all day if I have to," I said.

Gino sighed and closed his eyes. "So what do you want to know about David?"

"For starters," I said, "where is he?"

Gino pulled out his VISA card and laid it on the bar as the bartender set the stinger in front of him. He took a sip as he thought about the question. "If I had to guess, I'd say he's in Brazil."

"Answer his questions, dammit!" Josh said. "We don't need any of your smart mouth, we're trying to help you."

"Help me do what?" He chuckled to himself and kept on sipping the drink.

"We're trying to find out who killed Rulon."

"Are you saying I know something about it?"

"Do you remember where you were when he was killed?" I asked.

"Oh, so that's it. You're gonna try to pin murder on me." He tensed up and tapped the bar with the side of his fist. "He tears my heart out, and now I'm the one who's gonna take the fall? Well I don't think so."

"Hush your mouth," Josh said. "You better lay off the booze and start trying to figure out where you were and who can back up your story. You've threatened to kill Rulon a hundred times in the past few months and everybody in the French Quarter has heard you say it at least once."

"When was the last time you saw David?" I asked.

"Why don't you ask Rance?"

"I don't have the first clue," Rance said. "And I couldn't care less about your personal life."

"Yeah, right." Gino tossed back the rest of the stinger and pointed at the empty glass. Rance took it and made a sour face at him.

"Those things are strong," Josh said. "You better slow down."

"When did the piece of shit get killed?" Gino asked. "What was the exact minute? I want to mark it on my calendar."

"Probably yesterday," I said.

"Where was I yesterday, Rance? Was I in here?"

Rance rolled his eyes and groaned as he reached for the VISA card.

"Why did you say Stratton-Hume might be in Brazil?" I asked. "Were you serious?"

"Isn't that where fugitives go?"

"Watch what you say," Josh warned. "Let's not be making accusations."

"I figured he was going to try to sell me a piece of the Havana casino that fool Richie Leggett kept talking about," Gino said as Rance wiped the water off the bar with a dish towel and set the fresh drink on the bar. "But he wanted to talk to me about Rulon."

"Where did this happen?" I found myself watching Josh as if I needed his approval to ask questions.

"At the restaurant. Right at lunchtime. I was really busy, but when he said why he had come, I turned everything over to the help and we got a private table. He didn't beat around the bush, he told me straight out that he had been Rulon's lover over in Monaco."

"So you knew!" Josh said. "Why didn't you tell me you knew that?"

"You've got room to talk," Gino said. "Did you bother to tell me one word?"

Josh bit the inside of his cheek and reached across me to touch Gino's hand that he was resting on the bar. Gino snatched it away and took a big sip of the stinger. "I'm sorry," Josh said. "I should have told you. But I was only trying to keep you from getting hurt again." I could see the tears welling in Gino's eyes. I felt as if I were intruding on some private moment.

"So what did he tell you after that?" I asked, trying to sound crisp and businesslike.

"The first thing I wanted to do was put my fist through his face. But then I thought it's not his fault." He swallowed, took a deep breath and blew it out. His eyes had taken on an aspect of brooding. "I know how bad Rulon can mess with your head."

"So are you saying David Stratton-Hume drove over here just to tell you that?" I asked. "Was he trying to rub it in or something?"

"Jack!" Josh said. "Can't you be a little more sensitive?"

"It's all right," Gino said. "It's a good question. Damn good question. He said he came over to let me know that Rulon didn't send those e-mails."

"Well," Josh said, "I have heard that it could have been the Gay Pride Alliance."

Gino pounded his fist on the bar. "Bullshit! That's just like the sorry bastard to slip a knife into my ribs and then try to act like somebody else did it!" He knocked back the rest of the drink and slammed it down on the copper surface so hard that the stem of the glass snapped in two. His shift of mood came so quickly that I had to believe the whisky was already working on him.

"That's enough, Gino!" Rance said. "You're going to have to leave!"

"Just give us a minute," Josh said. "Everything's under control here."

"He's paying for that glass, and for the one he broke last night." I looked all around the room. There were four tables with seated customers and two guys playing bumper pool. Every eye in the place was on us. The guy who had stuffed the paper napkin in my pocket was still looking at me, still smiling. "This crowd doesn't come in here to get into fights," Rance said, "and they don't like to see fights."

Josh pulled out another twenty-dollar bill and tossed it on the counter. "Fifteen minutes. That's all we need."

Rance put on a less than convincing act that he was actually debating with himself about whether to take the money. Thought about it all of two seconds before he slipped the bill into his pocket. "You can stay, but no more outbursts. And I mean it."

"So why did you say that David might be in Brazil?" I asked, trying to right the ship.

"He told me that he and Rulon were getting back together and they planned to leave the country. He talked like they might go to France, but that was before Rulon died."

"But you said David was a fugitive."

"Well, isn't he? Isn't that the reason you're here asking questions?"

"I don't buy this story," I said. "He wouldn't come here just to tell you they were leaving the country."

"Give me another stinger," he said to Rance, "and put some brandy in this one."

"You've got to come up with something better than that," I said.

"I swear, he was trying to get me to believe Rulon's damned lies about those e-mails."

"Gino, David hardly knew you," I said. "Why would he care whether or not you believed anything Rulon had to say?"

"He'd care," Josh said. "When I told David what Rulon had done, it really bothered him. He said he was going to ask Rulon about it. He was genuinely shocked to hear that Rulon would have done such a thing."

Gino let out a dead laugh and shook his head. "Do you remember how Rulon had me fooled for over a year? Hell, I felt sorry for David. I could see that he had fallen for all the lies just like I did."

Gino took a fresh drink from Rance and stared at the amber liquid as he swirled it around. Josh stood up and walked around me and sat on the other side of Gino and reached for his hand. It was time for me to wrap things up; I figured one more of those stingers and Gino would be calling for Rance to put some Billy Holliday blues on the speaker system. Rulon Hornbeck really devastated the guy when he dumped him, but I didn't know how to remedy that.

"But you still believed that Rulon sent the e-mails," I said. "In fact, after David left you decided to go back to Bay St. Louis and track down Rulon, didn't you?"

Gino turned and glared at me, his eyes red and about to brim over with tears. Josh's mouth dropped, and he looked at me with the same outrage as he would if I had thrown a drink in Gino's face.

"You heard me," I said. "Why did you go back to find Rulon? Were you planning to tell him good-bye? No hard feelings? Or what?"

"I didn't . . ." his voice trailed off.

"Jack, I can't *believe* you're talking like this!" Josh all but shouted. "This isn't some police station, and Gino's not under arrest!"

"I didn't kill him! I didn't!"

"You tried to get Rulon's address from the casino," I said as I leaned into Gino. "You had been drinking. You wanted to confront him, and you . . ."

I had let down my guard because I had known Gino so long. Gino, the gentle defensive end from high school who never took a cheap shot, who never fought back in the locker room when the taunting came. But in all those earlier years I had never encountered him when he was depressed and angry and on the back side of a four-day binge.

His fist came up from down below the bar, below my field of vision. And it came up so fast that I never saw it. Smacked me square on the jaw before I had time to steel myself to the coming blow, rattled my brain and put the world into a spin just before the lights went off.

And in the next instant I was flat on my back on the floor between two stools, looking up at the ceiling, which appeared to be in a slow rotation, trying to focus in on the Atlanta Falcons pennant right below the dark oak molding. By the time all the lines were clear again Gino was out the door.

There was that old, familiar, metallic taste of blood and the sharp pain of a cut on the outside edge of my tongue where it got pinched when my upper and lower teeth got jammed against each other, and all the voices above me had a tinny echo to them.

As I pushed myself up, I heard Josh explaining to Rance why I wouldn't want him to call the cops and why I wouldn't be suing the bar. Why I damn sure didn't want any of this in the newspaper. When I sat up, there must have been ten guys standing around looking down at me.

Rance had jumped over the bar and was putting on a pair of latex gloves and pushing the guys back from the area where any of my blood may have splattered. The guy who had given me his phone number on the napkin was standing nearby and must have heard what Josh said. He was shaking his head and looked thoroughly disgusted.

I stayed down, resting on one knee and hung my head to let the blood flow back in and clear up the slight fainting sensation that still had my head spinning and had my gut on the edge of nausea. And as I felt everything clearing up, as the feeling returned to my throbbing jaw, I realized that poor, scorned, heartbroken Gino was more than capable of killing Rulon.

TWENTY-ONE

"What happened to your face?" Neal was behind his desk, all the way across the room. If he spotted the purple bruise all the way from there, it must have been more noticeable than I had hoped. "You enter some tough guy contest or something?"

"Something like that," I said. "Why are you still here at the office? I thought you closed at five."

"Seriously. What happened?"

"Our old friend Gino Stafford took offense at some questions I asked about Rulon."

"He hit you because of something you said about Rulon Hornbeck? I thought he hated the guy."

"I think he did," I said. "What did you want to see me about?"

"I can't believe you got into a fight with him. Where did this happen?"

"It was in a sports bar over in New Orleans."

"You mean you got into a fight in a public place?"

"It wasn't a fight. He sucker-punched me."

He tilted his head and smiled as he examined the side of my face. "Were you facing each other?"

"Yeah. Well, sort of."

"So it wasn't a sucker-punch."

"Whatever." Maybe he was right; maybe it was just reflexes slowing down. I don't think it would have happened with anybody else, not with some guy I didn't know and was ready for, so to me it was a sucker-punch. But I knew better than to start arguing definitions with him. He probably had some case where the Supreme Court had defined it, and I'm sure the definition would not have gone my way. "I'd like to stay and visit, but I need to get back to the house before that rain moves in."

"I've got somebody coming over who thinks he might need a lawyer," he said. "If I take the case, there's probably some legwork that'll need to be done. That is, unless you're tied up with Bayou Casualty."

"Would you quit staring at the side of my face?"

"I've never heard of Gino Stafford so much as swatting a fly. You sure bring out the best in people."

"You didn't call me over here to talk about Gino."

"Are you going to have time to take on any new cases?"

"Bayou Casualty only wanted me to keep Johnny Koscko and Tara from killing each other. Once she gets through with her report, my job is done. She says she's got the report done, but I haven't been able to find her to see where it is."

He snapped his fingers. "That reminds me, I called the Trent Lott Airport over in Pascagoula like you asked me to. Tara was over there yesterday. The guy I talked with didn't know her name, but when I described her he knew exactly who I was talking about."

I had forgotten about asking him to make that call. I guess Gino's uppercut had deleted a few kilobytes from my hard drive. "What was she doing over there?"

"Asking for directions to a jump zone."

"There are other blondes in this world," I said. "It might not have been her."

"The guy said she had the best set of legs he'd ever seen, no bra, and a pair of cutoffs so short you could see the cheeks of her ass."

"So did this guy talk to her, or what?"

"She was looking for Gold Coast Skydivers, which is located right by the airport. She chartered a plane and went up for a jump. He said the guy at the drop zone said she had also reserved a plane for today. Maybe you could call over there and see if you can tag along."

After a lifetime of practice, I can read my brother like a large-print novel. He's not all that subtle, and it's easy to tell when he's being sarcastic. But this time he was being serious. He really thought I might go over to that skydiving school. Whether he meant to or not, Neal had called my bluff. Hell, until he suggested that I go over there, I didn't realize myself that I had even been running a bluff. This don't-give-a-damn image that everybody in town has of me has taken root, and it's apparently gone even further than I would have dreamed.

So, I thought, if that's what everybody expects of me why shouldn't I go over there? I could take Interstate 10 and put the pedal down and be at the airport in less than an hour. Tara and I could jump out of that plane together and get a hell of a rush and check into one of those interstate motels close to the airport. With Tara that wasn't even speculation, it was a sure thing. And it was all waiting for me, just an hour's drive away.

But Neal had screwed up the fantasy when he called to my mind a clear vision of me getting into that pickup and driving over to that airport in Pascagoula and strapping on a parachute. Up to that point, all of Tara's thrill-seeking talk had been something that might happen somewhere else and some other time. The skydiving, the bungee jumping, and the hang gliding all sounded good when it was somewhere way out there. In other words, when it was a fantasy. And nothing kills a fantasy as fast as getting yourself into a position to act it out.

So the more I visualized that parachute jump, the more I realized that there wouldn't be any death-defying antics for the sake of a thrill. Hell, if the whole idea is nothing more than to jump my heart rate up and get me breathing faster, I can think of better ways to do it.

"I never thought she was your type," Neal said. "But then I've been wrong about what your type is before."

"Whatever," I said. "I need to find her pretty soon."

"You mean you're actually thinking about jumping out of an airplane?"

"I need to give her a heads-up about something," I said. "I've got a feeling she could be in danger."

"Tara looks like she can handle herself." He put his elbows on the arms of his chair and touched his fingertips together forming a tent. "The guy at the airport said he saw her jump yesterday. Most jumpers pull the cord at three thousand feet. He said she was down to no more than a thousand before her chute opened."

"Did that guy at the airport happen to tell you what time he saw her?"

"I called mid-afternoon, I'd say three o'clock. He said she had been there less than an hour before then."

"So did you ever find out where Clyde is?"

"Haven't heard a word."

"You're not still representing him, are you?"

"I handled his case when he shot Robert Earl Bailey. He hasn't called me since then, which is just as well." There was a rumble of thunder from the approaching storm. "So why are you asking me about him?"

"Our friend Johnnie the Dime told me that Clyde had discovered how Rulon and Robert Earl Bailey had been ripping off the casino. Said they had this plan where they cooked the books and dummied up a bunch of purchase orders and charged the casino for stuff that never got delivered. That's where all the leakage was coming from."

He shrugged and gave me this "so what" look. "And I assume since Clyde figured it out and Tara couldn't, you think she might lose her contract with Bayou Casualty? Is that what you're saying?"

"Clyde was lying to his uncle," I said. "He didn't discover any fake invoice scam. He was the one who started the whole thing. He got that Robert Earl Bailey to write out the purchase orders for twice the amount that actually got delivered. They were probably keeping two sets of books, but I don't know the details. When Rulon came in as the new manager, the whole scheme would have come to light, but he decided to keep it going. I mean, Clyde sure couldn't tell his uncle about it."

"Tara told you all this?"

"Sort of. I heard it from Tara and from Robert Earl's cousin, who seemed to know a lot about his personal business."

"So Rulon and Robert Earl just cut Clyde out of the action?"

"Rulon had him over a barrel. It was going to cost Clyde his ticket on the gravy train if Uncle Johnnie found out about the scheme. So Rulon took over and told Clyde he'd still have to pay Robert Earl the thousand or so a month he had been paying."

"And that's the seven hundred bucks Robert Earl was coming to get from Clyde the day he got shot?"

"Clyde must have decided that if he wasn't going to get any of the money, there was no way he was going to keep paying Robert Earl to write out the fake papers. I suspect he threatened Robert Earl and told him to keep his mouth shut. But Robert Earl wasn't going to sit still for that."

Neal pursed his lips and rubbed the point of his chin the way he does when he's mulling something over. "So from what you're saying, Clyde had a reason to kill Rulon aside from the fact that Rulon stole his job. You got any proof for all this stuff you've been telling me?"

"Nothing but hearsay. Did I use that word the right way?"

"Save the country boy act for your next investigation," he said. "I'm guessing Tara is the one with the proof against Clyde."

"She's knows he had a motive, but that's all. I still don't think Clyde killed Rulon, but Johnnie Koscko must think that he did, or he'd have never called in the mouthpiece from Vegas. I'm betting that Rulon's death had something to do with the stolen money from the Snow Mountain concert, and I don't think Clyde was in on that. And even if he was, they'll have twenty alibi witnesses lined up before they set foot in the sheriff's office. No way Clyde's taking the fall for murder."

"Wait a minute," Neal said. "If you don't think Clyde could get tagged with killing Rulon, why do you think he'd be such a danger to Tara? I can't see him trying to kill her just because she might have evidence that he'd been skimming from the company. He wouldn't get any more than probation on an embezzlement rap."

"But it might cost him a hell of a lot more than any probation," I said. "Even if Tara's investigation shows nothing more than a strong chance that Clyde was stealing, that might be enough to ruin him. Johnnie the Dime doesn't have to have proof beyond a reasonable doubt. If he thinks his Clyde, his own nephew, was ripping him off, he might kick him out the door even if he is flesh and blood. As it stands now, I think Clyde realizes that one day Uncle Johnnie's going to turn the whole operation over to him. That's why I don't think Clyde killed Rulon. It doesn't do him any good. He knows that sooner or later, he's going to get everything no matter what."

Neal nodded. "That is, if he doesn't get cut out of the will."

"Uncle Johnnie would overlook a murder or two, but stealing from family might be going a little too far."

"So if Clyde didn't kill Rulon," he said, "who did?"

"I think it was either our new friend the Earl of Stropshire or our old friend Gino Stafford."

"Gino?"

"He's in a deep trough right now. He's been trying to kill himself with booze ever since the breakup, and the more he drinks the more he blames Rulon for his troubles."

"I don't believe Gino could do it," he said.

"Sure he could. Don't fool yourself."

"What about the earl? Is he capable of murder?"

"He and Rulon pull off a big heist together," I said. "Then he decides that all of the loot looks better than half of it. People have murdered for less."

"But Clyde had a big reason for killing him too. Like you said, Rulon could have really shafted him if he ever decided to tell Uncle Johnnie about the fake invoices."

I rubbed my tongue against the cut inside my cheek from Gino's sucker-punch. He was right, my gut still wasn't telling me who killed the guy, and the deeper I dug the more murky everything became. "People were waiting in line to take a shot at Rulon, and we can sit here and make a case that any one of them did it. But Clyde is the only murder suspect who's also got a reason to want Tara Stocklin out of the way."

"Why don't you call over to that skydiving school and see if she's scheduled to go on a jump?" He started picking through the pink call-back slips scattered about the top of his desk. "I've got the number here somewhere."

"So why did you want me to come over here?" I asked. "You said something about a new client."

"Yeah, it's somebody who says he knows you. It's that radio preacher who bought Shorty Evans's old place out by the interstate," he said as he slid one of the pink slips across the desk toward me. "That's the number for the airport over in Pascagoula. You can use this phone."

"What does Billy Joe Newhart want to talk to you about?"

"He wants to see if I can speed up the process of getting him cleared. He's still a suspect, and it's costing him money every day the case drags on." He glanced over at the big wind-up wall clock. "He ought to be here any minute. Why don't you go ahead and try to call Tara?"

As I was talking, his secretary stuck her head in and said that Reverend Newhart had just come in. The guy I spoke with at the skydiving school had not talked with Tara, but he checked the schedule and she had lined up a plane for a jump that afternoon. I gave him my phone number, and he said he'd get the pilot to pass it along to her. Neal had already stepped out front to show Newhart to his office and to get a fresh pot of coffee brewing. I heard the preacher as he introduced himself.

"I believe you know my brother," Neal said as they walked back into the room.

"Reverend," I said, with a slight nod.

He brushed the raindrops off the shoulders of his sports coat as he stepped over to shake my hand, his deep-set brown eyes glowing with self-assurance. "We met the other day, the same day they found poor Rulon."

"Jack does some investigative work for me. If you don't mind, I'd like to have him sit in on this meeting."

"Might as well," he said. "He already knows most of what I need to tell you."

Neal sat behind his desk with a notepad, and the preacher and I sat side by side across from him. Neal was right, Newhart wanted us to light a fire under the sheriff's office and get his name cleared. He had temporarily stepped down from the pulpit while the investigation was going on, and the love offerings from the radio show had fallen off quite a bit.

He told us about the days back in Tomball and the wreck. Seems the casino had drawn both him and Rulon to Bay St. Louis, but for different reasons. He got a call from Rulon shortly after the billboard went up, and that's when Rulon started the blackmail. He laid it all out for Neal, right up to the day he came clean with the deacons and decided to stand up to Rulon. That was the same day I went to see him at the church.

"I'll need you to get your deacons to give me a statement about where you were the day they found Rulon," Neal said. "Jack can go to them if you think that would be faster."

"When was the time of death?" I asked. "Does anybody know that?"

"It's a sad story," Newhart said. "Just a case of the devil taking over somebody's life. I pray that the Lord will have mercy."

While the preacher told Neal the history on what happened back in Tomball, my cell phone went off. It was a voice I didn't recognize, a country boy who must have been in an auto repair shop or a construction site. Wherever it was, somebody in the background was operating an electric impact wrench, sounded like they were tightening lug nuts. "You the man I need to talk to about that reward?"

I was halfway listening to what the preacher was telling Neal and it took a second for what the guy was talking about to register. Before I could reply, he said, "Well, are you the man, or ain't ya? Ain't this the number they got on that poster?"

"This is it," I said. "What you got for me?"

"That dude the cops are after, I know where he is."

I held my hand out to get Neal and Newhart to hold down on the conversation so I could hear the guy on the phone over the racket of that pneumatic drill or whatever it was going in the background. "So where is he?" I jotted down the number that was showing on my caller ID.

"I'm gonna get that reward 'fore I tell you anything."

"Give me your name," I said, "and if it pans out, you'll get the money."

"Uh-uh, Bubba. No names. Ain't givin' ya my name."

I handed Neal the number and put my hand over the receiver as I told him to see if it was listed in his cross directory. The guy on the line asked if I was still there.

"If you don't give me your name, I can't get the money to you," I said.

"You better quit wastin' time," the guy said. "He's just about to leave town."

"I can give you a number," I said. "You can call back after we catch him and claim the money by giving us the number."

"How do I know you'll give it to me?"

Neal scribbled on a notepad and held it up for me to see. The call was coming in from the Stennis International Airport, maybe ten miles away from Neal's office. "That's the way it works, friend," I said. "You'll have to trust me."

There was a silent pause, punctuated by the pneumatic drill that had cranked back up. "What's the number?"

"Eight eighty-eight. As soon as we catch the man on that poster you can call me back and give me that number and the ten thousand is yours."

On the other end of the line a voice amplified by a loudspeaker called for somebody named Jimmy to pick up on line two. "He's here at the Stennis Airport right now. General aviation hangar."

"I can be there in twenty minutes," I said. "Thirty minutes tops."

"Well you better get your ass in gear."

"How do you know it's him?" I asked.

"Y'all described him on that poster you put on the bulletin board out here. And he talks like he's from England. We don't get too many of them in here."

"What's he doing at an airport hangar?" I asked.

"He's got this plane that flew in here from Pascagoula a coupla hours ago. It's a white Cessna with a red stripe along the side, twin props. He's gettin' ready to make a jump."

"A parachute jump? In this weather?"

"Maybe if you're on the run," he said, "you ain't got a lotta time to wait for perfect conditions."

"I didn't say he was on the run."

The man sighed into the phone. "Bubba, when the cops send a BOLO to the airports to be watching for some British dude who's on the run, and the same day somebody else puts out a reward for a British dude, it don't take much to put the two together. Especially when that guy comes out here dresed up in a parachute and a jumpsuit and has him a private plane ready to go. Means he's tryin' to skip town. You better get out here in the next thirty minutes, or they're gonna get in that plane and be long gone."

"*They're* gonna get in the plane? You mean sombody's with him?"

"The plane takes off at six o'clock. That's twenty-seven minutes from now."

"Tell the tower to hold the plane until we can get the cops," I said.

"Make that twenty-*six* minutes, Bubba," he said, and he hung up the phone.

TWENTY-TWO

There was a gap in the line of cars coming toward me on Highway 90, so I stepped on the gas and ran the red light. I speed-shifted as I raced west toward the Stennis Airport. The highway is a four-lane that cuts right through the city, and it's lined on both sides with shopping centers and convenience stores, so there's lots of traffic. It was raining, a steady drizzle from a dim, low-hanging sky, and my truck kicked up a cloud of white mist. It was dark and getting darker, and the taillights reflecting through the water on my windshield twinkled like Christmas lights.

I stayed in the left lane, popped on my emergency flashers, and rode the bumper of anybody who didn't get out of my way fast enough. The sight of the grille of my big Dodge Ram in their rearview mirror and the pulsating yellow flashers was enough to scatter most of the cars I came up behind, so it was mostly a clear dash all the way to the turnoff to Stennis. Still had nineteen minutes to go when I turned off I-90 and headed north and floored it so hard that I fishtailed.

I had tried to call the sheriff's office before I left Neal's place, but I got this desk sergeant who didn't seem to know much about the search for David Stratton-Hume and wasn't about to dispatch any car to the airport until he could verify what I was telling him. He said he'd check with the shift captain and call me right back.

But the clock was running so I left Neal with instructions to keep the line open and wait for the return call.

Got stuck behind two tractor-trailer rigs that were taking up the whole road as one of them creeped past the other one. The spray they were kicking up coated my windshield and overwhelmed the wipers. I snugged in behind the first trailer, right on his tail, too close to see anything but the rear doors of the trailer and even that was blurry. I started shouting at the guy to get the hell out of the way. I rode his bumper and kept my foot poised to hit the brake pedal just in case he got a case of the smartass and decided to tap on those airbrakes.

I hit puddles in the contours of the asphalt and they made the steering wheel tug in that direction. Through the soles of my shoes, I could feel the splatter against the underside of the truck. I was sitting straight up, my back not even touching the seat, gripping the wheel and cursing at that slow-assed truck. I was down to twelve minutes until the plane took off.

Was anybody there with Stratton-Hume? That's the way I understood what the caller had said, but I could have been wrong. Maybe he had been talking about the pilot. I tried to remember exactly what he had said. "They're gonna get in that plane and be long gone." But there was a lot of noise in the background, and I couldn't make out what he was saying. He could have said they're gonna get in that plane and *he'll* be long gone. I know he said *they* were going to get in the plane. But that would fit even if he were talking about Stratton-Hume and the pilot. I mean, he had to have a pilot.

But I couldn't fool myself. The guy had said somebody was with Stratton-Hume, and he said they were going to get on the plane with him. Of course, it could have been anybody. I sure didn't know how many connections the guy had over here in the States.

Aside from David Stratton-Hume, the only person connected to the case who knew anything about skydiving was Tara. And

Tara and Stratton-Hume had talked about going up for a jump, and she had been seen in Pascagoula at Gold Coast Skydivers. Had she arranged for a plane to take them up from the Stennis Airport? The last time I talked with Tara was before I saw the tape and figured out that Stratton-Hume had been in on the Snow Mountain heist. She wouldn't have any way of knowing that he was in on it.

The truck in front of me finally got beyond the one he had been passing for what seemed to be the past thirty minutes. The slower truck flashed his brights, that universal trucker's signal that your rig has cleared the front bumper and it's okay to pull back in. The truck in front of me flipped on a turn signal and creeped back toward the right lane. The guy was messing with me, he could have gotten over faster than that. I stepped on the gas and straddled the inside shoulder of the road and zipped past him before he even got his wheels across the center stripe. He blasted his airhorn, laid down on it good, and flashed his brights a few times. No telling what he was saying about me over his CB.

So with the cops bearing down on his ass, why would Straton-Hume call Tara for what was in effect a date? Answer: He couldn't go to the airport and rent a plane with a BOLO out on him. He would need for somebody else to book the plane, and since they had already talked about lining up a jump, she'd be the perfect one to get the plane. But then what would he do with Tara when it came time for the escape? He could just jump and try to get away in some remote area. But, more likely, he would decide that he didn't need to leave any witnesses, including the pilot and Tara. Just plug both of them and jump out of the plane.

I opened the big console beside me and pulled out my new 9mm automatic. Laid it on top of the dash. Tried to call in to Neal to see if he had heard from the sheriff's office. The line was busy.

The rain was picking up and the tops of the trees swayed. A flurry of pine needles blew across the road. My windshield wipers were running at top speed in a steady drumbeat, but not fast enough to give me anything but a glimpse of the road in that instant when the wiper blade crossed my narrow line of sight.

I watched for the tiny reflectors set along the center stripe so I could at least stay on the pavement. My phone rang and I nearly spun out as I tried to find the right button to receive the call.

"I finally got a call back from the shift captain," Neal said. "He wanted to know who called in the report."

"Dammit, they've got six minutes until that plane leaves! See if you can get Roger on the line."

"They said . . . federal facility . . . not about to . . ."

"You're breaking up," I said. "Can't hear you."

"If you'd charge up . . . every once in a . . ."

"Try to get them to call the tower and stop the flight!"

The phone was dead, and I didn't have a plug in for the cigarette lighter. They didn't have time to get a squad car there anyway.

I turned into the airport at four minutes until six. The general aviation hangar was off to the right. At the far end of the tarmac, where the planes taxied to get into takeoff position, sat this big twin prop, one of those top-wing Cessnas that carries about eight passengers. White with a red stripe, just like the caller said. Had both engines running and the strobe lights flashing. The rain had slacked to where it was just heavy enough to drop, a step above mist. The sun was a white smudge low in the western sky hidden by a blanket of soupy clouds, and the mercury vapor lights set high on poles at various points around the terminal and hangar had begun sputtering and popping to life.

Two figures with backpacks were standing on the concrete maybe fifty feet from the plane. The taller of the two stood behind the other one and appeared to be fastening a utility belt or something around the waist of the shorter one. After the guy behind pulled on the belt to see that it was snug, they started walking single file toward the plane, the shorter one in front. The guy in back was craning his head around, looking over his shoulder, and stopped and turned toward the gate as if waiting for someone. It was almost straight-up six o'clock.

I jammed down on the lever to engage the four-wheel drive. I shoved the gear stick up into first, and showered down on the gas. The big Dodge roared and leaped ahead and the tires spun and squealed on the wet surface.

I drove straight at the gate's weakest spot, the point where the gatepost opposite the hinges meets the fence. I burst through and heard the sides of my truck scrape against the broken, jagged chainlink wall that I was piercing like a spear.

I turned on my headlights and flashed them to bright. I cut through a space between two parked and tethered planes and sped toward the twin-engine Cessna and the two dark figures walking toward it. I flashed my lights and pressed down on the horn.

Off to the side, I saw a whirling blue light on the roof of a golf cart heading toward me. The two skydivers noticed the noise and the lights. They turned and faced me and my headlights hit them straight on. The tall one was Stratton-Hume. The shorter one was Tara.

Stratton-Hume hit the ground and spread out as flat and still as a rug, but Tara bolted toward the plane. I wheeled the truck around so that my door was on the side opposite from them. I hopped out and laid across the hood of my truck.

The whirling propellers of the Cessna were rising in pitch and sending out ripples across the huge puddle of water gathered behind a seam in the concrete behind the plane. I drew a bead on Stratton-Hume who was facedown on the tarmac. "Stay down, David!" I shouted as I scooted around my truck. Don't know how he heard me, I could hardly hear myself. But he didn't move. I ran toward him, staying low and watching him for any movement of the hands, keeping my gun cocked and ready.

By the time I got to him, Tara had already made it to the plane's gangplank. "Tara!" I yelled. "Stop!" The pulse of the sirens of the security carts were growing louder and the rain came down harder.

"Stay down!" I yelled at David. "Hands straight out!"

"What's the bloody problem?" he shouted. "We're just out for a jump!"

I did a quick pat down but didn't feel anything. I figured the security guards were close enough and could figure out what was happening and take over. I sprinted toward the plane where Tara was halfway up the little five-step gangplank. "It's okay, Tara! It's me!"

She was up at the door of the plane by this time. I stopped and waved my hands over my head, trying to get her to recognize me. But she ducked inside and started pulling up the gangplank. "Hey!" I shouted. "It's okay!" I started running toward the plane again, still waving my arms. "Tara! Stop the plane!"

The props revved up higher and the plane started moving, even though the gangplank was only halfway up. I chased after it with the winds from the props blasting the water into my face and blurring my vision. Over the whine of the Cessna's engines I could hear the siren of a security cart and a voice through a bullhorn telling me to stop. I had just about caught up with the plane, was just about to grab whatever I could and try to pull myself on board, but I couldn't quite reach it.

I made a final lunge and with one hand I grabbed a cable that served as a hand-hold for the gangplank. The plane was now moving barely faster than I can run. I moved my other hand forward and got a two-hand grip on the cable and held on as my feet began dragging along the wet concrete. Tara was on one knee just inside the doorway. She had pulled out a pistol from somewhere and was holding it with both hands.

"IT'S ME, TARA! GET HIM TO STOP THIS THING!"

Even though the water in my eyes made it hard for me to see, I could tell she was surprised when she recognized me. But I could also see that it didn't matter one bit. She was wound tight and ready to shoot anybody who was trying to get on that plane. Her eyes were squinting, almost shut, and her pupils were two black dots. Her hand was gripping the pistol so tight her knuckles had turned red.

And then I did something really stupid. I held on to the damn cable. I kept staring up at her, kept shaking the rain off my face. The cable was cutting into my palms, I knew from the feel that it had broken the skin. But I just couldn't believe she was going to blow me away.

"LET GO, BY GOD!" she shouted. "LET GO OR I'LL SHOOT!"

I held on long enough for the plane to drag me a few more yards. She closed her eyes for a moment, then she raised the pistol to draw down on me. The cable slipped out of my hands, and I fell to the ground. I slammed down on my shoulder and rolled over a few times.

The Cessna built up speed on its taxi to the main runway and roared as it lifted off the ground. I lay on my back, the rain stinging my face, as the golf cart wheeled up beside me and the guards hopped out with their revolvers drawn.

TWENTY-THREE

The first thing the desk sergeant at the sheriff's office asked me was if I needed to see the counselor they had for victims of violent crimes. Reasonable question considering the way I looked. The side of my face was already purple from the sucker-punch I had taken from Gino Stafford two days earlier, and now I had both hands bandaged from what amounted to rope burns from trying to hold on to the steel cable on that gangplank. I was in a flak jacket to protect the two ribs I cracked when I hit the tarmac, so I was stiff and trussed and couldn't twist my upper body.

I had big patches of white gauze taped to various points along my arms to cover the raw spots where the skin had been scraped off from the slide across ten feet of airport concrete. In some places there were red spots on the gauze where blood was soaking through. I told the sergeant why I was there and he motioned for me to go down to the end of the hall.

The Darvon or Darvocet or whatever they gave me the night before at the hospital had worn off sometime during the night. I had to shuffle as I walked because it hurt to swing my arms. I had sharp pains under my arms every time I drew in a breath, and the scrapes felt like they were on fire. The hospital pharmacy had given me a whole bottle of pain pills, but they were out in my truck. I've seen them mess up too many people even when they're prescribed, so I'm scared to take them.

I had been so doped up at the hospital that they delayed the questioning overnight. Neal had worked his magic to get the airport authorities to overlook that pistol I had carried onto the runway, and he assured them that Bayou Casualty would be picking up the tab on the chainlink gate I had rammed. But Roger still wanted me to come in and give him a full report and statement. He also wanted me to file a complaint for assault against Tara so they could get the nationwide manhunt into gear.

The night before, Tara held a gun on the pilot and forced him to fly north, directly into this two-hundred-mile-wide band of rain that was inching across the state. When I checked out of the hospital that morning, some fourteen hours after the plane took off, that same front was still dropping a sporadic drizzle on us. The plane was ten minutes out of the Stennis Airport, and ground control was screaming at them over the radio, when Tara shot the radio dead, busted up the GPS with an empty wine bottle, and, in doing so, also knocked out the lights on the instrument panel.

They flew above the cloud cover, and judging from the direction toward the sunset, the pilot knew they were headed on a course roughly north-northwest. No idea how high they were. She was plotting the course on a hand-held GPS and telling him where to go. He couldn't say for sure when she jumped because he was so scared she was going to shoot him in the back of the head that he wasn't paying attention to what time it was when she jumped.

Of course, the pilot had no idea where they were when Tara left the plane. After she jumped, he flew without a radio or a GPS for an hour before the clouds broke below him. He set down on this crop duster strip up past Vicksburg on the Arkansas side of the river near this little town called Tillar. Had to walk a few miles before he could find out where he was and get to a phone.

Roger wanted to see what I could add to the pilot's story, so there I was, sitting in this wooden chair against the wall outside the door of his office. I was waiting for him to get through with whoever he had been talking with in there for the past thirty minutes. With the dope wearing off and my head clearing up, I tried to think about what I was going to tell him. But I kept drifting off into a bunch of "what ifs."

If my grip hadn't failed me the night before, if I hadn't fallen to the ground, would Tara have pulled that trigger? I was having a hard time admitting to myself that she was on the verge of blowing me away, regardless of the look in her eyes. I mean, she had a chance to and didn't. She could have popped a couple of slugs into me any time I was holding on to that cable like a fool and dragging along with that plane. So that means she wouldn't have shot me, right?

But then, I didn't actually have a prayer of pulling myself up into that plane, so why should she? Why add a murder charge to the grand theft and whatever else she would be charged with, especially since there was nothing to be gained? So the decision to hold up on pulling the trigger, the decision to let me live, was probably nothing more than a quick assessment of the benefits and the risks, with no emotion or feeling coming into the equation. And if the equation had come out the other way, I'd be dead now.

It hurt my feelings to think that. After all, wasn't this the same woman who came on so strong that day I picked her up at the airport? Hell, she wanted me bad that day, didn't she? Or did I just happen to be the closest man on the scene that evening?

There was obviously a lot I didn't know about Tara. I never realized she was in on the Snow Mountain job until she pointed that gun in my face. But I had been trying to piece her story together all morning and a few things had become fairly clear. As much as I hated to admit all of that, there was another conclusion about Tara that I found really disturbing. And try as I might, I kept coming back to it.

The door to Roger's office opened and out stepped David

Stratton-Hume and Josh Hallman. Josh was all business, pinstripes, and wingtips. David was wearing a pair of off-white baggy pants, the kind with a drawstring at the waist, and a short-sleeved, solid black knit shirt open at the collar. He was shaved and fresh and smiling as he stepped toward me.

"Jack, I'm so glad to see you're out of the hospital already," David said. "Is everything all right?"

"You look like hell," Josh said.

"Thanks for noticing," I said. "What are you doing here?"

Josh studied the purple bruise on the side of my face. "Gino really felt awful about hitting you. He called me and said that when he hit you, he realized that he was out of control. He's decided to check into Clearview Rehab up in Hattiesburg."

"The sheriff will be with you in ten minutes, Mr. Delmas," the receptionist said. "He has to make a few phone calls."

"You need to go down to the evidence room and pick up your things," Josh said to David. "We're going to have to hurry or you'll miss your flight."

"Wasn't that a shock about our friend Tara?" David said to me. "I had no idea she was the violent sort."

"I hate to rush you," Josh tapped the face of his Rolex, "but you really must hurry."

"Quite a nasty fall you took. I do hope you're feeling better," David said as he turned and stepped down the hall. The soft rubber soles of his shoes squeaked down the slick, terrazzo floor of the corridor.

"Where the hell is he going?" I asked.

"He gave his statement and they're through with him."

"They're not charging him with anything?"

"They wanted to know what he could tell them about Tara Stocklin." He swept the seat of the chair beside me with a sheaf of papers he was holding before he sat. "What on earth would they be charging him with?"

"How about stealing over a million dollars? How about the murder of Rulon Hornbeck?"

"Where are you coming up with all of these outlandish ideas?"

"Why is it outlandish to suspect that he'd steal money if he got the chance? You said yourself that he wasn't a real earl."

"Everyone has their fantasies," he said. "That doesn't make them criminals."

"He and Tara were wearing parachutes and boarding a plane in the middle of a rainstorm. That sure sounds like they were running from something."

"They're both 'D' licensed parachutists with over five hundred jumps. They wanted to try a foul-weather jump just for kicks. So Tara lined up a plane out of Pascagoula and invited David to jump with her. It may sound crazy, but it's not criminal. Besides, he had no idea she had done anything wrong, and had no way of knowing that she planned to use the jump as a means of escape."

I have dreams like this. The dreams don't come as often as they did when I was working in my ex-father-in-law's bank in Memphis, but still often enough to wrench me out of a light sleep a few times a year. I'm always the only one who can see that a disaster is about to happen, and no one will listen to me. In most of these dreams, a bridge has washed out from floodwaters, the river is swollen and running fast. A car full of teenagers is racing toward it, laughing, oblivious, their radio blaring. The driver is turned toward the back seat, not watching the road. I'm on the side of the highway waving my arms, but no one in the car ever looks my way. I can't quite catch their eye, can't quite get there. I'm trying to scream, but no sound is coming out.

"Josh," I said, "David Stratton-Hume and Tara and Rulon got together and stole that money from the Snow Mountain concert. Somehow Rulon ended up dead from a gunshot to the head. Don't you see where I could assume they'd be holding him on some type of charges."

Josh laid his head back and sighed. "Do you have any evidence whatsoever that links David to a murder, or even to that robbery?"

"First of all, when the money disappeared so did he. And besides that the surveillance tape shows him in the room when they made the switch."

"Oh, yes. I heard about that. After hours of studying this grainy and poorly lighted tape, no one seems to recognize this person who claimed to be an auditor for the Snow Mountain band. But you think it might be David because of the way the person on the tape put his hand in his coat pocket. Is that the evidence you're talking about?"

I had started breathing harder and the pain was increased around my ribcage. I took a few short breaths and tried to calm down. Josh had taken on this sweet, confused, I-just-want-to-help kind of smile and that didn't help matters any.

"None of this is going to matter when they find Tara," I said. "I'm sure that once she tells them what happened, they'll track him down and arrest him."

"God," he said, "I'd hate to think how mushy she would have made your brain if she had actually got you in the sack."

"What's that supposed to mean?"

"It means that despite of the fact that she pointed a gun at you and threatened to kill you, despite the fact that she hijacked a plane, you still can't see that she was the one who killed Rulon." He glanced at the secretary to make sure he wasn't talking too loudly and leaned in toward me. "There's no evidence David was involved in anything wrong. None."

I winced as a pain shot along my chest from my waist to my armpit. I wasn't up to any argument with Josh. Those things wear me out like I've been boxing with him or something. I eased back into the chair and extended my legs to where only my heels were resting on the floor. "I thought this whole thing over this morning," I said. "I've come up with a theory about what happened. That is if you care to hear it."

"Were you still on Demerol at the time?"

"Once Tara remembered Rulon and Stratton-Hume from the days when they were all three in Monaco, she knew right away that David and Rulon were setting up for a big score. And once she heard about Snow Mountain's unusual method of handling cash, she knew what the target would be. She could have screwed up the whole deal for them, so they had to cut her in. Am I right so far?"

Josh drew his lips into a tight line and sniffed. "Have you forgotten that I'm the attorney for David? I wouldn't agree to what you just said even for the sake of argument."

"I'm not wearing a wire, Josh. Nobody's going to hear a word of this conversation. I'm just trying to talk this thing through."

He didn't say a word for a few seconds. He gave me this rolling motion with his hand to tell me to countinue and leaned back in his chair.

"They planned to switch the bags of cash for bags of paper," I said, "and they planned to put the paper on the armored car to Nashville. But the switch would have to be a two-man operation, one to set up a diversion and the other one to make the switch. So David played the part of an auditor sent down from Snow Mountain's main office in Nashville, and that put three people in the counting room, David, Rulon, and Clyde. Now remember, Clyde had never met David so he had no reason not to believe that the other guy counting the money was a representative of Snow Mountain."

"I must register a continuing objection to the use of my client's name in this fantasy."

"Objection noted," I said, "but that's a fact. Clyde had heard of the Earl of Stropshire, but he never met him."

"Get on with your story."

"Rulon was the manager, so he could find out exactly when the surveillance tapes would be switched out. It takes three minutes to rewind the old tape, pop in an new one, and queue up the new one. So they had a three- or four-minute window to make the switch where it would not be caught on film. And just to make sure they could get Clyde distracted at the right time, they hired this bimbo to drop in a minute or two before the change out occurred. When Clyde and Rulon left the room, David was supposed to get the fake bags out of this big cardboard box that was in the corner of the room and switch them with the real bags on the desk. Then he'd close the cardboard box and Clyde would never notice a thing."

"So, am I to assume you've eliminated Clyde as a suspect?" he asked.

"I wouldn't say eliminated. But it doesn't seem likely that Rulon would team up with him."

"If he's not a suspect," Josh said, "that leaves Tara, Rulon, and whoever was that Snow Mountain auditor as conpirators in the theft. You insist on calling this mysterious auditor David, but I think he sounds more like a Jack."

"I think David sounds better."

"Okay," he said, "but as a hypothetical only."

"Once the switch was made, Clyde and Rulon left their female distraction behind and walked back into the counting room. David closed the ledger book, and they all left the room together. They locked the door behind them, loaded the bags onto the armored car, and Clyde took off for a few days in Gulf Shores. Rulon was supposed to come back to the counting room later and pick up the cardboard box full of the real cash."

Josh, who had been listening with his head resting against the wall behind him and his eyes closed, straightened up when he realized I had stopped talking. "So you still haven't told me which one of them pulled the trigger," Josh said. "First of all, you haven't come up with any proof that my client was anywhere near that money. And second, you're trying too hard to deny the obvious. You know it was Tara, but you don't want to admit it."

"I never said it couldn't be her," I said. "In fact, now I'm sure that she's the one who did it."

His eyes widened and he broke into a smile. "Now we're getting somewhere. Tell me just how you know that."

"I went back in my mind and started piecing the story together. I remembered that the man I talked to at Snow Mountain's Nashville office had said the bogus shipment came from Gulfport. Didn't say it came from Bay St. Louis, he very clearly said Gulfport. You hear what I'm saying?"

Josh nodded.

"I didn't think much about it at the time because Armadillo Couriers is located there. I figured the name Gulfport must have been printed somewhere on the shipping tags and the guy in Nashville assumed the shipment came from there. But I called Armadillo's home office earlier today and got them to check their records. The shipment from Jackpot Bay Casino was never supposed to go to Nashville. The tags and the shipping order clearly stated that all those bags were to be stored overnight in Armadillo's Gulfport vault to be picked up the next morning."

"So who sent the fake shipment to Nashville?"

"The next morning a man came to Armadillo's office accompanied by a pair of uniformed security guards and picked up the shipment from Jackpot Bay. Then he sent a different set of sealed and tagged money bags to Nashville. Armadillo even called the Snow Mountain headquarters while the man was standing there to let them know the shipment was on its way. The man was convincing, the guards appeared to be professionals. It all seemed very believable."

"But doesn't the armored car company take inventory of what goes into their vehicles?" Josh said. "Couldn't they see that the bags they were loading for shipment to Nashville contained nothing but paper?"

"They take in their shipments already tagged and sealed, and they deliver it in that same condition. A courier company never breaks the seal on a shipment. That way, they don't leave themselves liable if a customer claims some of the money has been taken out during transit."

Josh scrunched his brow as he rubbed his fingers together. "So you're saying that there was no switching of the bags at the casino?"

"There was a switch, all right. But it didn't involve the bags. David switched the shipping tags. He left the fake money bags in that big cardboard box. On the real money bags he put new tags that directed the shipment to Gulfport for overnight storage."

"So Rulon went back to the counting room and retrieved the bags from the cardboard box thinking there was money in them," Josh said. "And he and Tara were literally left holding the bag."

"That's the way I see it."

Josh closed his eyes and pinched the bridge of his nose. He sat still and quiet for a minute or so and when he looked at me he was clearly puzzled. "But how does the fact that Tara and Rulon were both victims of a double-cross lead to your conclusion that Tara killed Rulon?"

"By itself, it doesn't," I said. "The reason I think Tara killed Rulon is because David didn't leave town after he pulled the switch at the armored car headquarters."

"Would you please stop talking in riddles?" Josh sighed and slumped into his chair. "Lord, give me strength."

"Tara had threatened her way into a cut of the loot," I said, "and hadn't done anything to deserve it. So David decided to swipe the whole bundle and skip town. He may or may not have planned to send for Rulon later. You're in a better position to answer that than I am."

"I'm sure he would have," Josh said. "Hypothetically speaking, of course."

"But he underestimated Tara's capacity for violence. She was waiting for them at the motel room where they had agreed to meet. When Rulon got there first with the money bags, and there was nobody there but Rulon and her, it was a perfect chance for her to take the whole bundle for herself. She pumped a bullet into his brain before he had the chance to sit down. It was strictly a crime of opportunity."

Josh raised his eyebrows. "So at last you've come to your senses about that wench."

"You know what Sherlock Holmes said about eliminating the impossible."

"Do that and whatever remains, however improbable, must be the truth," he said. "I follow that rule every time I prepare a case."

"Tara didn't take the time to break the seals and open the bags. She just grabbed them and ran. David was off somewhere taking his time and making plans to launder the cash or at least to convert all those bills into something easier to handle. There was no need for him to run because at that point, no one was chasing him. No one knew he was involved in the theft."

"There's still no proof that he was," Josh said.

"So he was holed up in some motel in New Orleans, Mobile, Hattiesburg. Somewhere he could relax, maybe lay out by the pool. He might have even planned to call Rulon and meet up with him so the two of them could leave the country together. But then he heard the news that Rulon's body had been found in the motel room, and he knew immediately what happened. Clyde Dubardo, Gino Stafford, and Billy Joe Newhart all had plenty of reasons to kill Rulon, but Tara is the only one who knew where he was. Eliminate the impossible and the signs point to Tara."

Josh pushed up and crossed his legs. He frowned as he drummed his fingers on the armrest of his chair. "So in your scenario why didn't David just leave the country? If he had all that money to himself, why would he go back for Tara?"

"Good question. There was no reason for him to go back. Even if he planned to give Rulon half of the take, it would have been a lot safer for them to meet up someplace a thousand miles away."

"So why did he?" Josh asked. "Why didn't he just leave the country instead?"

"Two possibilities. First, he went back to get Tara because they were lovers and wanted to run off together with a fortune in cash."

Josh laughed out loud. "No way! That much I'm sure of."

"The other possibility is that he wanted to make Tara pay, and pay dearly, for murdering his lover Rulon."

His smile faded as he sat back to consider all the angles.

"You've told me many times that Stratton-Hume was Rulon's protector," I said, "the only person in the world who thought he was worth a damn. If David put Rulon in danger, if he was the one who underestimated Tara, wouldn't he feel an obligation to settle the score?"

"I suppose he would."

"Of course he would! David loved Rulon. He loved him so much that he drove to New Orleans to talk to Gino because he couldn't stand the idea that Gino thought Rulon was some kind of monster. David would have done anything to protect him."

Josh sighed. "I never knew what David saw in Rulon. But you're right. He would have done anything."

"So let's say David hears that Rulon is dead," I said. "He immediately figures Tara did it. And he decides to make her pay. So he calls Tara and acts like he's scared half to death. He tells her that somebody has discovered the plot and killed Rulon because they thought he had that stolen money. He makes up some excuse why he took the money and didn't meet Rulon and her at the motel room that day. He tells her that he's hiding out and that she's also in danger and needs to get out of sight. Then he comes up with this plan for them to lay low and skip town together with the money."

"And Tara buys all of this?" Josh asked.

"Why wouldn't she? If he was lying to her, why would he call her? Sure she bought it. To her, getting David's phone call was like money dropping into her lap."

"So he was going to just hand the money to her?" Josh asked.

"Stratton-Hume wanted to set her up, but that would mean she'd have to get caught with the loot in her hands."

"Jack, he wouldn't dare come back to give it to her. She'd just kill him like she killed Rulon. Besides, he was already home free. If he came back and got caught with the proceeds of the theft, he'd be risking jail time himself."

"Not if he gave her all the money. If he doesn't have any of it, not a penny, who's going to believe he stole it? Let me ask you this, when he was arrested at the airport how much cash did he have on him?"

"Not a cent," he said.

"I assume the police found out where he was staying and searched the premises. What did they find there?"

"Nothing."

"David got Tara to line up a plane and a couple of parachutes. All in her name, of course. There was an all-points bulletin out on him by this time, so he told her they couldn't take a commercial flight and even in a car there was a good chance they wouldn't make it out of town without getting pulled over. But they could charter a private plane and drop down in some cow pasture miles up in the country. And he was smart enough to realize that it was a plan with enough danger in it to really get Tara's juices flowing."

"I don't believe a word of this," Josh said.

I started to turn to face him, but a stabbing pain along my ribcage stopped me short. "You believe that David was ready to jump out of a plane into a thunderstorm just for the hell of it, but can't believe he'd do it to set up Tara?"

"But if what you say is true, she would have probably shot him while they were up in the air. Besides, where's this setup you're saying he pulled off? If you hadn't been lucky enough to receive that call from that mechanic at the airport, they would have boarded that plane."

"I didn't get the call because of luck, and it didn't come from any mechanic. It came from David Stratton-Hume himself. He could imitate Elvis Presley and Burt Reynolds, remember? He's the one who made the call for me to come to the airport."

"Too dangerous," Josh said. "That would be cutting it too close."

"He had to cut it close. He couldn't give Tara the money ahead of time, or she'd probably kill him. And he couldn't hang around inside the airport or somebody may recognize him from the description in the BOLO the sheriff put out. So he was in the hangar where they do maintenance on the planes, where he was less likely to be spotted. That's where he called me from. The plan was for Tara to walk to the plane, and he'd run out from the hangar to join her where the lighting wasn't too good. So they met up on the tarmac just seconds before they were supposed to get on the plane. He strapped the fanny pack on her right there on the spot."

"That's another thing," he said. "Are you saying that all that cash fit into a fanny pack?"

"By then it was a manageable size. It had been converted into big bills and maybe even jewels. But the point is, Tara was the one who was carrying it. Every bit of it."

"But what if you'd been a minute or two later in getting to the airport?" he asked.

"I don't think that would have mattered too much."

"Of course it would," he said. "If you had been a minute later in arriving he would have been in real trouble. She would have shot him inside the plane the minute it took off."

"There was no way David was getting on the plane even if I never showed up. He kept looking all around like he was waiting for the cavalry to come. The instant I raced out on that tarmac and yelled for them to stop, he hit the ground like a sack of cement.

Didn't hesitate a second. That's because he wasn't the least bit surprised. If nobody had shown up in time to stop them, he would have let Tara get aboard first and then he would have turned and hauled ass. And if that happened, what could she do but go ahead and stay on the plane? She couldn't just shoot him in front of witnesses."

Josh pulled down on the knot of his tie and undid the top button of his shirt. "Now let me see if I understand what you're saying." He held up one finger. "One, David wants to cut Tara out of the deal so he pulls a switch and runs off with the money. He plans to call for Rulon later."

"That's right."

"Two, the three conspirators are supposed to meet in a motel room and split up the loot. But when Tara gets to the room and finds Rulon alone with the money bags, she sees her chance to take all of it. She shoots Rulon and runs off with what she thinks is all the money. Later she discovers that the bags are full of newspaper."

"Exactly."

"Three, when David hears that Rulon has been killed, he knows that Tara did it and comes up with a scheme to get even with her. He plans to set her up so she'll get caught with the money and take the rap for the theft if not the murder of Rulon."

"You've got it."

"But wouldn't he have a lot of explaining to do if he got caught at the airport with her?" Josh said. "What if Tara claimed she was being kidnapped and they believed her story instead of his?"

"That's where the timing came in," I said. "David fully planned to plant the loot on Tara and make sure she got on that plane by herself. Like I said, there was no way he was getting on with her. As soon as they took off, he was going to call the cops and tell them where she was."

"But she had a parachute," Josh said. "All she had to do was jump."

"Sure she could. But with a pilot telling the authorities exactly where they were when she left the plane, there wasn't a chance in a thousand she'd get away."

"But apparently she did."

"He misjudged her," I said, "By now she's living it up somewhere on the other side of the world. The money is in some safe-deposit box and the only crimes she can be charged with are damaging the airplane with a wine bottle and pointing a gun at the pilot."

Josh smiled and shook his head. "Of course you can't prove any of this. It's a fascinating tale, but there's no way you can back it up. My client had nothing to do with any theft from that casino." He glanced at his wristwatch. "David has to catch a flight out of New Orleans in a few hours. I wonder what's taking him so long."

"I'm not trying to put David behind bars," I said. "I'm doing a job for Bayou Casualty and I just want to recover that money. I need to know if my theory was right."

"If you want that money you need to find Tara Stocklin," he said. "That's all I can tell you."

Down the hall the door opened and David Stratton-Hume, the Earl of Stropshire, came toward us pulling this suitcase on wheels behind him. I pulled my feet in and leaned forward to position myself for the painful process of standing. "You know, this story I've come up with only works if what you've told me about David Stratton-Hume is true. Unless he would put himself in danger and give up over a million dollars to even the score for a dead friend, none of it makes sense. Are there still people walking around this world who would do something like that?"

"Don't get so melodramatic," Josh said. "I said he was protective of Rulon. The rest is a fantasy you've come up with."

"I understand that you've got to protect your client. But you've got to admit the pieces fit."

"Are you planning to tell the sheriff about this theory you've concocted?"

I shook my head. "What's the use? They wouldn't believe me. And it wouldn't help me recover the money. If my version of what happened is right, David Stratton-Hume doesn't have a penny of it. And he wouldn't have any better idea of where Tara is than we do."

"Well, in that case, I'll say once again that you need to get to work and track down Tara Stocklin." He smiled and stood and brushed the seat of his pants. "And do tell your brother I said hello."

TWENTY-FOUR

The Mississippi Highway Patrol and the sheriff's offices of several counties in southwest Mississippi searched for Tara for the next two weeks. The pilot from the skydiving service couldn't say with any certainty when she had jumped, and with a plane moving at an average rate of 130 miles per hour, that meant the jump could have happened almost anywhere in south Mississippi. To make matters worse, most of his navigation equipment had been knocked out, so he didn't know within forty degrees the direction in which he was headed when she left the plane. She could have bailed out in any of a dozen counties covering an area of six or seven thousand square miles.

The search team flew planes over the pine forests and river bottoms, the pastures and the cornfields. They set up roadblocks and put out wanted posters and got a lot of coverage on the TV news reports. But a search like that costs a lot of money and when it looked as though Tara probably had gotten away clean, they scaled it down to a general lookout by local law enforcement agencies and a listing with the FBI. The speculation was that since she had a handheld GPS she knew exactly where she needed to drop and had a car waiting for her. The summer passed and so did the fall, and no trace of Tara was ever found.

After the fiasco with the Snow Mountain money, the directors at Bayou Casualty decided that the insurance market for casinos was not something they were ready to jump into, so they dropped coverage on Jackpot Bay. But that didn't get them off the hook for the missing $1.3 million, and Snow Mountain had already filed suit in federal court at Biloxi. I hadn't been called in for my deposition yet, but I knew that was coming.

Johnnie the Dime scaled back his plan to run the classiest joint on the coast and started concentrating on new car giveaways and a seafood buffet, all you can eat for $8.99. From what I can tell he's making money and pulling in a pretty good drive-up crowd on the weekends. Mutual of Chicago is carrying Jackpot Bay's coverage. I say they can have it and more power to them. Clyde is running the casino's security full-time, but he still takes the time to greet the tour buses. This friend of mine who runs the Gator's Den on Bourbon Street says she sees him over there a lot. Says Clyde and this redheaded exotic dancer named Lola seem to be getting serious about each other.

Billy Joe Newhart "got the call," as they say, to take the pastorship at this big Pentecostal church in Beaumont, Texas, the first week in September. He's got a prayer line show on a Christian FM station over there, and it's going so well there's talk of syndication. He left the Narrow Path Church in good hands, and every time I drive by when they're having services the parking lot is full. But the new preacher isn't as flashy as Newhart, so the radio ministry has quieted down considerably and so have the protests. Mama tells me that Brenda Bailey, Robert Earl's widow, has been seeing this big-time highway sodding contractor out of Gulfport and that the guy really loves her kids. Mama has her ways of finding out such things.

On the coldest day in the past fifteen years, a raw, gray Saturday in January seven months after Tara and the money flew off together, I was laid out on my couch wearing a threadbare sweatsuit, eating homemade chili and watching the Ole Miss–Mississippi State basketball game on ESPN, when I got a call from Roger Partridge. The call came a little after two o'clock. We hadn't seen the sun in three days, it was twenty-eight degrees outside with a wind out of the northwest, and there was even talk of snow that night.

Roger had just got off the phone with the sheriff of Marion County, seventy or eighty miles to the north of Bay St. Louis. Earlier that morning, in a swamp where Sandy Hook Creek empties into the Pearl River fifteen miles south of Columbia, a pair of hunters were push-poling their floating duck blind through a flooded stand of cypress. One of them happened to glance between a pair of trees into a clearing off to the side and spotted the shredded end of a broken rope dangling a few feet above the knee-deep water that had been standing in the clearing for the past few days.

The trees were so close together that if you put your right hand on one of them, you could touch the one beside it with your left. Their branches intertwined, and the canopy of limbs and leaves was so thick that the hunters couldn't see what the rope was attached to. They snaked their way through the maze of cypress knees and tree trunks, cracking the wafer-thin sheets of ice that had congealed at the feet of the trees, and soon they floated into the clearing. Up above them thirty feet in the air, hanging at the end of six or eight nylon ropes entangled in the highest trees, was a human carcass in a dark blue jumpsuit, looking for all the world like a life-sized marionette.

"Come on and drive up there with me," Roger said. "I need somebody from the insurance company to inventory the money."

"You're assuming it's Tara hung in those trees," I said.

"She's the only missing skydiver I know of in the past thirty years or so," he said. "Besides, we might need you to identify the body."

Roger and I piled into a dark green four-wheel-drive Chevy Z71 pickup that belonged to the sheriff's office and tossed our duck hunting gear, waders and all, into the back of the extended cab. We headed north only three hours before darkness was to set in, not that there was all that much daylight anyway.

We drove under a mottled sky the color and texture of smoke, white here and gray there. Smudge pots, with their black-tipped yellow flames, warned drivers of ice forming on the bridges where road crews in orange vests were spreading sand with shovels out of the beds of county-owned flatbed trucks. When we reached Sandy Hook the day had darkened, and the sky glowed with a uniform dimness, equally dreary in all directions. Although we couldn't see it, we could tell that the sun was slipping below the horizon.

A half dozen steel-gray Highway Patrol cruisers and at least that many cars from the Marion County sheriff's office were parked in a row along Highway 35. White clouds of exhaust rose behind three of the cars that had been left with their engines running and their parking lights on and one of them had the blue lights flashing. A trooper had been posted along the side of the road to wave the rubberneckers along. He saw our Hancock County markings and told us to park on the gravel shoulder in front of the last patrol car up ahead.

We walked back toward the trooper, and as we approached one of the parked squad cars, a deputy lowered his window. We could smell the coffee that he had just poured from a Thermos and hear the crackle from his radio. He pointed us ahead to an abandoned logging road we had just walked past. Said they were using the old road as a foot trail to cross the Illinois Central tracks and get into the woods. No way a truck could get through there, four-wheel drive or not.

"But I'd just go back to your truck if I was you," the deputy said. "Highway Patrol's done dispatched a copter outta Jackson. Oughta be here any minute."

"The body's still up in those trees?" I asked.

"Cain't get to it," he said. "It's done rained for three solid days. The water's backed up to the other side of them tracks. Ain't no way to get a cherry picker through that muck."

"This man's here to make an ID on the body," Roger said.

"Well y'all might as well get on back to your truck and get comfortable. They're gonna set the body down right here on this highway. It's the only solid ground anywhere close. Besides, I got the body bag in my trunk."

We were walking back along the asphalt when we heard the soft bubbling of a far-off helicopter. It was dark by then, and through the tangle of tree trunks and bare, twisting vines we would catch an occasional glint from a flashlight where the rescue team stood around, helpless in the deep woods. My ears and fingers had started stinging from the cold. There was a dank and moldy odor where the troopers and deputies had walked down the logging trail and stirred up the two-inch layer of rotted leaves that had fallen back in November and now clung to the ground like wet newspaper.

"You still think that Stratton-Hume guy was in on the robbery?" Roger asked.

"What does it matter?" I said. "Whatever money was stolen is probably hanging up in those branches right now."

"Maybe I shoulda charged him with something," he said, "but that lawyer he had was some kinda smart. And all I had to go on was what you were saying about how he put his hand in his coat pocket."

A mist had begun, so I pulled up the hood of my parka. "I might have been wrong about that. Maybe it wasn't him."

"You got any idea where he is now?" he asked.

"If I had to guess, I'd say Europe."

We climbed into the truck and Roger flipped on our headlights. The mist dotted the windshield along with white specks of snow that fluttered around because they were too light to fall in a straight line. Every ten seconds or so, he'd hit the wiper switch for a double sweep so we could keep a clear view of that spot in the treetops where the guys on the ground had trained their flashlights. When the copter got closer, the pilot popped on the searchlight and trained it on the suspended corpse.

The mist stopped, so we killed the headlights and got back out of the cab to sit on the front bumper for a better view. The heat radiating through the grille kept our backsides warm. There was a sweet odor from antifreeze that had spewed into the overflow tank when the engine stopped, and a harsh smell of scorched motor oil that had splattered onto the superheated manifold during the hard run from Bay St. Louis. In the still, cold air the hollow beating of the helicopter's blades sounded like someone was doing a drumroll on a tympani and we were inside the drum.

They lowered a man in a harness from the open side into the treetops. The supple limbs flailed around under the chopper's heavy downdraft, and made it nearly impossible for us to see the trooper as he maneuvered through the cypress branches and girded the body with a canvas strap attached to a cable. We stepped away from the truck and found a spot that gave us a clearer view. Once he had fastened the canvas strap, he cut the parachute ropes that for seven months had held the carcass like a bug caught in a spider web. They pulled the trooper back up and the pilot showered down on the throttle and the copter roared and began a slow rise.

As soon as the body cleared the trees, snow began falling once again. Big flakes this time, some as big as puffs of cotton, and coming down hard. There was no movement in the air so they floated down evenly and at ground level, under the blue and white lights of the patrol cars around us; it seemed as if we were on some New York sidewalk during a ticker tape parade. When we looked upward the flakes disappeared as they blended into the deep winter sky, a sky as opaque and black as chimney soot. And against this backdrop, the corpse in the blue jumpsuit, glowing under the white glare of the helicopter's searchlight, drifted toward us like an illuminated angel.

The pilot lowered the body to the asphalt, set it down with a gentle touch, and as soon as he was unhooked he ascended and banked and took off for Jackson. They kept one lane of the highway open, but it still backed up, and in both directions there were headlights and clouds of exhaust vapor. The winter silence was broken by the sounds of windshield wipers beating like metronomes and police radios with their sporadic, hissing messages from headquarters. Every one of the dozen squad cars flipped on its lightbar so the surrounding swamp was painted blue. The body lay flat on its back on the rain-darkened asphalt lit up by a dozen flashlights. Snow was gathering on the folds of the jumpsuit, but around the body the snow melted as soon as it hit the pavement.

Roger moved me to the front after explaining to the local sheriff why I had come up with him from Bay St. Louis. We stood with the supine body at our feet as two troopers with white latex gloves snipped the strap of the fanny pack and pinched one end of the strap to lift it. There was a tiny brass padlock on the zipper of the pack, the kind you use on luggage.

"The money's inside that pack," I said. "Keep a close eye on it."

"We're taking it to that van to tag it and open it," one of the troopers said. "It's still evidence."

"It looks pretty full," the other one said.

Roger beat his gloved hands together. "Hurry up and get this over with so we can get out of this snow."

"So what do you think happened to her?" I asked.

"She miscalculated the altitude and the wind and drifted into that swamp by mistake. I'd guess she hit a tree and broke her neck."

The maggots and vultures had done their work over the past months. The hands had been picked clean of flesh and a few bones were missing. There was still some mummified skin on the skull, but the nose and ears appeared to have been ripped away and the eye sockets were hollow. There were a few sprigs of hair sprouting from what was left of the scalp. They were three or four inches long and dark brown except for the tips which were yellow blond.

"Can you tell if it's Tara?" Roger asked.

"I hear that hair keeps growing after you die," I said.

He held his gloves to his ears to shield them from the snow. "How in the world do Yankees live with this stuff every single winter?"

"If the snow's bothering you, go on over to the van and keep an eye on that money," I said. "I've got one thing I need to check out before they have to send off for the dental records."

The Marion County sheriff gave the go-ahead for a deputy to open up the jumpsuit. He used a set of wire cutters and started where the corroded zipper reached the neck. Everyone who had been standing beside their squad cars stepped over and ringed the body to see what was going on. They stood in silence, some smoking cigarettes and some sipping coffee, watching each careful snip that the deputy made as he worked his way down the front of the suit.

So this is how it ends, I thought. A bunch of strangers standing around wondering what's under the jumpsuit. I was having a hard time even imagining what Tara had looked like. I tried to picture those firm and perfectly shaped legs, now rotting and falling off the bone. Tried remembering her voice, but couldn't do that either. And now there was nothing left. The thrill of danger, the easy sex, and even the money, all those things she said she lived for were gone. And what good was that money or jewelry or whatever was in the fanny pack going to do her now? If she had made it a few more years maybe she would have found other, more permanent things to live for. But then maybe not.

She had great legs and a flashy smile and just the right amount of bad-girl allure to make me start thinking with something other than my brain. But was there a demon hiding behind those gray-blue eyes? Hell, she had murdered a man for nothing more than a bigger slice of the loot. Is that the kind of cold-blooded greed that you can ever grow out of? I never have been able to figure out just how much control any of us have or what we can do if Beelzebub decides to take over our souls. I couldn't decide if she had just made some awful mistakes, or if the lovely and vivacious Tara Stocklin was the devil in human form, beyond all hope of redemption.

Either way it was one hell of a waste.

"You see what you're looking for," the deputy asked, "or do you need for us to cut this jumpsuit all the way off?"

"See if you can open up that bra," I said. "I need to take a look at the breasts."

"You plannin' to ID her boobs?"

"Just hurry up and cut the damn thing open," the sheriff said. "I'm ready to wrap this up and get my ass next to some heater."

The skin had saponified and taken on a gummy appearance. Gave me this queasy sensation that I tried to supress. The jumpsuit protected it over the past months from the peckings of the carrion birds but it held in the moisture, and since the canopy of cypress blocked the sunlight year round the normal breakdown of flesh had been impeded.

The deputy placed the wire cutters at the point where the two bra cups are joined and with a sharp push snipped it in half. He pulled it away from the breasts. On the inside of the left breast, right where I knew it would be, was a faded, dime-sized tattoo of a red rose.

"That's her, Sheriff," I said. "That's Tara Stocklin. I'll give you whatever statement or affidavit you need."

"Hey, Jack!" Roger yelled from the van. "Get over here!"

"Get the body bag," the sheriff said to the deputy. "Let's load her up."

"Come on, Jack!"

The snow was now sticking and building up on the patrol cars and in the weeds beside the road. The puddles along the gravel shoulders were crystallizing, and I hit a few slick spots as I walked toward the van. Roger was standing beside the sliding door with two troopers wearing yellow parkas.

"You won't believe what we found in that fanny pack," Roger said.

"I'm guessing diamonds or emeralds," I said.

One of the troopers grunted; the other one laughed. "Take a look for yourself," the big one said.

Roger reached for the handle of the van's sliding door and pulled it wide open. Laid out on a the carpet were what appeared to be stacks of bills that were wrapped in butcher paper. Beside these stacks was this tin box, the kind throat lozenges come in. It had been wrapped in slick, black electrical tape, but they had sliced the tape and the little box stood open. The tiny colored rocks in the box sparkled green and yellow under the van's dome light.

"What is it?" I asked.

"Mardi Gras beads," Roger said. "Nothing but little plastic beads with holes bored through the center of them."

"And how about those stacks of bills?"

Roger handed me a pack of bills that had been opened. Someone had cut a hundred sheets of pale green copier paper into strips the width and length of American currency, slipped a rubber band around the stack, and covered it with white butcher paper.

"If Tara thought she was jumping out of that plane with a load of cash and diamonds," Roger said, "she got fooled even worse than we did."

I sat on the edge of the van's floor and put my feet on the ground. This feeling of lightness started in my gut and began rising with a tickling sensation. I had to hand it to the earl, he managed to screw over Tara and walk away with the cash at the same time. I never saw that one coming. I was there on that tarmac watching him as he strapped that fanny pack on her, and it had never crossed my mind.

"So where do y'all think the money is?" one of the troopers asked.

"Jack, I should have listened to you," Roger said. "But I didn't have enough evidence to arrest him."

"You still don't," I said. "There's still not one more bit of physical evidence against him than there was the day he walked out of your office."

"Shit!" Roger said as he kicked the ground. "That limey son of a bitch."

In the midst of all the cold and the snow that was pelting my hands, the troopers standing beside the van kept staring at those beads. I put my face in my hands and got this mental picture of David Stratton-Hume, or whoever the heck he is, resting on a chaise longue on a snow-white beach in front of this deep turquoise sea, sipping a tall orange drink and rubbing sunscreen on his arms.

"But I don't get it, Sheriff," I could hear one of them saying. "Why the hell would she parachute into a swamp for nothing more than a bunch of Mardi Gras beads?"

"My God, man," Roger said. "Can't you see it was a switch? The woman thought she had a load of diamonds."

"Well, why is that so funny?" I heard the trooper ask. "Why is that guy sittin' in that van laughing like some kind of fool?"

AUTHOR'S NOTE

Jackpot Bay is a work of fiction. Names, places, characters, and incidents depicted therein are products of the author's imagination or are used fictitiously. Certain liberties have been taken in changing the landscape of Bay St. Louis and the surrounding area to fit the story. Any resemblance to actual events at any of the locales is coincidental. Any resemblance to any person, living or dead, is coincidental.